I0819222

Books by Rita Mae Brown & Sneaky Pie Brown

WISH YOU WERE HERE • REST IN PIECES • MURDER AT MONTICELLO • PAY DIRT
MURDER, SHE MEOWED • MURDER ON THE PROWL • CAT ON THE SCENT
SNEAKY PIE'S COOKBOOK FOR MYSTERY LOVERS • PAWING THROUGH THE PAST
CLAWS AND EFFECT • CATCH AS CAT CAN • THE TAIL OF THE TIP-OFF
WHISKER OF EVIL • CAT'S EYEWITNESS • SOUR PUSS • PUSS 'N CAHOOTS
THE PURRFECT MURDER • SANTA CLAWED • CAT OF THE CENTURY
HISS OF DEATH • THE BIG CAT NAP • SNEAKY PIE FOR PRESIDENT
THE LITTER OF THE LAW • NINE LIVES TO DIE • TAIL GAIT • TALL TAIL
A HISS BEFORE DYING • PROBABLE CLAWS • WHISKERS IN THE DARK
FURMIDABLE FOES • CLAWS FOR ALARM • HISS & TELL • FELINE FATALE
SEALED WITH A HISS

Books by Rita Mae Brown featuring "Sister" Jane Arnold

OUTFOXED • HOTSPUR • FULL CRY • THE HUNT BALL
THE HOUNDS AND THE FURY • THE TELL-TALE HORSE • HOUNDED TO DEATH
FOX TRACKS • LET SLEEPING DOGS LIE • CRAZY LIKE A FOX
HOMEWARD HOUND • SCARLET FEVER • OUT OF HOUNDS
THRILL OF THE HUNT • TIME WILL TELL • FOX AND FURIOUS

The Mags Rogers Books

MURDER UNLEASHED • A NOSE FOR JUSTICE

Books by Rita Mae Brown

ANIMAL MAGNETISM: MY LIFE WITH CREATURES GREAT AND SMALL
THE HAND THAT CRADLES THE ROCK • SONGS TO A HANDSOME WOMAN
A PLAIN BROWN RAPPER • RUBYFRUIT JUNGLE • IN HER DAY • SIX OF ONE
SOUTHERN DISCOMFORT • SUDDEN DEATH • HIGH HEARTS
STARTED FROM SCRATCH: A DIFFERENT KIND OF WRITER'S MANUAL • BINGO
VENUS ENVY • DOLLEY: A NOVEL OF DOLLEY MADISON IN LOVE AND WAR
RIDING SHOTGUN • RITA WILL: MEMOIR OF A LITERARY RABBLE-ROUSER

Clawed and Dangerous

Clawed and Dangerous

RITA MAE BROWN &
SNEAKY PIE BROWN

Illustrated by Michael Gellatly

BANTAM BOOKS
NEW YORK

Bantam Books
An imprint of Random House
A division of Penguin Random House LLC
1745 Broadway, New York, NY 10019
randomhousebooks.com
penguinrandomhouse.com

Hardcover ISBN 978-0-593-87414-1
Ebook ISBN 978-0-593-87415-8

Printed in the United States of America on acid-free paper

1st Printing

First Edition

BOOK TEAM: Production editor: Andy Lefkowitz • Managing editor: Saige Francis
Production manager: Meghan O'Leary • Copy editor: Pam Feinstein
Proofreaders: Megha Jain, Allison Lindon, and Caryl Schwartz

Book design by Diane Hobbing

The authorized representative in the EU for product safety and compliance is Penguin Random House Ireland, Morrison Chambers, 32 Nassau Street, Dublin D02 YH68, Ireland, https://eu-contact.penguin.ie

For Holly, a Pomeranian mix rescue. She has never met with worldly disappointments. Her life is one joyful frolic and always by my side.

CAST OF CHARACTERS

Mary Minor Haristeen, "Harry" was the postmistress of Crozet right out of Smith College. As times changed and a big new post office was built, new rules came, too, such as she couldn't bring her animals to work, so she retreated to the farm she inherited from her parents. Born and raised in Crozet, she knows everyone and vice versa. She is now forty-five, although one could argue whether maturity has caught up with her.

Pharamond Haristeen, DVM, "Fair" is an equine vet specializing in reproduction. He and Harry have known each other all their lives. They married shortly after she graduated from Smith and he was in vet school at Auburn. He generally understands his wife better than she understands herself.

Susan Tucker is Harry's best friend from cradle days. They might as well be sisters and can sometimes pluck each other's last nerve as only a sister can. Susan bred Harry's adored corgi. Her husband, Ned, is the district's delegate to the General Assembly's House of Delegates, the lower house.

Deputy Cynthia Cooper is Harry's neighbor, as she owns the old Jones adjoining farm. Law enforcement is a career she is made for, being meticulous, shrewd, and highly observant. She works closely with the sheriff, Rick Shaw; adores Harry; and all too often has to extricate her neighbor out of scrapes. Harry returns the favor by helping Coop with her garden. It probably isn't an equal exchange but they are fine with it.

Tazio Chappers is an architect in her late thirties, born and raised in St. Louis. Being educated at Washington University, she received an excellent education, winding up in Crozet on a fluke. Just one of those things, as Cole Porter's song lets us know. Warned off a job at an architectural firm by many people back in Missouri, due to her being half Black and half Italian, she came to Virginia, anyway. No one can accuse her of being a chicken. Now owner of her own firm, getting big jobs, she is happy, married for two years, and part of the community. She is also terrifically good-looking, which never hurts.

Paul Sanchez manages Big Mim Sanborne's Thoroughbred stables. He is married to Tazio Chappers.

Dr. Wilson Anglin is a successful emergency room doctor. He invests his money in remodeling homes and selling them.

Bumpy is a former drug addict who works for Dr. Anglin. He's been to rehab three times. This time he swears he has it knocked.

Mac is another former addict. A big, powerful man, he works with Bumpy. He's been clean for years but Crozet is a small town. His reputation is ruined.

Shifty Brennan owns a gas station in town. He is helpful with the Halloween fundraiser for Susan Tucker's Seeing Eye Rescue Group.

Kyle Lawler assists Paul Sanchez. He's good at feeding and grooming the horses, and not much else. He never does anything extra.

Shauna Grayson, mid-thirties, is the director of Bootstraps, the local rehab center.

THE ANIMALS

Mrs. Murphy is Harry's tiger cat. She is bright, does her chores, keeps the mice at bay when need be. Harry talks to her but not baby talk. Mrs. Murphy just won't have it.

Pewter is fat, gray, and vain, oh so vain. She irritates Tucker, the corgi. She takes credit for everyone else's work. However, in a pinch the naughty girl does come through. She's also quite bright.

Tucker, the corgi bred by Susan Tucker, runs around everyone. She's fast, loves to greet every person once she has checked them out, and particularly likes to herd the horses. The horses are good sports about it, which is a good thing. Tucker is brave and she loves Harry totally.

Pirate is a not-yet-fully-grown Irish Wolfhound who landed in Harry's lap as a puppy when his owner died. Huge, able to cover so much ground, he can be dominated by Pewter sometimes. Tucker has to give him pep talks. Like Tucker, Pirate has great courage and loves being part of the family. He is trying to understand people. The others help. A sweet, sweet animal.

Haley is Carolyn Maki's fourteen-year-old yellow Lab. Smart and obedient.

Jeb is Carolyn Maki's Jack Russell puppy. Smart and disobedient.

Shortro is an athletic Saddlebred from Joan Hamilton's Kalarama Farm in Springfield, Kentucky. He's calm, likes trail rides. Most people don't recognize that he is a Saddlebred. His gaits are a bit high but he's not a showman. He's a terrific fellow.

Silver Silence is a Thoroughbred stud standing at Big Mim's farm. As he had a good track record he is not cheap.

Clawed and Dangerous

1

September 17, 2025

Wednesday

In theory mid-September should be good weather. Mother Nature is not interested in theories.

Fair Haristeen, DVM, drove through the cold rain to the elegant stables owned by Big Mim Sanborne. Built in the mid–nineteenth century, the two-story brick structure, with Dutch stable doors and trim painted white, had withstood worse than this over the centuries.

Parking on the south side, Fair grabbed his bag and his Barbour raincoat, making a dash for the stable doors, which he easily slid open.

Paul Sanchez, who managed Big Mim's stables, her large equine operation, shouted over the rain din, "Glad you're here."

A bay Thoroughbred stallion, seven years old, screamed in his stall while kicking the walls, fortunately made out of thick oak.

Kyle Lawler, Paul's young assistant, stood white-faced by the closed stall door. "He tried to kill me. Ran for me in the field. Wanted to roll me."

Neither Fair nor Paul replied. Rarely would a stallion attempt to knock down a human, pick him up with his forelegs, then rear up only to hit the ground hoping to crush the human to death. People volunteered many reasons for this murderous behavior on the few occasions when it occurred. A few may even have been correct.

However, both Fair and Paul blocked Kyle's babble. He could clean stalls, tack, lead horses in and out, but he evidenced no particular talent with the animals. He made sure anyone who met him knew he worked at Big Mim Sanborne's stables. She was known throughout the horse world.

"How long has he been in the stall?" Fair asked.

"A half hour. Got him in then called you," Paul answered.

"Let me grab some stuff out of the truck. I'll get him zoned out then check his legs."

"Bring the X-ray machine in case." Paul then added, "I'll go out with you. Help carry stuff."

"Thanks." Fair slipped on his old but still perfect Barbour raincoat as Paul pulled on his Filson.

Both brands cost money but they lasted forever. In the long run they proved cheaper. As Fair's mother used to say, "Buy the best then you only cry once."

Kyle moved in front of the stall door, which further set off Silver Silence, who screamed again.

"Kyle, step out of his sight," Paul ordered.

"He wants to kill me." Kyle whimpered but did step away.

"Just stay out of sight." Paul raised his voice.

At the truck Fair opened the locked back, which he'd had specially built to carry equipment and meds. The tall man climbed up to hand down the X-ray machine, a bit unwieldly. He then grabbed Banamine and a needle.

The two men trotted through the rain into the stable, now leaving the doors open a crack.

Fair filled a needle, flicked it with his finger. "I'd rather not use this but given his behavior I think drugs aren't out of order. Paul, I never know when I've given a horse a drug if it masks some pain. I always feel I can make a better assessment without."

"I know that. You do what you have to do."

"Okay. Open his stall door a crack." Fair kept his right hand, carrying the needle, up straight.

Silence snorted.

"There you go, big fella, there you go." Fair reached up to the impressive animal's neck, ran his fingers alongside his chest. "Let's see."

Paul, voice low, said, "I don't know."

Kyle, curious, began to creep over just as Fair reached up to inject Silence with the Banamine. Usually, horses paid him no mind, as Fair was a master at administering shots.

But, hearing Kyle's footsteps, the horse spun around, and kicked Fair high.

"Ahh." Fair held his chest but amazingly did not drop the needle.

Paul stepped in, put his hands under the six-foot-four-inch man, quickly pulling him out as Silence kicked again, this time banging against the stall door, which reverberated.

"Close the goddamned door!" Paul shouted at Kyle as he now put one arm around Fair's waist. "Can you take a step?"

Kyle closed the door.

"Yeah. Thanks for getting me out."

"You need to go to the ER." Fair shook his head. "Come on, Fair. I've broken my ribs, I know how painful it is."

"How'd you know he got my ribs?"

"He kicked high. Plus, I heard the crack," Paul said.

Paul gently lowered Fair into the tack-room chair, pale though he was.

The vet took a deep breath. "My bag is out in the aisle. When I get out of the ER, I can return to check his legs, I hope. I'll leave the X-ray machine with you, my bag and my truck."

"Don't worry about anything, especially Silence. I'm taking you to the ER." Paul was polite but firm.

"Silence has won some big races. He's worth a lot as a stud. I don't want to take any chances with him. Mim needs him breeding sound. Cracked or broken ribs won't stop an X-ray. I'll call my wife. She'll take me. When I get back, I'll take the X-rays."

"Fair, please. None of us will be any good for anything if something happens to you."

"That's flattering." Fair winced. "Let me call my babydoll." He punched the button on his cell. "Honey, pick me up at Mim's. I need you to take me to the ER."

Paul grabbed the cell from Fair and gave Harry a more detailed explanation.

"I'll be right there," said Harry.

As Fair sat there, he asked Paul, "When did this behavior start?"

"About a week ago. He's gotten worse."

"Any change in his routine?"

"No."

Fair reached into his pocket, handed Paul the keys. "Lock the back, will you?"

Paul nodded then told Kyle to go to the other barn and bring another bag of sweet feed.

As Kyle left, Fair said, "I don't really know him, Paul. I wouldn't trust anyone I don't know with some of the drugs in the truck. They can bring big money on the street."

"Right." Paul sighed just as the doors opened on the other end and Harry walked in.

"Honey."

"He's here." Paul raised his voice. "You talk some sense into him. He wants to come back from the ER and do X-rays on Silence."

Attractive even in her wet, muddy jeans, Harry looked at her husband. "Come on. We can figure out what to do once the doctor fixes you up."

"If Silence has a leg problem I want to get on it."

"Fair, do as your wife tells you." Paul did so like Fair and Harry together.

Fair rose, unsteady, Paul immediately went over, put his arm again around his waist. He carefully walked him out to the old Volvo station wagon. Harry opened the door as Paul eased him onto the passenger seat, then knelt down, picked up his legs, and slid them in.

They all got wet.

"I'm not crippled," Fair groaned.

"Not yet." Paul closed the door as Fair lowered the window, for Harry had left the motor running.

She was already behind the wheel.

Paul leaned over. "Don't worry about the truck. Taz and I will bring it to you." He named his wife.

As she backed out, Fair noticed. "You didn't wear a raincoat. You'll catch a cold."

"I'm fine, but I will turn on the heat, low. Every time I hit a bump, it's going to hurt."

"Where are we going?"

"Augusta." She named a hospital close by, over in the Valley. "I called and told them we were on the way just before I picked you up. They wanted to send an ambulance and I said I was on my way and the ambulance wasn't going to do any better in this rain than myself. Plus, it was only broken or cracked ribs."

"Okay. Uh." He felt that bump.

"I'm sorry."

"Damn roads," he cursed.

"Where the hell does our state tax money go?" She peered intently through the windshield.

"There's a subject that hurts more than my ribs." He smiled a bit. "Although I do think we're better off in Virginia than a lot of other states. I mean, what if we were paying state taxes in New Jersey?"

"Even Mim with all her millions would have a fit." Harry smiled. "Does it hurt to wear a seatbelt?"

"A little," he answered.

"The weather is bad. Buckle up. I know it will hurt but just in case."

He did as he was told.

"That was obedient," she praised him.

"Women have secret weapons." He smiled then grimaced as it did hurt.

"I'm glad to hear that." And she was glad to hear him tease her. He might be in pain but he hadn't injured an organ, and his mind was fine.

She pulled under the hospital canopy, cut the motor, and got out to help him as two orderlies walked out of the building. She provided his name, told them she'd park and be right back in.

As Fair leaned on the desk before the nurse could call them back, Dr. Wilson Anglin, who also lived in Crozet, came out.

"Fair, sit in a wheelchair. Make it easy on yourself. Come back with me. Knew you were coming. Good staff here."

"I am not sitting in a wheelchair."

"Bullhead." Wilson now walked beside him, his hand under Fair's elbow.

"I'm sure there are people here who need you more than I do," Fair replied to the man he had known socially for years.

"Actually, it's a light day but I fear not for long. People fly on these roads regardless of weather. You know, buddy, it's four-wheel drive, not four-wheel stop."

"That's the truth." Fair could see the room up ahead, glad he didn't have far to walk.

"Sharon." Wilson summoned the nurse. "Call X-ray. Help me get his shirt off."

Fair winced as Sharon pulled off his sweater then unbuttoned his shirt.

Red marks showed, two perfect hoofprints. Those would turn darker later.

Wilson carefully felt Fair's chest. "Take a deep breath." Fair did and it hurt.

"Another." Wilson continued to feel his chest. "You got nailed."

"I did. What do you think?"

"We'll take X-rays to be sure. Shouldn't be painful, as they can do it with you sitting. Okay, another deep breath. I see. Now lift your arms up."

"Uuuhh," Fair grunted.

"Down slowly. Okay, now bring them out to your side, out and up." He poked around. "I don't know as you have clean breaks. Need the X-rays to be certain, and as I am sure you are aware, it's more than one rib."

"Right." Fair grimaced but obeyed.

A wheelchair was brought out.

"I'm not getting in a wheelchair."

"Fair, you will get to the X-ray room a lot faster. Time. Time, buddy. Now get your ass in the chair."

Put that way, Fair sat down and was in and out of the X-ray room, impressive in itself, in twenty minutes. He couldn't believe how fast and careful those technicians were.

Wilson had the X-rays on his computer by the time Fair was back in the room. "Cracked but no complete breaks. Six ribs. Hell of a kick."

"What do I do?"

"We'll wrap you up. You can't take a shower for a few days. Go to your family doctor Monday, and then you should be able to take a shower. But I don't want you or Harry unwrapping you just yet. No lifting anything over a pound. Could you lift five pounds if you had to? You could, but don't. It might be painful to lie on your lower back to sleep, so put some pillows behind you and lean against them like you do when you read in bed, and you'll fall asleep eventually. I wouldn't bend over to touch your toes, either. All in all, you're in good shape. I didn't have to set anything. I'll give you a prescription for a mild sleeping pill. You need sleep. You'd be amazed how much healing happens when you sleep."

They could hear sirens outside at the front door.

"Think you'll have more patients. Can I go?"

"Yes." Wilson handed him the prescription.

The two men walked out as the front doors opened, a gurney was rolled in followed by another. Lots of blood. Wilson left Fair without a word as Fair looked at the two young men; must have been a car wreck. He was glad he wasn't an ER doctor.

When Harry came up to him, she, too, was mesmerized by the upsetting sight.

Once in the car, Harry was wet all over again from going out in the rain to get into the ER area, they sat for a minute as she turned on the heat.

"Those are two kids who will never be the same," Fair said.

"If they live," she said.

"Need a prescription." He would be glad for it, as it would lessen the pain, which he was determined not to show.

"Okay." She drove up one side of the mountain then down the other into Crozet.

Once at the pharmacy, Fair opened the car door, and winced.

"Honey, give me the prescription," Harry said. "Everybody knows me, and you, too. You stay in the car, I'll get it filled."

"The pharmacist knows us, but who knows what crap you have to produce to release the drug?" He looked at the prescription. "Not an opioid. Diclofenac."

"I'll get it. If worse comes to worst whoever is behind the counter can come out in the rain and you can give him or her your driver's license."

As it was, the owner, who knew everybody, gladly filled the prescription.

"Hey. Anything wrong with you?" a familiar voice sounded behind Harry.

Harry turned around. "Shifty, I'm fine. Fair got kicked. He'll be fine, too." She looked at him, a wry smile. "And what's wrong with you?"

"Bet you thought I was going to say I need Viagra." He was maybe sixty, just.

"Never occurred to me." She laughed at him.

"My diabetes. Doing good, but I gotta watch it. But I'm fine, really."

"Shifty, you're always fine." She paid for the drug package and as she walked out she spoke to the skinny fellow, "I'll tell Fair I saw you and you looked good."

He smiled.

Once at the old station wagon she got in the driver's seat, dropped the drug bag in his lap. "Shifty's in there getting his diabetes drug. You know, I always thought diabetics were fat. He's skinny as a rail."

"Takes some people that way. The body can't metabolize the sugar. It's funny about his nickname. He was out of high school by the time you and I were in it but his glory was still double-shifting old cars when the guys would race."

"Nicknames stick." Harry turned on the engine. "Okay. We're going home."

When the Haristeens reached the farm, Fair's big truck sat in front of their stable.

Cutting the motor, Harry remarked, "Paul and Tazio are good friends. That was nice of them."

With difficulty she helped Fair out of the station wagon, as his ordeal was telling on him. He was more tired than he cared to admit.

As the humans walked into the kitchen, the corgi jumped up and the huge Irish wolfhound came over, eager to love on their people.

"No jumping," she admonished them.

"I'll help you," Tucker, the corgi, promised.

Pirate, not quite two years old, observed, *"He's moving slow."*

Pewter, on the kitchen table, a fat gray cat, told him, *"He hurts."*

Mrs. Murphy, the tiger cat, told the animals, *"We'll have to take care of him."*

"Are you hungry?" Harry asked.

"Not so much. I'm tired."

"I'm hungry," Pewter declared.

The others agreed. Harry, looking down at four upturned faces, opened the cabinet door, took out cat and dog food. While up, she also removed a container of chicken soup from the refrigerator, pouring the contents in a pan, then fed the pets.

As the soup heated, Fair took a diclofenac, a sort of super Motrin. "Meant to tell you, while Wilson was poking and prodding, he told me about the Dunkin House, which he bought to remodel. He's done a lot of that. Obviously making money. Says he loves it."

"A relief from crisis, I would think."

"We all need things that rejuvenate us." He took a deep breath, and regretted it immediately.

"We do. That old place is haunted." She mentioned the gossip.

"Sweetie, every third house in Virginia is haunted." He smiled. "So many of our old homes still stand." He paused, began to rise.

"What do you want? This is almost ready."

"Tea. I feel like I'm going to fall asleep."

"Stay put. I'll do it. If the Dunkin House isn't haunted, it ought to be. Looks the part."

Quite so.

2

September 18, 2025

Thursday

"Slow down," Harry instructed her best friend since childhood, Susan Tucker.

The well-appointed new Highlander SUV slowed as they approached a true Victorian house. "Wonder what he paid?" Susan stopped. "Dr. Anglin has a knack for judging property. He probably got a good price for this."

"Fair said that, too. He's making calls today." Harry exhaled. "There's no point telling him to take it easy." She then opened the door. "Let's take a closer look."

The two women, coasting into early middle age, stepped out, followed by Tea Tucker, Harry's corgi, female, and her brother Owen, Susan's corgi.

"Doesn't it look scary to you?" Susan remarked.

"Well, it looks like it needs TLC, bushes trimmed, but it looks sturdy. Victorian architecture lends itself more to ghosts and goblins." Harry's voice lifted a bit.

Harry took a few steps closer, peering in the window. "It's been empty a couple of years. Enough to look forlorn. You'd think it would be more dusty."

"If Wilson, Dr. Anglin, I suppose I should be proper, I don't know him that well," Susan paused, "would let my Seeing Eye Rescue group use this for a fundraiser for Halloween, I could put ghosts at the windows."

"Corgis should be used as seeing eye dogs." Tucker meant that.

"We're too small. We can do support work." Owen proved more practical than his sister.

"What about Pirate?" Tucker mentioned her Irish wolfhound friend left at home with the cats, as Susan's car was a bit small for Pirate.

Then again, most vehicles were too small for Pirate.

"Best to find out how much cleaning you'd have to do." Harry had a vision of washing baseboards, vacuuming, keeping windows open during daylight hours to freshen the smell.

"We'll do what has to be done. Dr. Anglin gave generously to Ned's campaign." Susan's husband was the delegate to the statehouse from District 55. "I think he'll help."

"You know he has to make a good salary." Harry respected any physician working in the emergency room.

"Good enough, I guess." Susan looked up at the turrets. "I would reckon there are expenses in medicine of which we are unaware."

"No doubt, but at least you don't have to pay for that expensive hospital equipment. Don't doctors have to take long tests every ten years to stay in practice?"

"I think so." Susan studied the gray stone house. "We could put witches on the roof."

"We?"

"Harry, I need you. You always have good ideas and you're strong."

"There have to be strong women in your Seeing Eye Rescue group." Harry knew she couldn't wiggle out of this, but she could try.

"Not as strong as you. All that farming. You're tough." Susan paused. "Harry."

"Yes."

"Yes what?"

"I'll do it." Harry grinned. "If I don't, you'll send the Halloween ghouls after me."

"I knew you'd see reason. Oh, look again at this."

"Hmm." Harry studied the house. Which looked more downtrodden than frightening. "From the outside, I'd have at least two people inside, lights behind them, pulling a curtain back to peek outside. You have to have things, like Frankenstein, beckoning people to come in or somebody to woo them in."

"I like that."

"I should growl, that's better," Tucker said, but Harry and Susan heard only a little bark.

"Corgis aren't scary." Owen realized their breed was seen as adorable.

"We have to do something." The dog, low to the ground, pouted.

"Maybe they'll put us in costume. Like a ghost?" Owen, like Tucker, didn't want to miss anything. *"We'll figure it out. There has to be something we can do to frighten people."*

"We could carry human bones," Tucker said. Owen laughed. *"Like an old hand."*

Susan looked down. "Don't you love it when they make that puffer sound?"

"I do." Harry smiled. "Okay. Back to Halloween. We'll need some weird sounds. A false guillotine would be great. We could have a head on the floor. Have the blade fall. People come into the room and the head falls into the basket."

"Gross. But effective. The blade has to be fake. Too dangerous."

"What was it, seventeen thousand people killed by the guillotine?" Harry's brow wrinkled.

"Someone can be hanging, a dummy."

"Can't do that, Susan. Remember Chloe Sandford's father hanged himself in 2008. When he lost all his money."

"Oh." Susan's face fell. "You're right. You know, this is harder than I thought."

"Stuff will come to us. Plus Tazio will help." She named their architect friend. "Babs, now that she's retired from her radio show, she'll be full of ideas."

An unexpected stiff wind hit them while rattling the shutters.

"Cold." Susan headed back to the car, the dogs leading.

Harry, rubbing her arms, took another look then trotted back to the car. "What is it about wind that can make sixty degrees feel like the low fifties?"

"Feels divine on a hot day but otherwise it gets right to you." Susan turned on the motor. "If Dr. Anglin doesn't allow us to use his house, any suggestions?"

"Not a one."

"An old barn?" Susan thought out loud.

"Barns aren't scary. You don't think of ghosts. What about an old house on an estate?" Harry thought anything old was better than anything new.

"Aunt Tally's uncle's house has wear on it." Susan named Mim Sanborne's aunt, who had tipped over one hundred and who put a former political aid, hired from Richmond, in the old house.

"Haven't been over there in a couple of weeks. Better make a call. She's becoming more frail."

Susan sighed. "What a life."

Harry nodded. "Come on, Boss. Take me home. Want to have supper ready for Fair and I want to have a painkiller pill by the plate. If I bug him, he'll take it."

As they drove to Harry's farm, a simple clapboard house, Susan said, "It's not like Mim's horses to break bad."

Harry agreed. "I expect something went wrong."

"Me, too." Then she added, "What if we could figure out how to have a Headless Horseman?"

Perhaps.

3

September 19, 2025

Friday

Rolling over the low bridge, water below, Harry stopped on the other side to admire Carolyn Maki's pastures. Tidy, fences weed-whacked, the farm road, in the middle of this green heaven, was free of potholes. A depression or two gave her a little bump in the old Ford F-150, but what it really gave her was envy.

"Tucker, I have got to scrape our road, smooth it. The fillings in my teeth tell me I have to do this before winter comes."

"*What are fillings?*" Pirate, young, asked the corgi.

"*Humans get holes in their teeth. They fill this with metal or some kind of white stuff.*"

"*Eew. Sounds awful.*" Pirate sniffed.

"*Mother has good teeth. A few fillings. The only reason I know this is she mentions them every time she hits a bump.*"

"*Thieves. Criminals. Stay where you are!*" Jeb, Carolyn's Jack Russell, charged out of the barn as Harry parked.

"They're friends," Haley, the fourteen-year-old Lab, informed him. *"You've seen them before."*

"I'm defending Mother and the farm. I don't care who they are." The little fellow stood foursquare waiting for the truck door to open.

Haley offered no more details. As far as the yellow Lab was concerned, Jeb didn't have sense to come in out of the rain. Might as well save his energy.

Carolyn stepped out of the barn.

"Death to intruders!" Jeb jumped straight up three feet.

"Jeb, that's enough," Carolyn admonished her puppy.

She'd be admonishing him for years. Jeb would be a puppy until his muzzle was totally gray.

"You never know, Mother." The handsome little fellow stepped back.

The two friends hugged then Harry opened the door. Pirate stepped out and down. Harry lifted Tucker.

Jeb craned his neck to fully view the Irish wolfhound.

Haley, now with Tucker, sighed. *"The young."*

"Tell me about it. Pirate is calm but he can't put two nickels together."

The two older dogs followed the humans into the barn.

Jeb, realizing Pirate was close in age, decided this was better than hanging around with old pooches. *"I have a dead bird. Wanna see?"*

"Yes!" Pirate enthusiastically replied.

The little fireball blew past the humans and darted into a stall, emerging with a hard used toy that once looked like a duck.

As the two pups ran off, Jeb carrying the duck, the other two stayed in the center aisle.

"What do you think?" Carolyn switched on the lights, which she'd redesigned.

"Great lights." Harry thought the placement so practical. "Bet it cost plenty."

"Not as bad as you would think." Carolyn walked into a stall. "I couldn't take another winter in the dark. The center aisle was okay but dim. Couldn't see much in the stalls."

"Sure can now." Harry inhaled the perfume of fresh straw covering the stall floor.

"I don't know what's worse. Dark at 4:30 P.M. or wearing myself out at 8 P.M. doing another outside chore. Get blisters fixing fence boards even when I wear gloves."

"The dark, well, it doesn't depress me, but the sun goes down and I get sleepy. Don't forget the cold." Harry smiled. "You put on another layer. Summer, you can take off your clothes and still sweat buckets." She picked up some straw. "Good stuff."

Carolyn heard Jeb barking. "Well, here's to another adventure."

"Mom, it's Bumpy." Haley knew who it was walking toward the barn, not that Carolyn understood.

"Miss Maki, does this big dog bite?" Bumpy asked.

Harry hollered, "No. It's the Jack Russell you have to worry about."

The two friends walked out into the sunshine, where Jeb was guarding the farm. Pirate stood next to him. He was impressive.

"Pirate, come to me."

The sweet dog obeyed Harry.

"He's all right, Jeb," Carolyn said to the little fellow, reluctant to walk away. Bumpy, rough around the edges, was in his early fifties, a man who clearly worked outside.

"Bumpy, you remember Harry Haristeen."

"Fair's wife. I do." He slightly inclined his head to the lady.

"Haven't seen you in a long time," Harry replied.

"Miss Maki, I could paint your shed. Paint the back fences. It helps hold off the weather damage."

Carolyn hesitated. "When can you start?"

"Monday. Finishing up a little job at Basic Necessities, back parking."

"Fifteen dollars an hour. I'll get the paint. Will take two coats."

"Yes, Ma'am." He smiled reflexively. "Monday. I'm clean, Miss Maki. I'll do a good job."

Then he walked to his truck, newer than Harry's 1970s Ford. His was a 1984 Chevy with a 454 engine.

The dogs and humans watched him go down the drive.

"Think he can do it?" Harry asked.

"I think he can. He's been sober three months now, so I hear." She whistled for Jeb, who was leading Pirate into the woods at the bottom of a hill. "Does anyone ever ask Fair if he's Harry's husband?" She laughed.

"I don't know. I'll have to ask him." Harry smiled. "I don't take offense. Especially from Bumpy. I heard he did some remodeling work. Most people won't take a chance on him."

Jeb ran up.

Haley looked down. "*Don't go off.*"

"*I want to show Pirate rabbit dens,*" came the quick reply.

"*He has plenty of rabbit dens at home. Stick with him, she's probably going to go into the house. Treats.*"

"*Really?*" The bright dog lit up.

"*You only get them if you behave.*" Haley had Jeb's number.

As Harry and Carolyn walked to the house built in the 1830s, Harry told her about Fair's ribs.

"How is he today?" Carolyn asked.

"Bullheaded."

"Back at work?"

Harry threw up her hands. "Yes, he can visit patients but he can't bend over and lift their legs up. Can't carry bags of grain, either."

Carolyn opened the door. All the dogs went in first. The two sat at a cozy table off the kitchen. Carolyn had brought iced tea plus snacks. They caught up.

"Don't let me forget the horse feed for the older horses. Fair said to try it."

"Great."

Harry's mind drifted back to Bumpy. "I haven't seen Bumpy, I don't know, in a year. Thinking about it because you gave him a big job."

"I'll buy the paint myself tomorrow. If I sent him out, no one would give it to him."

"Would he buy cheap stuff, charge you for more expensive brands?"

"No. But no one trusts him. I don't feel like making a lot of calls. Easier for me to get the stuff. Bumpy, loaded, lost his temper in the hardware store. They threw him out. That's when he went into rehab again. Mmm, maybe six months ago. I want to believe he's clean; if not, I'll have gallons of paint on my hands."

"The hardware store looks great. New owners transformed it." Harry liked the place and the owner.

"Yes, it does. The owner said he was so glad Wilson Anglin has been remodeling houses as he buys a lot of stuff at the store."

"Wilson worked on Fair."

"I guess Bumpy shows up in there regularly, too." Carolyn tried to ignore the Jack Russell's imploring eyes. "You know he has good hand skills, just blew up his life. They say three times is the charm. That's three for him." Carolyn didn't understand addiction but then who does? "Maybe I'm talking about this hoping he really is okay, now thinking about those gallons of paint."

"I expect any ER doctor has regulars. Drunks. Drug addicts. People with mental problems and nowhere to go. Dr. Anglin has to know Bumpy's history. Has probably treated him. And correct me if I'm wrong, doesn't ER staff have to take anyone who walks in?"

"They do," Carolyn responded, handing out treats, which she had on her plate. "We pay for it." She also had biscotti for Harry and herself.

"Carolyn, we'll pay one way or another." Harry grinned. "Were you going to eat those?"

Carolyn handed her one. "Those imploring eyes distract me."

The biscotti disappeared. The iced tea was refilled. Harry enjoyed a delightful visit with an old friend. Time goes by so quickly in the company of a good friend.

Walking back to the truck, she dropped down the tailgate, climbed up, carried the horse feed to the edge. Carolyn brought it down.

"Have to see how this picks up my golden oldies."

Harry jumped down, lifted up the tailgate. "Thinking about what you said about the ER. Can we solve the problem of the homeless or those people who show up at the ER?"

"I don't know. I expect we don't know the half of it."

4

September 20, 2025

Saturday

Harry scrubbed the last water bucket, hanging it back in the stall. The cats, up in the hayloft, looked out the back upper open doors mirroring the front. These doors helped air flow in the warm months, allowing hay to be stored. Harry had an old hay elevator. She'd put her square bales on it and push it upward. Worked. Anything was better than actually throwing the hay bales.

Mrs. Murphy and Pewter stared out at the cut fields, the hay now off those fields behind them. The entire second story of the barn was filled, a walkway through the center, a crossways also. It helped if a human could get in the hay from time to time. As it was, a black snake was in there on mouse patrol.

The opossum, Simon, also lived up there. Late afternoon and Simon, a touch overweight, was sound asleep on his old saddle pad.

"*He snores,*" Pewter complained.

"Not as bad as Tucker," Mrs. Murphy replied. *"I love him, but sleeping close to him keeps me awake."*

The two observed the crows sitting in the trees alongside the pastures, bands of hard woods beyond that. The Blue Ridge base touched the back of the property. The swells announcing the higher land behind it were covered in lots of black walnut. Susan owned all that, having been willed it by her uncle, who had been a monk.

"Crows are happy birds," Mrs. Murphy noted.

"I think most birds are. Except blue jays. That terrible jay nesting by the house, that's the worst."

"He is a smart-ass," Mrs. Murphy agreed.

"Dust. Someone's coming."

Tucker and Pirate rushed out of the barn to announce the vehicle, which Tucker knew to be Susan's. The corgi could recognize the tire tread sounds even from the barn.

Harry wiped her hands on her jeans, walking outside.

The cats crossed the wide hayloft, reached the ladder nailed to the side of the wall by the office door, turned around, sunk their claws in, and backed down. They, too, walked outside.

"What a beautiful day." Susan hugged Harry, greeting her.

"Is. Just finished my last chores. It's the day to scrub the water buckets. Gets easier as the heat subsides. Got to do it every day in high summer."

"It's how you keep your figure."

"Susan, that's one way to look at it."

"Was driving around. Owen, wait a minute." Her corgi was barking in the car, so she opened the door.

The dogs rapturously greeted one another. The cats were polite but not rapturous.

"How many miles on this car?" Harry always wanted to know mileage, if people liked their cars. If it had wheels, she was interested.

"Can you believe I've put eighteen thousand miles on it this year alone? It's all that damn driving to Richmond."

"Well, it is one hundred miles one way. That adds up. The apartment you and Ned have there is nice."

"You flatter me."

"You have a gift for decorating. I really don't. The only reason my house looks decent is after I got married you took pity on me and decorated."

"Oh, Harry," Susan smiled. "You were lucky to inherit the house from Mom and Dad. Who could afford a farm this size today? Ned and I were talking about that last night. We couldn't buy our house today, and we aren't poor."

"I keep thinking this will end. All this rising cost, inflation." Harry sighed. "I don't understand the economy but I sure understand paying bills."

"Hear, hear."

"Standing out here blabbing. Want a drink? Anything to eat?" Harry offered her childhood friend.

"Actually, Harry, if you have an iced tea, I would like it. Then I thought maybe we could ride over to the old Dunkin House."

"Sure. Getting more ideas?"

Susan beamed. "I am actually, for which I can thank my wonderful husband."

"I expect he's under the gun," Harry noted as Ned Tucker was the representative from the 55th district to the state House of Delegates.

"Big funding cuts. He says he doesn't see a way out, but he would have chosen different targets than our governor. But that's what makes a horse race."

"Glad I'm not the one cutting the funding. Our library's going to get it. The rural libraries will all be slammed. We've got a good library." Harry continued, "That started at the national level. And all those government workers who lost their jobs. Virginia is top heavy with government workers."

"This gets me to my Seeing Eye Rescue fundraiser. With all this economic stress, people will give less. I understand that. Anyway, I've been thinking more about the haunted house."

"Okay." Harry knew she was going to be doing more than just helping.

"Are you really willing to be the Headless Horseman? I know that will be a big hit."

"If we can figure it out. If Dr. Anglin will let us use the house."

"That's where my husband comes in. He spoke to Wilson. They are on a committee to create more halfway houses for those people winding up in the ER over and over again for drug use; mostly drug use, but Ned said we've got some pretty stubborn alcoholics, too. Maybe I shouldn't say stubborn. But they stop drinking then start again. Some never stop."

Harry sipped her tea; she'd poured herself a glass, too, as Susan talked about her idea and Dr. Anglin agreeing to allow them to use the Dunkin House.

"You're so big, you could scare people without a costume," Pewter told Pirate.

"I don't want to scare anybody," the Irish wolfhound stated.

"I could be a demon." Tucker thought. *"You know who would be great? Jeb. He's a little devil."* That Jack Russell could create havoc.

"Now, there's an idea," Pewter agreed, for she had observed the dog on the few times she'd been in the car when Harry had driven over to Carolyn's. She much preferred Haley, whom she thought sensible like herself.

Harry picked up the glasses, putting them in the sink.

"Come on. Let's drive over there." Susan, refreshed, looked down at her corgi and Tucker, littermates. "We can take the dogs, including Pirate. I made room."

Within twenty minutes, driving slow, they pulled onto a side street in Crozet. The Victorian house was bathed in late-afternoon light. Cars were parked along the street. The front door was open.

Susan, taking the lead, walked up the sidewalk, dogs and Harry in tow. "Anyone home?"

"Yeah," came a man's voice.

"Bumpy." Susan recognized that voice.

Harry smiled at him. "Seeing you again is good luck."

He looked down. "Well, I don't know about that."

"Come on," Tucker urged her companions. *"Let's explore."*

As the three trotted down the wide hallway. Harry called out, "Hey."

Bumpy shrugged. "Can't hurt nothin'."

"Dr. Anglin said we could use his house to raise funds for Seeing Eye Rescue. For Halloween."

"Be good. Kinda creepy." He nodded.

"Dark." Susan glanced around. "Going to take some time for Dr. Anglin to really get it shiny."

"Yeah. At least the plumbing still works. He turned the power back on. Needs work. But Mac and me," he gestured to a heavyset man coming out of one of the back rooms, "are moving out some old furniture. Not much of it."

"Do you mind if we stick our heads in the downstairs rooms?" Susan inquired.

"No. Go ahead," Bumpy agreed. "Mac, is there anything left upstairs?"

"No. Bedrooms. No chairs even."

Two women, wearing scarves over their heads, came down the steps. Each carried a large rolled-up bag that looked like a sleeping bag. One was older, prodding the younger. They said nothing to Bumpy, averting their faces from Harry and Susan. Bumpy paid them no mind.

Harry and Susan walked down the hallway. A room that was an empty library could have been lovely. A library without books is sad. They walked back to the kitchen. No stove. Sink was one of the old double high sinks. Water still ran. Then they poked their heads into more bare rooms, one of which had to be the formal sitting room. Finally they reached the ballroom, which had an upstairs mini platform, iron railing, for an orchestra.

"Must have been grand once upon a time." Harry imagined musicians up there.

"We can use it. We can have an ongoing ball, the dancers being witches, warlocks, you name it. Oh, this is perfect."

"Susan, who are you going to get to do all this stuff? We have a month."

"Leave it to me. I'm calling in all my favors. I am determined to raise a bundle. Why, we can even raise the dead."

"Susan." Harry laughed at her just as the three dogs came into the ballroom.

"We met some rats. They said people come in and out of here."

Harry and Susan didn't understand a word.

The little crew walked out of the back, remembering the back door, then around the house to the front.

"We could hide ghosts in these bushes," Harry suggested.

"No. The ghosts have to be in the upstairs windows."

"Right." Harry did think it a better idea.

Walking around to the front, Bumpy and Mac carried an old trunk to the back of Bumpy's truck.

"Thanks." Susan then asked, "Anyone live here that you know about?"

Mac answered. "Sometimes people down on their luck would stay here. No one really lived here. No electricity. No heat."

"Dr. Anglin uses Mac and me to clean out the houses he buys and rents out or sells. Do repair work, too. I'd really like to work on this. They don't build 'em like this anymore," Bumpy enthused.

"You're sure right about that," Susan agreed.

Back in the car, the two drove back into town, which took all of five minutes.

Susan took the road to pass Chiles Orchard. "Ever hear how Bumpy got his name?"

"No."

"I think his real name is Jonathan Haden. He's had so many ups and downs, he earned his nickname, *Bumpy*.

"No one ever thinks addiction will happen to them. You'd be surprised how many secret alcoholics there are in the statehouse. Probably a few druggies, too. But I expect those druggies have a prescription from a doctor."

"They'll be the first ones to vote against measures to help people," Harry, a bitter note in her voice, replied.

"It's one way to look clean, I suppose. Ned works with everyone but he has said a couple times that drinking is part of the job. I mean, if you want it to be. All those meetings, dinners, fundraisers."

"How does he do it?" Harry admired Ned.

"Part of the process, he says. It's the ones caught up in rigid ideology who get really stuck. No ability to compromise, and all government is compromise."

"Susan, this is a terrible thing to say, but I don't care about politics anymore. I care about Ned, don't get me wrong, but as far as I'm concerned, everyone else in politics can go to hell. My energy is going toward my farm, my husband, my friends, and those causes in which I believe. I look at these bloviating toads, and that's an insult to toads, and I figure whatever happens to them, they deserve."

"Now, Harry." Susan was the granddaughter of a governor as well as married to a state representative.

"Mom's being crabby," Tucker remarked.

"Maybe she has a reason." Pirate loved his mother.

"You're probably right, Susan, but I'm tired. Just so tired. On the other hand, I'm glad we got to peek inside the Dunkin House. We can scare people."

"Let's hope we scare some money out of them."

A happy thought.

5

September 21, 2025

Sunday

Harry climbed up into her husband's big dually. Her old Volvo station wagon was in the shop. It needed a new battery.

"Ugh." She grabbed the sidebar on the outside of the door, put her foot on the small, lowered step, and swung herself up. "Not easy in a skirt."

Fair laughed. "No, but fun to watch. Are you hungry?"

"Not yet. I do think Reverend Jones gives the best sermons. He used the equinox tomorrow, the coming of fall then winter as his starting point. Given that most of us have large suburban yards or, like us, a real farm, we have to prepare. And now I'm thinking about preparing spiritually. The Romans thought those days had a spiritual importance."

"Yes. For me, as you know, it's a bit easier, although some people feed too much pellets, causing colic. New people."

"Right. New horses. They often don't realize horses like cool weather. Maybe not the bitter cold, but low fifties, high forties, perks them right up. Say, anything new about Silver Silence?"

"Paul says he's fine as long as Kyle isn't near him. Breeding will pick up after January. Let's hope things settle down."

"Your ribs are healing fast."

He smiled. "I have somewhat listened to Wilson Anglin. Home?"

"Let me call Carolyn to see if we can drop by. I want to see what she's done in her stable."

Harry fetched her cellphone out of the center console, hit the number for Carolyn, which she had on speed dial. "Maki, we're just leaving St. Luke's. Might we drop by? I'd like Fair to see what you've done. And if it isn't convenient, forgive me for calling on short notice."

"Well, did you pray for me?" Carolyn laughed.

"No but I prayed for Jeb and Haley and for your patience."

"Good. I need all the help I can get. Sure, come on by."

Twenty minutes later the Haristeens bumped down the long farm road, parking by the house, which was across from the barn. Bumpy's old truck was parked by the big shed. One side had already been painted.

"Boy, he's working fast. I told you we ran into Bumpy and Mac yesterday."

"Did." Fair cut the motor, hurried around to lift Harry down. "Easier."

"You can always lift me."

Carolyn emerged from the barn, flanked by Haley and Jeb. "I hardly ever see you dressed up."

"Well?"

"You look very nice."

"How come your dogs didn't notice us?" Harry was curious.

"They were chasing mice. Big deal."

"I terrified them. I would have caught them but they had a hidey-hole in the back stall," Jeb bragged.

Haley, next to Carolyn, said nothing.

"Bumpy came a day early. Good." Harry walked into the barn with Carolyn, Fair, and the dogs.

"Surprised me but said he was getting more work on restoring houses. It's a good thing I get up early. He pulled in at six-thirty. So, Fair, I rethought my lighting." She flicked on the overhead lights.

"I see." He scanned the center aisle then the stalls. "Ahh, you've got a dimmer."

Her hand on the switch, she bumped up the brightness. "Max."

"This will be such a help in the winter. I wish more people paid attention to the lighting. Makes it easier for me. Who did the work?"

"Carsell Lighting," she answered. "We spent a lot of time going over what I wanted in the barn. As to the stall, Kit Carsell suggested a center bulb. Then far smaller ones in the corners. This way I can see everything. I just assumed we'd up the wattage with a big bulb covered by wire in the center. Anyway, the real test will be on December twenty-first."

"Well, tomorrow's the fall equinox, so we have three months." Harry admired the lighting.

"The other thing is, I put up a railing along the hayloft except for where the ladder is. I have to throw down over the ladder, but it's safer. As you know I fell out of my hayloft. Never again."

"You were lucky you didn't break every bone in your legs and pelvis. Was a miracle." Harry shuddered.

"What was a miracle was I landed on my feet but it drove the bone up. Lost two inches in my height." Carolyn would never forget the moment she tipped over.

A simple farm accident, although the results of farm accidents are never simple, and they are common.

"Sometimes I wonder what would happen if my hand got caught in the twine. I'd go over with it." Harry could toss her haybales right into each stall. Convenient, but could be tricky.

"I can show you how I've helped in the garden." Jeb wiggled his butt.

"You haven't helped." Haley looked down at Jeb, who had dug a lot of holes in a short time this morning.

"Thanks for letting us stop by." Harry really liked the new setup.

"You're here. Come on and look at the big shed, the run-in shed."

"Sure." The two followed Carolyn to the side of the shed facing the farm road.

"Just painted it the same color. White. Helps in the summers reflecting the light a bit. The problem with white is you have to repaint more frequently, as you know." Carolyn noted how tidy the work was, no big spills.

"I've always admired the green barns and outbuildings at Montpelier, but like you we keep stuff white." Harry looked up. "All that wood trim, so tidy and white."

"I don't hear Bumpy. Let's walk around the back." Carolyn reached the other side of the useful run-in shed.

Fair, now standing next to her, observed the ladder still in place.

"Maybe he is inside the shed," Carolyn thought out loud.

"You'd think he'd hear us." Harry peeped inside the roomy shed.

Three horses could fit in with no problem. Four if they got along. A run-in shed is golden in bad weather.

"Bumpy," Carolyn called out.

No response.

Jeb and Haley, noses down, began to follow a line of scent. Harry squinted to watch them.

"Carolyn, the grass is tamped down a bit."

Both Carolyn and Fair focused on what looked like drag marks. Quietly the three humans followed the dogs.

"Dead!" Jeb barked, quite thrilled with himself.

Haley, no talk, walked a bit faster until coming upon Bumpy, on his back, eyes closed. Bumpy had seen his last fall equinox.

Carolyn, in front, saw him first. "Bumpy!"

Fair, behind her, knelt down to take a pulse. "Gone."

"He's clutching his paintbrush." Harry was horrified, as when Fair reached for his hand, Bumpy's head flopped a bit to the side.

Carolyn studied the body, shocked though she was, she could keep thinking. "Not a mark on him."

Fair examined Bumpy closely. "I don't see anything. If he'd been choked, there'd be fingerprints on his throat, some kind of red mark, plus his eyes would be bloodshot. I see no blood anywhere. My guess is a massive heart attack." He paused. "That doesn't explain the drag marks."

Jeb bragged, *"If there were blood, I'd know."*

"Jeb, shut up," Haley grumbled. *"You've never seen a dead human before."*

"Yes, I have. I have, too. On Mother's TV." The little fellow had raised his voice.

"Jeb, I mean it. Shut up. The humans are terribly upset. You aren't helping."

Jeb made a face, that Jack Russell I-can't-stand-you-right-now face, but he did shut up.

"Should we turn him over?" Harry asked. "Just in case we see signs of life. Or at least turn him over onto his side?"

"Honey, it won't do any good. He's gone." Fair stood up. "Not a mark that I can see."

"Stroke." Harry spoke without thinking.

Carolyn pointed to the grass. "Drag marks, remember?"

"You're right." An involuntary shiver ran over Harry as the situation was becoming more clear. He may not have died of natural causes.

"It doesn't look as though he struggled. Carolyn, you didn't hear a truck or car?"

"No. You are the only people who have driven up here."

"So someone walked in from the road." Fair looked out onto the farm road.

"Maybe," Carolyn answered. "Someone could have come over the ridge or even up from far back through that old orchard." She paused, shaken. "I figure whoever did this knew the territory."

"And knew Bumpy." Harry finished Carolyn's thought.

"He'd screwed up a lot in life," Carolyn added. "Not that he deserved to be killed. Poor Bumpy. What a way to have your life end."

"Murder," Fair said low.

The three of them looked at one another.

Jeb and Haley carefully sniffed the fresh corpse. They could smell the fading scent of human male, a slight cologne scent under Bumpy's left arm.

"Whoever did this was strong enough to move him," Harry said.

"No sign of struggle. No marks on his knuckles. No torn clothing." Fair again knelt down. "He knew his killer."

6

September 22, 2025

Monday, First day of Rosh Hashanah

Standing by the back door of Cynthia Cooper's old farmhouse, Harry swept her arm toward the door. "Masses of stargazer lilies on either side. It's sunny here and well drained."

Cooper, as she was usually known, or as Coop, stared down. "Are they hard to grow?"

"No. The bulbs are big. We need to plant them deep."

"How deep?"

"I'd say eight inches. This is the best time to plant. I brought my shovel and edger. So let me edge this. Herb's people used to have little shrubs."

"He mentioned that when I bought the place. I'm no good at landscaping. I have no ideas. If I have ideas, I don't know how to make them happen."

"That's why I'm your neighbor." Harry looked to see her dogs racing around the family plot, going back to Monroe's time. "Hey. Hey, you two, calm down."

Mrs. Murphy and Pewter, by the two women's feet, observed the wild, happy dogs.

"Fat chance. Tucker loves graveyards." Pewter sniffed.

"So many bunnies visit the graveyards. I think that's it." Mrs. Murphy took a guess.

The cats and dogs rode with Harry in the old Ford truck even though the properties touched each other. As this was the country the drive from Harry's house to Cooper's covered two miles. The two could walk to each other's houses, but that covered three-quarters of a mile and one had to cross the fast-moving stream dividing the properties. If it had rained, that was difficult. Driving was better.

Harry fished a spool of twine out of her back pocket. "Here. Walk this to the corner of your house. I'll hold the end."

"Why am I walking string?"

"Because we are going to stake it down. The line will be straight. I need straight." She fished two little round twigs, roughly the size of Popsicle sticks, from her other pocket.

Cooper did as she was told, placing the twig in the ground as Harry did the same on her end. Cooper then looked up.

"Thanks."

Harry had handed her a penknife to cut the string. "When are you going to learn to carry a penknife? You can't live in the country without a pocketknife of some kind."

"All right. All right." Cooper smiled at her neighbor.

The tall, slender, blonde woman was a deputy with the sheriff's department. She had moved here, taking a job as a young woman in the county's department. She worked her way up to deputy. She had rented the Jones family's house, as the good reverend lived in the beautiful house behind St. Luke's Church. Over the years she improved the property, tended the graveyard. Harry helped with this as well as teaching her how to use different types of mowers and urging her to buy a small John Deere tractor, small as in a 25 horsepower. Harry and Fair owned two tractors. One a powerful 125 horsepower, and the other a smaller 80 horsepower. They could and did drive over to do bigger chores for Cooper, who in turn would let them use the little tractor. Not that it was truly little. But compared to the Haristeen tractors with their many implements, the 25 horsepower was modest yet so very useful. It had a short turning radius, proved good on gas, and could mow a big patch if one was inclined to do so.

The whirr of the edger made the blue jays in the trees by the house squawk.

"*It's bad enough I have to put up with that hateful blue jay at our house. Now I have to hear them here,*" Pewter grumbled.

Mrs. Murphy agreed. "*Bossy birds.*"

Harry finished her straight line on the one side of the door. "Let's do this first then we can do your south side. You've got that wonderful skylight in the kitchen on the south side. Perfect in winter."

"I haven't done much to the old homeplace but wanted more light, especially in the kitchen," the tall woman replied. "The longer I live on this land and in that house, the more I love it."

"Know what you mean." Harry started digging, so Cooper picked up her spade and imitated her neighbor.

"Anything I should do?"

"Just turn the soil over. We'll use hand claws to get it as we want, put the bulbs in, then pull earth back over. It's good here. Good soil is a form of gold." Harry spoke like a true farmer.

"Smells wonderful."

"*Let's sneak into the house,*" Pewter suggested.

"*Okay.*" Mrs. Murphy liked Coop's kitchen. The deputy had treats.

As the humans concentrated on the dirt, the bulbs in a big bag on the ground, the two cats walked to the back door, where Pewter wedged her paw behind the screen door. It opened just enough for the two cats to slip into the open kitchen.

"How many dead bodies do you see? I thought of that yesterday after we found Bumpy. Would it be just another day's work for you?" Harry asked, as moving dirt made her think of graves, death. "You came after Carolyn called the department."

"No. I do see a fair amount of death. I wonder what their last moments were."

"Yeah." Harry had dug a trench parallel to the edge of the flower bed. She knelt down to place the bulbs then pull the moist dirt over them.

"You're fast." Cooper worked on the back trench.

"Farm girl," Harry simply replied. "Any more information on Bumpy?"

"No. Sheriff and I got to you as fast as we could. Bumpy was still warm but cooling. We sent the body back, obviously. You know the rest of the team was there in twenty minutes. When I took your statements I was impressed with how calm and observant you all were."

"Thanks. He owe his drug dealer?" Harry responded.

"They say he was clean. Sheriff Shaw said Bumpy was a regular at Augusta's emergency room. He thought his last rehab visit made a big difference."

"Like how regular?" Harry's mind was beginning to whirr.

"Mmm, last time six months ago. He was recommended to rehab again. His third time, but seemed clean. We'll know more after his autopsy, but Rick," Cooper called her boss by his first name, "said he didn't look like he was on anything."

"I guess he'd seen everything."

"Sort of, but many times we know because of the position of the body. Fentanyl deaths, usually young men, sitting or slumped over or in bed. Sniffed it at a party. Bumpy wasn't on that stuff. He'd get arrested for coke. Uppers," Cooper informed her.

"Carolyn allowed as he was a good worker. He came early, as he told her he'd gotten more work redoing a house bought for rent. Maybe he was really coming back."

"If you can get a good renter for your property, it's a nice stream of money each month. Of course, one needs to keep the place up.

Carolyn said Bumpy was good at that. Could fix anything. She has a house next to her, up by the ridge. He got it in shape."

"I asked her if he ever stole anything," Harry said.

Cooper's eyebrows rose. "And?"

"No. She said the problem she had with him over the years was he'd start a project then disappear or show up days later."

"I don't have any ideas. The ladder wasn't moved. There was no struggle. He wasn't even dirty, other than some paint on his T-shirt. Whoever dragged him away from the shed must have been fairly strong.

"Again, we'll know more after the autopsy. We've had two murders this year. Those were domestic. When you think about it, this place is safe to live in comparatively."

"Until it's you." Harry stood up. "Okay, next side."

As Harry double-checked the straight line and fired up the edger, they both heard noise from the kitchen. Harry cut the motor.

"Stinkers." She opened the back screened door, Cooper in tow.

There, so innocent, sat Mrs. Murphy and Pewter on the floor by the table, one chair overturned.

"Who did this?"

Not a peep.

"All right, you two, outside," Harry commanded.

"Oh, let me give them a treat. I bet that's why they came in." Cooper, a big softie, opened a cupboard door, pulling out delicious munchies.

"*Thank you. You are so pretty,*" Pewter meowed.

"*Gilding the lily.*" Mrs. Murphy daintily took her treats.

"*Well, they're planting lilies.*" Pewter crunched the tidbit in her mouth.

"Coop, you don't have to spoil my cats." Harry watched her two felines rub on Cooper's long legs.

"Isn't it you who tells me, what's the point of loving something if you don't spoil them? Look how happy they are."

Blushing a bit, Harry opened the back door to the porch; almost all the old farmhouses had a back porch. "All right. Out."

Very slowly the two cats left the kitchen.

The humans returned to their planting.

As they finished the south side, the two dogs raced up.

"*The graveyard has had everybody,*" Tucker enthused. "*Rabbits, raccoons, possums. Everybody had visited the place.*"

"*We had treats.*" Pewter puffed up.

"*I want some.*" Tucker ran to the door, followed by the giant dog.

"*Maybe you'll get some and maybe you won't.*" Pewter tormented the dogs.

"*How'd you get some?*" Pirate asked.

"*Opened the door and waited them out.*" Mrs. Murphy then gave Pewter credit. "*Was her idea.*"

Harry and Cooper finished planting fifty bulbs. Harry had bought plenty, and when the stargazer lilies bloomed they'd be spectacular. As long as they were well tended, watered, they'd multiply. Harry loved lilies, all lilies, but she thought Cooper could use a pop of color and this would do it. The two put their tools away and walked into the house, the dogs shooting in.

Cooper poured a cold co-cola for Harry. "Caffeine." She then opened the cabinet cupboard and gave the dogs treats, plus more for the kitties.

"You are such a sweetheart to keep treats for my beggars," Harry thanked her.

"I enjoy them. I'd like some pets of my own but my hours are so terrible. I can't keep a dog or cat locked up all day. It isn't right."

"Well, maybe some kitty or pup will walk into your life; I can help. They can stay with me and you can pick them up when you come home."

"That's a lovely offer. If I find a dog or cat or they find me, I'll remember that."

"This is good and cold." Harry drank more co-cola.

"I'm drinking Assam tea. Got hooked."

"Do you think Bumpy's murder will be top priority?" Harry changed the subject.

"For now. And it is odd. My hunch is he owed someone money. Guys like Bumpy usually do."

"Would he threaten a dealer? Like expose him?"

"I doubt it. He could be unwittingly endangering a dealer but a threat would be a death sentence," Cooper remarked.

"But that's just it. He is dead. He was murdered."

7

September 23, 2025

Tuesday, Second day of Rosh Hashanah

"Do you feel people come of their own free will?" Cooper asked the woman in charge of the rehab center.

"Yes. As you know, you can't place them in rehab. All you can do is arrest them. The various ER doctors at UVA, Augusta, and Martha Jefferson all recommend us. We, as you know, deal with individuals with multiple relapses." She sat across from the woman, each in a comfortable chair in Shauna Grayson's small office at Bootstraps.

"How many times did Bumpy reside here?"

"During my tenure, three times in the last two years. I went over his records, of course, he was here in 2022, when William Sarceran was director. He's now director at Richmond Hope Rehab."

"Thanks. I'll track him down."

"No need, I'll give you his information. He'll want to help. We know our people, I don't think of them as patients, can live volatile lives, depressed lives, but they're rarely murdered." Shauna looked pained. "An awful way to die."

"Yes. What did you think of Mr. Haden?"

"First off, Deputy, I am not a doctor but I do believe based on my work that all these illegal substances change people's brains, change the pathways to pleasure in the brain, to put it in simple terms. Once someone comes off OxyContin, say, they may not experience happiness. They may feel flat. For many that's worse than courting an overdose."

"I believe there is some truth to that. As a law enforcement officer, I see so much of this. I know I can't change anyone. But each time I arrest the same individual, I lose hope for them. It's a short step from getting high to losing your job, your marriage, if you have one, your money. And then it can be a short step to criminal activity."

"Bumpy, he'll always be Bumpy to me, was clean, I assure you that. He'd talk about it in our group talks. Some people won't participate in group therapy, but they'll talk one-on-one. He had no problem with talking. As you probably know, he was highly skilled."

"I do." Cooper kept making notes in her notebook, a journalist's notebook, the paper lined.

"When he left here the last time, he was upbeat, had work repairing, remodeling houses. And he said the pay was good."

"Did he come back to visit?"

"He did. He'd bring pizza for everyone. Encouraged our people to stick it out, shout, even sing, but get it out. Find out you aren't alone. He was very convincing."

"You thought he was a good guy?"

Shauna Grayson smiled, nodding. "I did. His murder is a terrible shock."

"Do you think he had relapsed?"

A long silence followed this. "No. Perhaps that's overly hopeful but he worked so hard to clean himself up and this was the longest time, no arrests. No sleeping rough or in empty houses. That was before my time. But I don't think he was back on ketamine, OxyContin, fentanyl, you name it." She paused. "He did mention that sometimes he'd sleep in houses he was working on. He needed to save money so he could rent a place, if someone would rent to him. His reputation wasn't helpful."

"Any idea why he would be killed?"

Shauna breathed in, the light coming from the windows now shining in her eyes. She stood up, moved her chair a bit, sat down again.

"Deputy, he wasn't inclined to women problems. If he was, we never saw it here and he never spoke of women except to say he blew up his engagement eight years ago. As for money, he did owe money. He was afraid about it and that was one of the reasons he was happy about getting a job where he could use his building skills. Decent money, he would say. He wanted to pay off his debts. He'd borrowed too much from family and friends over the years."

"Another common thread with addicts," Cooper simply stated.

"Yes. One of his sorrows was that his mother died before he was clean. He wanted to pay her back."

"Did he ever discuss the size of these debts?"

"No."

"Out of curiosity, why did you go into this line of work?"

She smiled. She was maybe thirty-five at most. Attractive. Cooper was curious, for Shauna surely had other options.

"Oh," she paused, "I had no direction in college. I was at Tech. Lots of friends. Lots of parties. Lots of drugs. I had the sense to see what drugs were doing to some of my friends. I stopped partying. I'd see the gang at football games, basketball. To make a long story short, one of those friends OD'd. It hit me hard. I went into psychology. Here I am." She laughed lightly, a bit self-conscious. "Obviously, I'll never make money. I like to think I'm doing some good."

Cooper, liking the woman, stated, "I'm sure you are." She

handed Shauna her card. "If anything occurs to you, call me. Don't hesitate."

"Let me give you William Sarceran's number at Richmond Hope." She rose, pulled up the information on her computer, writing it on a light blue notepad, "Bootstraps" printed across the top. "He's a good guy. He'll be happy to help, too. We have three locations. The organization is familiar with Bumpy's record."

Driving away from Bootstraps, Cooper thought the county was lucky to have such an organization.

Whatever drove people into relapse wasn't incompetence at Bootstraps.

8

September 24, 2025

Wednesday

On Susan's worktable in her special room at the back of the house, she had a large white heavy paper, not as heavy as cardboard but heavier than typing paper. On this, she had carefully drawn the Dunkin House's interior, the first floor and, above it, the second floor. She'd also indicated where the road was and where she thought parking could be organized.

Harry, Tucker, Mrs. Murphy, and Pewter were at or under the table. Susan was so used to Harry's animals. Tucker liked playing with her brother, Owen. Pirate liked it, too, but he was so big, each time he turned around, the two corgis were already chasing each other yards away. Always a good sport, the big fellow would be upon them in four strides. Along with rolling around on the ground, there was chat.

"*I hope they stay outside. Those dogs' voices grate on my nerves.*" Pewter batted at the pencil in Harry's hand.

"Pewter."

"*I'm helping.*" But she did take her paw off the pencil.

"How did you do this? We didn't take measurements," Harry asked.

"I have a good eye. For instance, the ballroom is about two times the length of our garage and two widths, too. It's not exact but enough so we can plan."

"As in what to do with each room."

Susan hovered over the paper. "And how many people can we move through it at any given time. You know the fire department will be on our butts."

"Forgot about that." Harry tapped the pencil on Pewter's butt. "That's why you're such a good organizer. You think of these things."

"I try. Okay, we can have people walk around the outside of the house first. We'll have ghosts with lanterns at the window, maybe people dressed in costumes from different times. I'm pretty sure the Dunkin House was built around 1870—I'll check at the courthouse—so we could have late–eighteenth century attire, World War I, flappers, you get the idea. A few moans here and there might help." She smiled. "But we don't want people to go upstairs. Just too much moving about and it will be hard to police two floors, especially since the second floor will be mostly in the dark."

"How will you keep them out?" Harry thought the wide stairway quite inviting.

"Every so often, a ghost, male, can appear at the top of the stairs, say, dressed in early clothing, and he carries a head by the hair. Mouth open. Just awful."

"Blood?"

"Harry, they'd pass out," Susan teased her. "Well, it would be scary, but then we'd have to clean the upstairs hallway and the stairs. Best to keep our cleanup to the first floor. As it is lots of dirt will be tracked over the floor."

"You're right. What happens if people want to go to the bathroom?"

"Porta-potties outside. It's the only way. The last thing we need is plumbing damage. Dr. Anglin would be very unhappy and we'd be unhappy at the price. It will cost to rent the outdoor toilets, but not as much as damage would. I think so, anyway."

Pewter smacked a round eraser on to the floor. *"Whee."*

Harry walked to that side, bent over, and picked it up. "These two have been busy. The other day they opened the screened door to Cooper's, got into the kitchen, looking for treats. And, of course, Coop went inside and gave them goodies."

"She learned it from you. Okay, back to this. If people walk around the house before or after, I'd like to have a werewolf hiding in the bushes. That'll give them a fright. For the kitchen, how about a mannequin with its head in the open stove?"

"Gross."

"Well, it's supposed to be a little outrageous. We can have a sign next to the body creating a story about how her death looked self-inflicted but it was really a murder. Then I thought we could have someone, a man, in the basement, screaming, 'She deserved it.' "

"Does he have to be in the basement? I mean, what if he appears and, say, her husband or boyfriend from the time, the classic lover's triangle, appears and he chases the killer? Could have them run through the house shooting pistols in the air."

"Yes." Susan drew out the *yes*. "Cap guns."

"Let me see if I can find some cap pistols. Look up what my great-great-great-grandfather's flintlock rifle is worth? The one hanging over the door to the living room. We can use real guns, rifles with blanks. I have my flintlock pistols. I'll use one. Will stick one in my belt. Be from the time of Ichabod Crane."

Susan sat down in the director's chair by the table.

"Does she have any catnip?" Pewter rubbed against Harry's arm as Harry leaned over the drawing.

"Pewter." Harry rubbed her ears even though her voice carried a note of censure.

"Wait until they leave this room. Then maybe we can lure them into the kitchen," Mrs. Murphy suggested.

"How long is that going to take?" The fat gray cat lifted her silky eyebrows.

"I don't know, but if you irritate her there goes the treat," the tiger prudently remarked.

"Bother." But Pewter did sit quietly.

"We have to move them through the house in the same direction." Susan had spent a lot of time thinking about this. "The last place they should come to is the ballroom. Music is playing. We also have to find who will do this. Musicians have no money, so I figure we'll have to pay and they'll have to learn waltzes, the classic waltzes."

"Okay."

"People will be dancing in costume, everyone wearing a mask."

"That sounds wonderful."

"I think the two dancing schools we have here might allow us to ask for volunteers. Yes, we will have to pay for the music, but we need to get a lot donated. Money in, not money out." Susan sounded serious, which she was.

"That's possible, and the dancers can sit on the sidelines when they get tired. We can have shifts. If you allow the dancing schools to have signs on the wall or cards to pick up, might not be scary, but could bring them customers. We could all use a tune-up." Harry felt a tail swish over her forearm.

"You're right. Here's the best part. The dancers ask people coming through to dance. So anyone that wants a spin gets it. Of course, they have no idea with whom they are dancing. All the dancers, male, female, are masked."

"Some with elaborate masks?" Harry was entering into the spirit of this.

"Sure. Our dancers can make their own masks. Anyone who

doesn't want to do that, we'll have general generic bandit masks for them. And I want there to be promenades. Those that don't want to dance can watch that, which then breaks into dancing. Will be unique."

"I'm willing to bet most anyone will dance. Be easier for the women, as the male dancers will ask them. But I think some of the men on the side might be emboldened if a dressed-up lady approached them."

"Right. I want this to be unforgettable." Susan rose. "Come on, I need a drink."

Wonderful words. Pewter raced to the kitchen, as Susan loved to cook and was good at it. Having spent so much time in Susan's house over the years, Pewter knew where the treats were. Mrs. Murphy followed at a more leisurely pace. Pewter parked her behind right in front of the pantry. Mrs. Murphy joined her.

"All right, you two," Harry chided them.

"You know where the fishies are. Give them a few. I'm going to have sherry. Do you want your usual iced tea, or hot tea? I'd love to pour you a sherry."

"Thanks, Susan. I really never learned to drink but I am in the mood for a hot tea. Draggy today."

The two beggars received ample fishies before the two old friends parked themselves at the kitchen table. Sooner or later everyone winds up in the kitchen, especially in Virginia. It's the same in Minnesota but Virginians like to think they started it. Given that the English came to what is now Virginia in 1607, no one wasted time arguing about it.

Harry took a much-needed gulp. "Whew."

"It's the Yorkshire Gold you gave me. Your eyes will pop." Susan laughed.

"Been tired." Harry looked out the huge kitchen windows, so much more modern than her kitchen. "Those dogs are crazy."

"I've been telling you that for years. Dogs have a screw loose." Pewter raised her voice.

Mrs. Murphy laughed. *"As long as they're losing it outside."*

Harry, who could and did say anything to Susan, confessed, "Finding Bumpy hit me. I think that's why I'm dragging. It wasn't gory or anything like that but it was a shock. I mean, you and I had just seen him, what, a day before at the Dunkin House?"

"I can imagine. Any idea why he was killed?"

"He didn't have a mark on him. Some paint on his T-shirt and jeans. Still had the paintbrush in his right hand. The ladder wasn't moved. No sign of violence except he was dragged. No blood."

"The dragging takes care of natural causes, I would think."

"Yes." Harry finished her cup in short order. "I needed that."

"I didn't know Bumpy. I mean, I'd see him at odd times. But I can't say I knew him."

"Me neither. Those guys live in a different world."

"What do you mean?" Susan felt a paw tap her knee.

"Pick me up. I want to see what you're eating."

Susan looked down to see the pretty gray face, whiskers forward, looking up at her. She scooted her chair back a bit, leaned over, picked up the heavy cat, placing her on her lap.

No food, but Pewter was satisfied to be with the humans. Mrs. Murphy jumped on the counter to look out the window. Susan, knowing these cats all their lives, accepted their comings and goings. What was a counter? You could always wipe it down.

"People that are hooked, seems to me, drink or drugs, cover for one another. There's no reason we would know much about Bumpy. Drugs, especially, bond people regardless of background. You need one another to score, and you need one another to lie for you. I expect it's a tight community."

"I wouldn't know. I am perfectly happy to live in a different world."

"Me, too," Harry agreed.

Different, yes, but they also lived in much of the same world that Bumpy did. They were freer than Bumpy and those like him, but they all lived in rural Virginia. Often when people from different ways of living collided, the results could be unpleasant, but in the country people worked it out or avoided one another.

"Funny how something like murder shakes you." Harry got up, poured more hot water into her cup, plopped in another teabag.

"Nothing we can do about it." Susan spoke with finality. "I want to concentrate on Halloween and make lots of money for seeing eye dogs. I'm not going to solve a murder."

"Then we'll concentrate on shaking money out of people's pockets."

"Yes." Susan beamed. "I'm still thinking about you as the Headless Horseman. Are you thinking about that?"

"I can't keep running up and down the street. I think it has to be a big finale."

"It could be tiresome, running up and down the street, but it does mean only those people at the end would have the experience."

"Well, true, but that could be part of the next day's gossip. The hurled pumpkin has to be a one-time thing. Remember it will have a light in it."

"Not a flame?" Susan's eyebrows raised.

"Too dangerous, but I'll have a light in it."

"You'll probably scare yourself."

Harry laughed. "Maybe."

9

September 25, 2025

Thursday

"You can get chlorine anywhere." Harry looked at Susan as they rooted through clothing to see if they had anything that could be used for Halloween.

The people who had agreed to help, many of their friends, were doing the same. While Susan would pay University of Virginia to use costumes from the theater department, better not to pay if she could help it.

"As tablets. Liquid for your pool," Susan agreed. "Ned had asked Sheriff Shaw if he felt there was danger to people. He said he didn't think so, but it never hurts to be observant."

The medical examiner, not much workload over the week, had gotten to Bumpy's body. The examiner found chlorine in his lungs.

Harry found a lacy negligee. "I see."

Susan snatched it back. "Older than dirt. Never got around to throwing it out."

"Did it work?" Harry teased her.

"Well—yes, back when. It's not that I've lost interest in sex, but Harry, I am tired. Ned's tired. I feel as though all we do is work."

"Comes with the middle years. You have to make time to do things that aren't attached to your job or to organizations, well, maybe I should say, nonprofit. We both are overloaded on community service. I thought dedicating the old segregated school would lighten the load."

"It did a little bit. Once I'm finished with raising money for Seeing Eye Rescue, I swear I'm taking a break. Ned's promised to do that, too."

"The only way it will work is if you take a foreign vacation."

"Oh, Harry, this isn't the time to go overseas."

"You're right. But there's no reason you can't start in Maine and travel down through New England. Might be some snow in Maine but I bet there will be color throughout those states. Or you could go in the other direction. A weekend in Charleston, drive through the Carolinas. No end of places to see."

"The advantage of a big country." Susan sighed. She shifted back to chlorine. "Chlorine as a liquid would be more effective than a tablet. Much quicker."

"Had to be liquid. And had to be a soaked handkerchief. Something to cover Bumpy's mouth. Also, whoever did this had to be strong. He was not a small man."

Susan threw selected items into a large carboard box. "Think about it. Bumpy climbs down the ladder. You grab him. Smash the handkerchief over his face. He starts to go. I think chlorine is quick. Bumpy was not a big man nor an overweight man, but it would take muscle."

"Right. I wonder if we surprised the killer? Did he intend to leave Bumpy close to the shed? Well, close enough. Maybe he had plans to drag him farther or even put him in a car or truck. I think this was done in haste."

"I do, too. It's unnerving to think we have a killer in our midst."

"Maybe we do. Maybe we don't."

"Yes, I've thought about that, too. But whoever did this knew the territory. I say local."

"Yeah." Harry picked up the box, walking it to the back porch.

"Thanks. I'll take these to the Waynesboro dry cleaner. They also do wash, dry, and fold, and I don't have the time." Susan hoped she'd have the discipline to get rid of these items once Halloween was over.

"What about Ned's stuff?"

"I don't fool with his clothing. I buy things for him, but that's it. And since he has become a delegate, boring. He always had such an eye for color, especially with sweaters. He still has the eye, but he can't wear anything like that at the statehouse."

Harry walked outside, plopped down in a Brown Jordon chair on the patio. "Need a short break."

"Me, too."

"Sheriff Shaw will inform the newspaper about continued law enforcement work to find the killer or killers. TV news, too. For one thing, gossip won't help and people spreading fear messages won't help. Knowing the killing substance is simple is important, I guess."

"Well, you know everyone with a pool has chlorine." Harry tapped the arm of the chair.

Susan sighed. "I know."

"The other thing we know is, this was premeditated. Thought out. We may have made him hurry, but it's not family violence or drunks in a brawl. Cold-blooded. Something was at stake."

"That's the thing about premeditated murder," Susan agreed. "Sheriff Shaw also told Ned to tell you to keep your nose out of this. Your curiosity can be near-lethal."

"Well, he shouldn't have told Ned about the chlorine, because Ned would tell you and you would tell me."

"But Ned is our representative, he did need to tell him. Also, what if he needs Ned's help? It's possible."

"I am not a busybody," Harry huffed.

"You are nosey. You are not a gossip, but you start poking around."

"I do not," came the heated reply.

Susan did not answer.

These two had been placed in the cradle together as infants by their mothers, who were best friends. As they grew, the cradle changed to the sandbox then the swings and so on. Neither one knew life without the other. Their love was strong, sisterly. They didn't really think about it. It was life as they knew it.

"I am insulted," Harry spoke, breaking the silence.

"Don't be. Your curiousity is a good feature. Gets you to read books, try new things, but in a circumstance like this it could be dangerous. I think that's what Rick Shaw meant."

"I'll think about it." Harry's voice had grown quieter.

"For what it's worth, I'm certainly curious. But given Bumpy's background, I doubt it will take too long for the authorities to find the answer."

"The killer could leave town." Harry thought out loud.

"I guess if things heat up, he will."

Harry's eyebrows rose up. "If he can. If this is someone who, like Bumpy, had a difficult past, drugs, the whole bit, that person could leave. Maybe already has, but what if this is someone who can't leave?"

"Like a respected person?"

"Yes. Or could be a woman, an affair that needs to be hidden."

"Harry, I don't think a woman killed him."

"No, but she could have paid someone to do it for her. She could have a lot to lose. I mean, what if he dumped her or wanted money? And what if her husband would hit the roof or divorce her if he found out? Who would tolerate an affair, regardless of circumstances, but especially an affair with a well-known addict, clean or not?"

Susan thought about this. "It's possible." Then she inhaled. "But anything is possible. Someone could have just gone off the rails. Or a drama was about to unfold."

Harry said with finality, "I just wish we hadn't found him. We came upon him so soon after he died that he looked asleep. If he hadn't been on his back with those drag marks, I don't think I would have thought he was dead. But Haley and Jeb sure knew he was."

"Dogs have such incredible senses." Susan shifted in her seat. "Speaking of which, here come our corgis, each one with a tennis ball."

"You must have pitched them far." Harry smiled.

"Those are lost ones. Guess they found them. I try to put Owen's toys away at night. He is capable of waking up and playing with them."

"Mine, too." Harry nodded. "Given my dogs and even the cats, who don't miss much, I'm not worried for myself, I mean finding a murder victim. People know we found him."

"I suppose the only people happy about the murder are the newscasters. It's been so quiet. Now they can blab on."

Susan took the ball Owen offered her.

Harry did the same with Tucker, but she pitched it onto the lawn, so Susan had to do the same or Owen would whine. "At least we aren't seeing AI-generated scenes. I guess that will happen in the next couple of years. You'll be able to see a corpse endlessly."

"What's happening to us?" Susan wondered.

"I don't know." Harry leaned back, the chair was so comfortable and the light breeze on quite a warm day felt fabulous. "But I do know if the killer is here, part of the community, he knows we found Bumpy."

Susan sat upright. "That's a bad thought."

"Well, it may not be dangerous, but I would be suspicious of anyone asking us questions."

"People can't help it," Susan said with finality.

"Here comes those tennis balls." Harry smiled, seeing the dogs.

As Harry again pitched tennis balls, Fair was again at Big Mim's farm.

Leaning over the fence, he watched Silver Silence. "Moves okay."

"He does, but he's draggy. Not like him," Paul said.

"Do you want bloodwork? Lyme? It's the middle of fall. That doesn't mean he can't pick up something."

"Anything passing through the county and anything you've heard about from other vets, say in Kentucky?"

"No." Fair continued to watch the stallion, a good mover.

"If you hear of anything, tell me. If this goes on, say, for another week, ten days, yes I will want bloodwork. Have to tranq him first."

"Not getting better?"

"No, he's pretty good, but he gets difficult if he's led to the breeding barn. Actually, he's no longer led to it. Wrong season, as you know better than anyone, but he doesn't want to go near it."

"Any mares kick him badly while breeding?"

"No." Paul looked up at Fair. "No problem at all."

"It is unusual. Keep me informed."

"How are your ribs?"

"Healing. Don't worry about it. It's part of my line of work. Yours, too. Sooner or later you'll get hurt with a horse. Dumped. Bitten. Kicked. Not much, but everyone gets something at least once. Have you ever noticed if you talk to someone who isn't around horses, the first thing they tell you is when they rode a horse. Often the tale involves parting company, hanging on while the horse runs off. It's rarely a good story."

Paul laughed. "Get it all the time."

"Maybe those people are smarter than we are," Fair mused.

"I'd die of boredom in another line of work."

"Paul, I would, too."

"You doing okay after finding Bumpy?" Paul, like most Crozet folks, knew who Bumpy was, but wasn't close to him.

"Yes, but I hope nothing like that happens again."

"I can imagine. But you know, Fair, I expect stuff is going on all around us that we don't see or even think about."

"Maybe you need a criminal mind. I often wonder, too, about what I'm missing, and now I really do."

"I know I don't have a criminal mind." Paul grinned.

"Yeah?"

"If I did, I'd have more money."

They both laughed.

10

September 26, 2025

Friday

Crozet's library, built in September 2013 at 18,300 square feet, served the small town and the surrounding area. Built to allow much natural light in, a large open space surrounded by bookshelves, it was pleasant and much used. Fridays, people doing their shopping often stopped by to check out a book or two for the weekend. Despite being engulfed by electronic media, many residents still wanted a good book, including the young.

The parking lot proved adequate, except for those occasions when a special event was planned. Today the lot handled an inflow and outflow of cars, busy, mostly full, but you could find a space.

Cynthia Cooper, standing next to Sheriff Shaw, looked at a 2017 Subaru Legacy. The head librarian had listened to reports from patrons concerning a car parked in the rear of the lot with a passenger who didn't move. People did fall asleep in their cars, others used the lot to make a few quick calls on cellphones, a few others were deeply glad to be away from everything and everybody for a bit. But after enough patrons reported this, the head librarian decided to take a look.

She'd knocked on the window. Knocked again and then turned on her heel, hurried back to her office, and called Sheriff Shaw. He did not hit the sirens but he was there within fifteen minutes.

The occupant was dead. The doors were not locked. Cooper opened the passenger door. A young Latina woman, perhaps just out of her teens, did not fall over. She sat in the passenger seat, her head back on the headrest, eyes wide open.

Both law enforcement officers wore medical gloves.

The first thing Cooper did was search for a pulse.

The sheriff carefully inspected the car. The only item in there was a small makeup bag in the backseat. Also no registration or insurance papers in the glove box.

Cooper felt the young woman's hand. "The small muscles in her hand are going into rigor."

"This car is in the back, somewhat secluded. Away from people. Well, we have one more body to send to the medical examiner." He blew air out forcefully. "Let's hope this was a heart attack. The small muscles go first."

"Of course, but how many people this age get heart attacks? A few do on the football field, but sitting in a car, I don't know, Boss."

"No. And no papers. Nothing to identify her." He was not a man to jump to conclusions.

Neither of them were, and their profession frowned upon jumping to conclusions. You dealt with the evidence, facts.

The facts were a young woman was dead, sitting upright in a Subaru in the Crozet Library parking lot.

Rick wisely had not turned on the lights on the squad car. He didn't need curious people in the mix. The Subaru could be towed after library hours. It would draw less attention and be easier.

Just in case, he'd have a plainclothes officer in an unmarked car in the parking lot. Someone might come back. They'd get the body out now.

"What about questioning people in the library?" Cooper asked.

"Once we get the body out, we can ask the women behind the desk if they remember who mentioned the car. As the library has regulars, this could be people they knew."

"We haven't had any missing persons reports."

"No, but as this happened today, I'll check with the city's department. Then the state. It's possible this is a traveler, but there are no signs of luggage. Just a makeup bag."

"People do have heart attacks when driving." Cooper then added, "Not that this is what happened but I don't know, Boss, I feel something's odd."

Sheriff Shaw didn't respond then he said, "When I give a statement, I can say the usual, if anyone has information to call us. Let's get her out of here. I'll deal with the press after that. We have a short amount of time before word spreads."

Cooper said, "She looks about twenty, at the absolute most."

"Young. Young. No wrinkles." He half smiled. "Young people can sometimes die of heart attacks, massive strokes."

"When we find people in that condition, they are usually slumped. She's sitting straight up, head resting back on the headrest."

"I know." He again let out a puff of air.

The ambulance arrived. By now people were coming out of the library to stare.

"Keep 'em back, Deputy."

Cooper walked toward the growing number. "Folks, if you'll stay where you are. We need the ambulance to be able to get in and out. Please, stay where you are."

Her tone, commanding, kept them in place.

On the way home, the sun setting later and later, Cooper stopped by Harry's house.

Joyously greeted by the crew, she knelt down to pet Tucker and the kitties. Pirate leaned his big head down to give her a wet kiss.

"Need anything? Food. Drink," Harry asked.

"No, thank you. Do you use the library a lot?"

"Once or twice a month. Why? I have my library card. I'm not overdue."

"I'm sure you're not. We found a young woman, dead, in an older Subaru parked in the back. No I.D., nothing. Well-dressed. A little makeup bag on the backseat."

"That's sad. So young, I mean."

"You don't know of any young women around here, maybe even working for Aunt Tally?" Cooper mentioned the centenarian who lived in the farm that was down the road from their homes.

"No. Tally has Luke. He takes care of everything now." She mentioned a fellow in his late forties who lived in a frame outbuilding.

"Thought so. What puzzles me is how well dressed she was, nice gold hoop earrings."

"Maybe she had money."

"Young, but she could've had a good job."

"Family could have money."

"No I.D."

"Well, Coop, all that could have been in her purse. Maybe thievery is part of this."

"I don't know." Cooper sat down in a kitchen chair and Mrs. Murphy jumped on her lap. "Strange."

"It has been a strange time. Let's hope things get back to normal."

The tall woman laughed. "Harry, they never do."

11

September 27, 2025

Saturday

"Next time someone asks you to do something, say no," Fair suggested as they walked down Dunkin House Street.

The dogs and cats walked with them. The only traffic on this street was usually people who lived there.

"Look who's talking." She lifted her face up to him, making him smile.

"Usually my beneficiaries are horses."

"In this case, it's Seeing Eye dogs. I had to say yes. It's Susan's big cause. Anyway, once this is over, I don't have to worry about anything except Thanksgiving—no gifts, just food."

"Then comes Christmas."

"True," she agreed.

"*The tree is the best part*," Tucker told Pirate.

"*It's the presents*," Pewter disagreed.

"*Only if you tear them up.*" Mrs. Murphy knew that would get Tucker blabbing.

"Oh, yes. One year, long before you were born, Pirate, the cats and I opened a big present. It wasn't in a carton, only wrapped. It looked fat. We couldn't resist." Tucker beamed.

"I tore open the paper," Pewter bragged.

"A new comforter was inside. Full of goose feathers." Tucker's face shone with rapture.

"Was the best. Tucker chewed it. I clawed it." Pewter blinked, happily remembering.

"The feathers floated up in the air, twirling around." Mrs. Murphy's whiskers swept forward.

"Think we'll ever get anything that good again?" Tucker wondered.

"You never know, but as you might recall, Mother had a fit, a running fit." Mrs. Murphy's whiskers now swept back.

"She fretted over the price. She told Fair that the goose down was super-expensive. But the best thing was, it wasn't useful for them after that." Pewter slowed as the humans stopped in the front of the Dunkin House.

"She folded it up, put it on the floor in the bedroom. The best snuggle bed ever. 'Course it's old now. We need a new one." Tucker felt a brand-new comforter was essential for the winter.

"The good thing, Pirate, is even you can fit on it. We can all fit on it." Mrs. Murphy liked being next to her friends, even though Tucker snored.

"How do we get her to buy a new one?" Tucker asked.

"I don't know. We'll figure it out." Mrs. Murphy stared at the empty Victorian house.

A Range Rover drove up, slowed then stopped. Dr. Anglin got out.

"Perfect timing. Wilson, thank you again for letting us use this." Harry moved a bit sideways as Wilson Anglin shaded his eyes from the sun.

"You can make this really spooky." He smiled then added to Fair, "You're moving a lot better than when I last saw you."

Fair tilted his head slightly. "I heal fast. Went to our family doctor, as you directed. Thanks again for your help."

"That was quite a kick. Glad I could help."

"Funny, that stallion used to be so well-mannered. He's changed."

Fair then returned to the house. He looked around and being a helpful husband said, "Anything you want us to do, we'll do it."

"No, just clean it up when you're done. I came by to see if any hedges need to be trimmed. I think Mac and Bumpy got everything out. They put it in another remodel. Well, I know they did. I checked it out that night."

"Terrible about Bumpy," Harry simply said.

Wilson's face dropped slightly. "He tried, he tried. I'd get him in the ER sometimes. Send him to rehab. Trouble followed Bumpy like a cloud. Think the sheriff will ever find the killer?"

"We hope he will," Harry answered.

"Best not to speculate." Fair looked again at the house. "You are good at picking properties. This is so distinctive."

"Thanks, but you know even a rancher will sell if you clean it out, spruce it up. People want to own their home. That's why I like rentals. Get them in the area, get them in a decent house, they'll often stay. And you'd be surprised how many times people buy homes they've rented. It's a win-win."

"Being out on a farm, we miss a lot of that." Harry admired people who found ways to make money.

She, herself, was not money-driven, but she did worry about costs. She would be inclined to buy land, farmland, if she felt she had some extra cash.

"Would you two like to come in?" He swept his hand toward the front of the house.

"Oh, no thanks, Doctor. Susan, the best-organized person on the globe, has drawings of the rooms. We were walking down the road. I'm supposed to close the fundraiser by being the Headless Horseman. Walking, I can really see what's on the street."

"Then I'd better clean up the bushes. You never know, Harry, there might be a goblin behind a bush." He opened his car door, got in.

The doctor drove off, Harry and Fair walked back to his truck. Harry turned back a moment to look. She swore she saw a flicker at an upstairs window. "Fair, there's someone in there." He looked. "I don't see it. Maybe a flicker of light through the trees."

Heading toward town, which they needed to go through to get home, Fair checked the fuel level. "Low. Let me stop and fill up."

He pulled into Shifty's old Mobil gas station displaying a red Pegasus as its symbol, now called Brennan's. Given its central location, business was always good.

As Fair pumped, Harry strolled inside to buy a twelve pack of soda.

Shifty had just walked out of his office. "Virtue is its own reward."

"Yes," she drawled.

"You and Fair." He looked out the window. "Need a cold beer."

"Let me buy two. I'll put them in the fridge." She peered into his office, door open. "Shifty, you still have your pinup calendar."

"Reissues of one from the '40s and '50s. Better than what's on your phone."

She laughed. "Hey, those pictures aren't on my phone."

He rubbed his chin. "No muscle men?"

"Shifty, I don't think they made calendars like that in the '40s and '50s. If they do today, they're for gay men. I don't know any women that look at stuff like that."

He stood taller. "I consider the girls art."

She had to laugh. "You are so full of it."

He laughed, too. "My wife would agree. But I love those old calendars. Dad always had them. When he ran the station, so many of the fellows would come here after work, sit outside in the summer, inside in the winter, and shoot the breeze. No one has time anymore."

"True. We miss out a lot. I guess you can make a case for the calendars being art. Kind of a dream of perfection. Now with plastic surgery, woman can pay for perfection."

He thought about that. "Gotta take a lot of money." He started to chuckle. "I look at these current movie stars, what pops up on my phone, and you know what I think?"

"I'm afraid to ask."

"I think I'm looking at a pair of thirty-thousand-dollar boobs."

Harry let out a whoop. They both dissolved in laughter.

Then she added, "No male equivalent yet. It's got to happen sometime."

"Oh Lord." He closed his eyes for a moment.

"How did we get on body parts?" she teased him.

"You started it. The pinup calendar in my office."

"Right."

Fair stepped into the building. "What are you two up to?"

"You don't want to know." Harry punched Shifty in the arm, leaving with her confused husband.

As they left the building two women walked by them, one older, one younger. Harry and Fair didn't recognize them.

Parking the truck in front of the house, they got out, carrying the drinks, the setting sun casting a warm glow over everything.

The humans stared at the copper-skied west.

"Should still be warmish tonight. I'm not bringing the horses in. Their barn doors are open if they want to go in."

"Won't be long before that first frost." Fair watched the clouds immediately over the mountains transform from copper to hot gold with splashes of red.

"That was one of the smartest things we ever did." Harry reached for his hand. "Putting the geldings in the north field, the mares in the south, each in their pasture but every horse can get into the barn if it rains, snows, whatever. Of course, when the nights get bitter, they'll have their coats on and, yes, as you know,

I bring them in at sunset, shut up the barn. It always amazes me how much body heat they throw off. It's rare that the water buckets freeze in the barn."

"Thank Heaven. Hate chopping out buckets in the morning. Maybe we did it last winter ten days total. The hay in the loft helps keep the temperature warmish. I don't know what's more difficult, keeping our animals cool in the summer or warm in the winter. I take each season as it comes."

"Beginning to feel like fall. The sycamores are showing a hint of yellow color, the willows, too. Fall doesn't come as early as it once did."

"Come on, I need my evening libation." He led her to the screened-in door, opened it, then opened the kitchen door. "After you, Madam."

He carried the drinks into the house.

He then put the twelve-pack of co-cola on the counter as she put two beers in the refrigerator.

Inside the kitchen, Harry watched as Fair made himself a bourbon and branch. He liked his evening drink. One. That was it.

She asked, "Are you hungry?"

"I'm not. Are you?"

"A little. You have your drink. I'll warm up leftovers. By the time they're ready, you'll be ready to eat."

A scraping noise caught both of their attention.

"What are you doing?" Harry asked Pirate, who was hauling the old comforter to the kitchen while Tucker picked up the hind end.

"We need a new one," Pewter told her as the dogs dropped the comforter.

"That's getting worn." Fair took a welcome sip of his bourbon.

"Remember, Honey, they destroyed it Christmases ago. A new goose-down comforter will probably cost three times as much now."

"I don't doubt it but we could buy a synthetic goose-down. Those things really do keep you warm."

"*We'll freeze.*" Tucker gave her a shiver for drama.

"Fair, you spoil these creatures. They have everything."

"*No, we don't. I want catnip and tuna. I want a comforter. I want more fishies,*" Pewter rattled on.

"Well." Harry hesitated.

"Get on the computer and find out what the synthetic comforters cost. Just for the hell of it." He knew he'd buy one but best to involve her.

"Okay." Harry stirred snap peas in a bowl then poured them in a water-filled pot on the stove.

Taking a deep breath, stretching his legs out, Fair promised, "I'll take down the screens tomorrow and put up the glass on the porch. Might as well do it on a nice day. We'll have a frost soon, I think. Frosts usually start mid-October now, but we might get an early one."

"Good idea. I'm glad I got my bulbs in. Got them in for Cooper, too. We did it together."

"Any word on Bumpy?" Fair asked.

"No, nothing new."

"What about the young woman found in the library parking lot?"

"Coop hasn't stopped by today. Nothing on the news. Unusual."

"As long as there isn't a murder on Halloween or evil spirits provoking mayhem." He finished his drink.

"Fair. Don't think about that. But these two deaths, one a murder, it's not good. Evil spirits."

"More likely evil people," he replied with finality.

12

September 28, 2025

Sunday

"You'll never catch me, Pokey, Pokey." Jeb raced through the barn and shot out to the pasture then back.

The cats watched from the hayloft.

Pewter sniffed. *"That dog is mental."*

Mrs. Murphy replied, *"No, he's just a Jack Russell."*

"Like I said, he's mental." Pewter was never one to take a correction or amendment to her statements all pronounced as though they were the God's honest truth.

"I can outrun him." Pirate raced after the little dog as he turned to blast out of the barn again.

Once in high gear, Pirate covered ground, but Jeb, those little legs pumping, could turn on a dime and give you a nickel's change. So he would turn, right under Pirate, turn, then do it again.

"No fair," the giant dog sputtered.

"I can outrun you," came the instant brag.

"You can't outrun me," Pirate fired back.

Tucker and Haley, sitting side by side in Harry's spacious barn, at the back doors, watched with amusement.

"*How do you stand him?*" Tucker asked the Lab.

"*How do you stand Pewter? That's a cat with attitude.*"

Tucker tossed her head. "*I ignore her. All she wants is attention.*"

"*Same with Jeb. He makes Mom laugh when he isn't digging up her garden. Then he pretends he did nothing wrong.*" Haley observed the trees bending.

"*What a gust.*" Tucker also noticed.

The force of the wind moved Jeb sideways. There wasn't a lot of him, but it even gave Pirate a moment.

"*Where did that come from?*" the big dog wondered.

"*I don't know, but it's getting worse.*" The little fellow braced himself.

"*Let's go back to the barn. Walk on my right side. I might block some of the wind. Must be a storm coming up. I didn't smell it,*" Pirate admitted.

"*Me, neither, but we were playing. I can smell it now.*" Jeb took a deep sniff. "*Let's hurry. It's going to rain.*"

As the two young dogs raced to the barn, Mrs. Murphy and Pewter moved back from the large open doors of the hayloft.

"*Look at the clouds rolling over the mountains.*" Pewter loathed rain.

"*Ugly.*" Mrs. Murphy walked back to the middle of the hayloft, bits of hay on the wooden floor, polished from years of human footwear.

"*The overhang on the open doors helps. But hay bales can still get wet and so can I.*" Pewter liked the fragrance of the hay bales.

"*They'll dry out fast enough.*" Mrs. Murphy licked her paw. "*Mom thinks she'll get one more cutting. That's unusual but it will save money come February and March. She grows good hay.*"

Pewter listened to the wind howl. "*Trees will come down. There's always a weak one that tips over. Looks fine from the outside.*"

As the animals focused on the weather, so did Harry and Carolyn both in the tack room.

Harry hurried out of the doors facing the house. She turned, walked briskly back to the tack room. "He's got the glass up."

Carolyn, sitting in one of the director's chairs, said, "Good.

This instant storm could have broken panels leaning against the wall."

"He works fast, plus he's been at it since ten this morning."

"It's time for me to close in my porch, too. I usually pay someone to do it. You know who likes doing this stuff? Lucas. He's gotten so handy working for Aunt Tally."

They discussed a newer resident in the community when the dogs started barking.

"That's enough," Harry called out.

"It's Cooper," Tucker hollered back.

Jeb and Haley knew Cooper, although not as well as Tucker and Pirate.

The minute Cooper stepped into the center aisle of the barn, the heavens opened.

Harry, standing in the doorway to the tack room, laughed. "Boy, are you lucky."

Walking toward her neighbor, Cooper agreed. "Out of nowhere."

"Hey." Carolyn called from the tack room.

Cooper walked in, pulled up another chair as Jeb jumped into her lap.

"You need attention," Jeb announced.

"Jeb, leave her alone," Carolyn reprimanded him.

"No."

Cooper laughed. "I can see how well trained he is. I don't mind. I was telling Harry a few days ago that I wish I had time for a dog."

"And I told her if she found a dog, or a dog found her I'd keep it while she worked. He or she would be happy here with this crew."

"I hope it's a Jack Russell," declared Jeb.

"The poor woman won't have a minute's peace." Haley lay down, putting his head on his paws.

"Not true. Not true," came the reply.

"Chatty." Cooper wiggled her toes, as her feet felt a little numb.

"That's a nice way to put it. All he wants is attention," said Pewter, who loved it.

Harry's pets didn't say a word to this.

"Need anything? Have my little fridge here and my teapot," Harry offered.

"No thanks. Thought I'd stop by. Worked this Sunday. Only half a day, for which I am grateful now that the kids are back in school." She meant UVA. "The freshmen are still getting lost or drunk on weekends. Sometimes we'll pick a kid up who has passed out, I presume on the way back to the dorms. Sooner or later they learn."

"What about the ones who don't learn until their fifties?" Harry grinned.

"Find that anywhere." Cooper exhaled, happy to be with friends.

"True," Carolyn chimed in. "You know, there are people who can drink whiskey all day, a sip here and a sip there, and work as though nothing affects them. I don't know how they do it."

"I think they have different systems than the rest of us." Harry listened as the rain thundered on the metal roof.

"Glad we're inside." Cooper had to raise her voice because of the din.

The wind whipped through the hayloft.

"I'm going downstairs. This wind carries a chill," Pewter complained.

"Does. It's the moisture, plus the mercury is dropping. Remember five years ago? We woke up one November morning and it was sixty degrees. Sixty. Mom kept talking about it. By three that afternoon a wicked storm came up, terrible winds like this one, and snow, so much snow." Mrs. Murphy backed down the ladder to the hayloft.

"I do remember that. I also remember Harry starting a big fire in the fireplace and Fair coming home early. Said he could barely see. You never know." Pewter, grumbling with every downward step from the hayloft, repeated herself. *"You never do know, but usually we know before they do. So this is a surprise."*

"Is." Mrs. Murphy waited for her best friend so they could walk into the tack room together.

"Hello." Harry greeted them as they jumped up onto the pads on the saddles.

Both cats liked high spots.

"Everyone is here but the horses." Carolyn then stopped herself. "Here they come."

The humans heard the horses hurry into their stalls, as they had all been at the far end of their respective pastures.

"We're all here. Safe and sound." Harry smiled.

"Thought I would stop by. Safe and sound provoked me." Cooper paused. "We got feedback from the medical examiner. Had a couple of people working Sundays. They are nonstop there. Well, they are responsible to the entire state, and fortunately not too busy right now."

"That got our attention." Harry sat up straight.

"Still no I.D. on the young woman. She was killed by chlorine."

"What!" Both women spoke at once.

Cooper shook her head slightly. "Unnerving. It really is unnerving. Anybody can get chlorine. Anybody. Two murders. Same method."

"Good Lord. And two people with nothing in common," Carolyn blurted out, still amazed at the report.

"We don't know that. We don't know anything." Cooper then leaned forward. "After we found Bumpy, the boss and I divided up the territory. I spoke to those who knew Bumpy from rehab and I tracked down some of the people he worked with. He was on a renovation project. Would have started, as you know, Carolyn, he was to start Monday, so he painted your big shed. Well, he was going to work on a house in Crozet, the town, not out of town. A couple of the other men were surprised, of course. A few weren't. Money troubles. They said he owed. The big fellow, Mac, declared Bumpy was paying his debts off. Why kill him when he was giving them money week by week? It's confusing, but these things are always confusing until piece by piece you fit it together."

"I hope you do." Carolyn quietly replied.

"I found him. If the killer had been there I would have brought him down," Jeb let everyone know.

"Jeb, you couldn't bring down a fly," Haley couldn't help but criticize.

"I would bite his ankle. My fangs would draw blood."

The other animals remained silent.

"What could Bumpy and a young woman have in common?" Harry asked.

"Maybe they both owed the same person money," Carolyn thought out loud.

"But like you said, Coop, why kill someone who was paying you back?" Harry again questioned.

"It may not have anything to do with debt. Mac, who had worked with Bumpy over the years, believed it was not money. Those two knew each other well enough, as both had been hitting up whatever they could find over the years, that and booze. Usually at the same time."

"How did Mac get clean? I assume he's clean," Carolyn asked Cooper.

"Shifted to rehab. He didn't need as many visits as Bumpy. He swore if he lived, as he was almost dead when they found him, he would do whatever it took. He did. It's hard to find jobs as a recovering addict, so most wind up in skilled labor jobs." Cooper listened again as another great gust blasted.

Harry rose. "I'm going to close the big doors."

"We'll help." Carolyn and Cooper, speaking together, also got up.

Turns out the doors weren't easy to close, with the wind hitting them. So the three took each set of open doors, finally getting them closed.

"What about your hayloft?" Carolyn asked.

"I'll trust on tomorrow being dry. I don't think we'd have an easy time closing them."

The women returned to the tack room, changed the subject and caught up with one another.

Then Harry piped up, "What if those murders were a lovers' quarrel."

"Bumpy would have to have been robbing the cradle." Cooper posed that idea. "Not that it couldn't happen."

"He didn't strike me as the passionate type," Carolyn interjected.

"People can fool you," Harry said.

Cooper crossed her arms over her chest. "Obviously, someone is."

13

September 29, 2025

Monday

A soft rain continued, no lightning or thunder. Days like today inspired Harry to clean out a closet or her cupboards. She chose her closet. With fall closing in, it was time to fold up her summer T-shirts, shorts, thin long pants, put them in clear plastic boxes, and carry them downstairs.

Throwing stuff on the bed, she divided things up. What to keep, what to donate or throw away. Ridding herself of objects, clothing, proved onerous. She was always sure the minute she parted with something she'd need it within ten days.

"*One pile is smaller than the other.*" Pewter watched from her spot on the bed pillow.

"*Never changes. Spring, fall, it's the same. Aren't you glad we don't wear clothes?*" Mrs. Murphy thought it sorrowful that humans had no fur.

"*They don't have a choice,*" Pewter wisely commented. "*They suffer in the winter. Women can't grow beards to warm their faces. The wind hits full force. That's why Mom has those scarves and turtlenecks. She still gets a pink face.*"

Tucker padded into the room. Pirate, on his side, never opened one eye to see the tough little dog get up and leave the living room.

"Anything we can steal?"

Pewter looked down at the dog. *"No. You know how she gets if any of us drag off a shirt or even an old towel. You'd think it was dipped in gold,"* Pewter replied.

Tucker sat, ears forward, watching clothing fly out of the closet, landing on the bed. *"This stuff costs money. You know how she is about money."*

"We know," came the reply.

Harry's cell rang. She pressed the button as Carolyn Maki's number popped up. "Hey."

"Hey to you, too."

"What are you doing?" Harry inquired.

"Got stir crazy so I put on my raincoat and walked halfway to the gate and then back. Needed to stretch my legs. Anyway, I then went behind the shed. I haven't been there since we all found Bumpy. I looked at what was left to paint, thinking maybe I'd do it." She paused. "I don't really want to. Not that I can't paint but well, I don't know. Creeps me out."

"Would me, too."

"But here's the thing," the tall woman responded. "You'll recall where the ladder was?"

"Yeah, sure."

"Well, when the team came to crawl over the place, after Bumpy was hauled off, they moved the two concrete blocks he had placed behind the ladder to stabilize it. The ground is a bit uneven. Anyway, they moved the ladder, examined everything. Nothing. But I found a coin buried in the mud. The rains made everything soft."

"Like a quarter?" Harry wondered.

"No. I don't know how they missed it, but maybe it was somewhat buried when the ladder was dragged away from the shed. The ground wasn't hard then, either. I picked it up. It's a Venezuelan coin. Called a Bolivar, I think. Looked it up on my computer. Maybe worth fifty cents. I'm not sure."

"Venezuelan?" Harry said. "Seems surprising for Bumpy."

"The only thing I can figure is this fell out of Bumpy's pocket."

"Maybe he was a coin collector."

Carolyn replied, "Could be, but I doubt it. I guess I'd better call the sheriff's department."

"Since you found it back there, yes," Harry agreed.

"You know, I've gone over that day in my mind a hundred times. Something like that keeps popping back in your head. I've known Bumpy from a distance. I guess we all did. I didn't know much about him. It's possible this coin isn't his."

"True, it could have fallen out of a pocket, but there aren't any people from Venezuela around here."

"Maybe there are and we just don't know it. I don't ask people where they come from."

"You're right, Carolyn."

Carolyn looked out the window. "It's getting cool again. The department has gone from car wrecks during early football games to murder. Poor Coop. Fortunately they don't have to cover the stadium. That's Charlottesville Police Department's territory. I'll show this coin to Coop."

"People that don't live in the Commonwealth don't understand the two law enforcement systems. One for the city. One for the county. It actually makes a lot of sense since the needs are different. I think they have something like this in Pennsylvania. There it's townships. Kind of fascinating how each of the colonies had its own form of local government. Great Britian loaded us with taxes and demands but those people over there had no idea what life was like here."

"Harry, people alive today in our country have no idea what

other people's lives are like. Well, anyway, let me get on this. I knew you'd be interested."

"Fascinated," said Harry truthfully.

As Harry and Carolyn talked Cooper took a phone call from a friend on the Richmond police force. "Dot."

"The one and only," the officer with the nickname replied.

She got the nickname because she was such a marksman that whenever she was at the range her card had little dots all in the middle of the bull's-eye.

"What have you got?"

"No missing persons report that corresponds with the body you found, but an interesting thing did happen this morning. One of the officers pulled over a white woman who was speeding. She had a New York driver's license, the car was registered to a ride-share company like Uber. She was one of its drivers. He asked her to pop her trunk, rain or not. She did. He looked in. Lots of cartons. He opened one. It was full of small makeup bags. And they sound like what you found in the car in the library lot. Small Sephora makeup bags. Easy to stuff in a purse, has the basics, not expensive."

"I see."

"She said she got a good price. She was taking them up to New York for her friends," Dot filled her in.

"Must have a lot of friends," Cooper noted.

"There's no law against taking advantage of sales and selling them elsewhere. It's not like carrying cigarettes or 'shine. But it's an odd coincidence. Sephora carries good stuff. Good prices."

"You went through the bags?"

"Did. Two lipstick colors, eyeliner, mascara, and a face crème. That's it. Oh, a roll of Life Savers."

"Huh. Let's consider if this will be resold. Maybe after gas costs,

each bag makes five dollars' profit, and say there are five hundred bags. Then again, who knows what that woman's circumstances are. Twenty-five-hundred dollars in cash is decent. No taxes if people pay in cash. Women look for a bargain. Men, too. Different products but people love a bargain." Cooper thought it one of those human peculiarities going on in every nation.

"Well, there you have it. If anything breaks, let me know. It's a strange case, as is the fellow pulled off the ladder. You all have gone from the usual to the unusual."

"We have. That's one of the reasons I really love law enforcement. I never know. And I am no longer amazed at how people think, or don't think, but I am still surprised that people think they can get away with things."

"They can. What was the classic movie with James Cagney? *Never Steal Anything Small*. In this case it doesn't seem to apply."

They both laughed.

But it did apply.

14

September 30, 2025

Tuesday

"Last year the drought hung on for months. This year it's rain." Harry checked the hay in the hayloft, the two cats also inspecting.

"Close the big doors," Pewter advised. *"The hay by the doors dried out from the last storm but another one is coming."*

Harry stood at the opened hayloft doors, inhaled deeply, then stood inside the left door, pushing it with her shoulder. She repeated the motion with the right door. They were closed with a thin opening, less than a half inch. There were no hay bales at the exact center of the doors. A little bit of wind could get through, maybe even some wetness, but not to the bales off to the side and others farther back. She headed to the big doors facing the house. Repeating the process, she brushed her hands on her jeans then climbed down the ladder, followed by the cats.

Simon, the opossum who lived in the hayloft, pretended to be asleep in his living quarters not far from the ladder. This way what heat there was would rise to him. He luxuriated in an old blanket, an old towel, plus toys. Harry left out plush little monkeys for him. Grateful though he was, he tended to hide when anyone but the cats moved about his hayloft. The great owl in the cupola didn't bother him and vice versa. Coexistence.

Her feet hitting the center aisle, Harry double-checked the horses, now all in, as this storm was also predicted to pack fierce winds.

Satisfied that all was in order, the main floor barn doors closed tight, she opened the door to the tack room. The cats followed. The dogs, asleep, didn't lift their heads. They'd spent the late afternoon chasing vultures who would fly low then climb upward to perch in the trees. The birds enjoyed tormenting the dogs. Unkind names were traded between species. Finally, realizing they would not be pouncing on a big bird, the two dogs came in, pushed the door open enough for Pirate to squeeze in, dropped on the old rug. Out they went.

"*Tucker snores like an old man,*" Mrs. Murphy laughed.

"*He is an old man.*" Pewter giggled.

"*Pewter, you and I are the same age as Tucker. Pirate is the youngest.*"

"*Pooh. Dogs age faster than cats. Look, Tucker's going gray around his muzzle. Old man.*" Pewter stood her ground.

"You know, it's cold in here." Harry checked the wall thermometer. "Fifty-eight. Well, it's almost October. I think the incoming weather has dropped the temperature." She announced this to her animals, who looked interested. At least the cats did.

Kneeling down, Harry flicked on the attractive propane stove Fair had given her a few Christmases ago. She'd used a wood-burning stove for years, dragging wood into the barn, piling it by the tack-room door. Fair didn't mind cutting wood. He did it for the big fireplace in the house, but he finally decided the tack room could be more efficient. He removed the old wood-burning stove, replacing it with a propane stove, the door being glass so Harry could see the flames. Then he took the old stove, transferring it to the enclosed equipment shed. He carefully placed thick slate underneath, fixed up a pipe to carry the smoke outside, again using nonflammable material where he cut the hole in the roof. Occasionally he worked on old tractors, or pulled in his truck when the weather turned. If he fired up the stove, it warmed the shed, making it much easier to use his hands. Both Fair and Harry, practical, liked to accomplish things, save money by doing the work themselves. As it was, Fair was handy. Harry could perform basic maintenance but her area, soil testing, rotating crops, overseeding, fertilizing, used up her time as repairs used up his. They were a good team.

The stove warmed the tack room in fifteen minutes. Harry took off her beat-up Carhartt Detroit jacket. Time for a new one. She'd never do it. She'd wear this until it was in threads.

The cats watched as she sat down at the desk, pulling out her notes. Then she pulled out a magnifying glass. Clicking on the computer, she held the magnifying glass up to the spot where they found Bumpy's body. Her curiosity had gotten the better of her. She'd check this against photos of the side of the shed and ladder. Cooper had the photos, had sent them to Harry. What if they had all missed something? Finding the coin fired her to keep searching. Carolyn had sent her a picture of both sides of the coin.

Looking over at the cats, each on a saddle with a plush saddle pad, she declared, "It's possible this coin belonged to someone else. Pockets have holes in them. Could have been Bumpy's killer."

The two felines appeared raptly attentive.

"Can't buy anything here with that coin." She clicked off her computer, glanced out the small tack-room window on the outside wall. The barn, built in 1905, possessed a few individual features. The window was at the corner of the outside wall, away from the saddle racks. Originally, whoever lived in here, and someone did, had the wood-burning stove where the propane stove now sat. Given that it was a small space, the rooms would be pleasant. The stable help probably slept on a cot, best to be raised off the floor. It would be cozy. The outside water pumps made getting wash buckets and drinks easy enough, although in winter, best to fill up buckets and bring them inside.

She noticed trees swaying.

So did Cooper, sitting in the squad car at Owensville Road and Route 250. She sat in the parking lot of Duner's Restaurant. Another half hour and she could go home. Often she was allowed to use the squad car or department SUV to go home.

She was clearly visible, so whoever passed her drove under the speed limit. She checked her phone.

Dialing the number, she heard Dot's voice.

"Coop, I got curious because of what you said about the makeup bag in the victim's car. The woman who was stopped with cartons full of those makeup bags is Kylie Mason. No marks on her driving record. She has an apartment on Hamilton Street, West. I cruised by. No car parked in front, no lights, but that's not unusual, as I drove by at three-thirty A.M. No record."

"Thanks, Dot. It is a serious thing. Nothing new here. Thanks again. Tomorrow I will go to Sephora; they have a shop in Stonefield. I'm curious as to the prices of makeup, lipstick, stuff like that."

"Think it's pretty affordable. Good stuff, so my girlfriends tell me when we get together. I stick to Clinique. Haven't the patience to try new things and this has worked for years. Doesn't hide the wrinkles though." Dot sighed.

Sitting in the car, temperature dropping, Cooper started the motor. Hung up the phone. The wind whipped up. This wasn't a particularly dangerous intersection, but traffic could get heavy as people drove home from work. Bad weather exacerbated that. She checked the time. She pulled out, heading west, going the speed limit. The sight of a cop car always slowed traffic. She was glad she wasn't working late tonight, as there were bound to be trees down.

Reaching home as the rain started, she dashed into her kitchen, picked up the landline phone. Being out in the country, keeping a landline was helpful.

"Harry."

"Yes, Madam."

"Can I pick you up tomorrow, oh, eleven? I want you to go to Sephora with me, the shop in Stonefield."

"Sure."

"Need to look at the products there. Do you think you know much about makeup?"

A light pause was followed by, "Well, about as much as the average woman. I mean, I use it when Fair and I go to a social event. Don't use it working. Can you imagine how ridiculous it would be to be made-up while driving a tractor? I'd sweat it off."

"What about moisturizer?"

"I don't consider that makeup," Harry replied. "Damn, I'm going to sit here until the rain lightens up. By the way, how did you know I was in the tack room?"

"You usually are at this time unless it's the depths of winter." Cooper watched the rain hit the windowpane over the sink.

"You're right. I'm a creature of habit."

"Jeez, raining hard."

"We're all snug." Pewter purred.

Tucker, half-asleep, thanks to the phone call, opened one eye. Pirate lifted his head then flopped it down. All were glad Harry wasn't heading for the house. They could all wait.

Fidgety, Harry picked up her cell, punching in Susan's number. "How is it over there?"

"Pretty ferocious."

"Here's a question for you. Do you think most women carry makeup in their purse? Loose or in a bag?"

"I don't know about loose or in a bag, but it's a rare woman who doesn't at least have lipstick in her purse or in the center console of the car," Susan answered.

"Think volume of makeup is age-related?"

This obviously stumped Susan. "I don't know. I think it's more culturally related," Susan replied.

"What do you mean?"

"I think women on the upper end of the class scale don't overdo the makeup. The goal is to look natural. When makeup is obvious, I always think that it's someone without much education. I'm prejudiced. Or someone in the media whose career depends on youthfulness."

"Never thought of that, Susan. See, I figure she's young or the reverse, she's trying to hide her age. Then again, some women think lots of makeup attracts men." Harry said this with finality.

"Now, what's this stuff about makeup?"

Harry told her about the woman stopped for speeding, her car full of boxes of small makeup bags, when the cop opened one it had basics in it. The items came from Sephora because she produced a sales slip for them so the cop wouldn't tear open every carton.

"Odd, unless she's in the business. Taking this to another store or somewhere." Susan doubted the importance of the information.

"So you think, say, if this was going to another state where the prices are higher, that's normal?"

"Harry, I didn't say it was normal. For all we know, the woman could be a crook, but the bottom line is, most every woman carries some makeup. Even you."

"What's that supposed to mean?" One of Harry's eyebrows shot up.

"You never wore a lot of makeup in school, but you did have blusher on."

"Susan, my mother would have killed me. You know how she was about how you presented yourself."

"I remember. She always looked terrific. Your mother was fun." Susan smiled, remembering the long-gone lady.

"Cooper wants me to go to Sephora with her tomorrow, so I'm going. She's focused on the small makeup bag in the backseat of the young woman dead in the parking lot. I don't know what I can add to it. She wants to look at the quality of the brands."

"Might help her determine the economic level of the woman still unidentified, I take it?"

"Yes. I guess I don't see how makeup can be so important." Harry flinched when a big bang of thunder roared overhead.

Susan jumped, too. "A biggie. Here, too."

Harry looked at her animals. "You all don't have to worry about blusher and eyeliner. I can't see that this will lead anywhere."

Then she told Susan about Shifty and the calendar girls. So they decided he'd like makeup. They descended into what attracts men, cracking up each other with vivid details about body parts.

15

October 1, 2025

Wednesday

"What do you think?" Harry held up a deep pink lipstick.

Cooper shook her head. "If I have to wear lipstick, I usually put on something dark. Actually, I hate lipstick. I always get it on my teeth."

"Me, too." Harry put the black tube back in place.

The Sephora store in Stonefield Shopping Center carried a lot of products, nicely displayed. The store was clean and bright. The young woman behind the counter, somewhat subdued by Cooper's presence in uniform, observed but didn't interfere.

"What about a morning face crème?" Harry held up a red bottle promising to erase your wrinkles. "Soaks in fast. Can't bear greasy ones."

Cooper felt a round ceramic jar plop into her hand. "Well, one can always use a good crème."

The young woman by the cash register spoke. "That's one of our best-selling products. People swear by it. I use it."

"You don't have any wrinkles." Harry lifted her eyebrow.

"If I keep using that I won't," the girl, good-natured, replied.

Cooper put the jar on the counter. "I'll take this. We'll keep looking."

The two perused blushers, basic face powders, all the products created to make women feel better by looking better.

"Hmm." Harry held a small jar designed specifically for wrinkles around your eyes. "Mine get deeper and deeper."

"Those are laugh lines, around your mouth, too. You don't want to be without any expression."

"You're right," the salesgirl agreed with Cooper. "That's the problem with facelifts. Of course, I can't say how many of my customers have had them, the lift was done by some of the best, but there is that sort of flat look, loss of expression, if the surgeon wasn't flawless, same for men. You know, more and more men are having facelifts, brow lifts. It's not such a big secret anymore."

"What's your name?" Cooper asked.

"Millicent Garcia. Named for my maternal grandmother. Everyone calls me Milly."

"You've been helpful," Cooper complimented her. "If I were to put together a small makeup bag, small enough to put in a purse yet not take up a lot of room, what would you choose?"

The young woman came out from behind the counter, walked to a display tilted at an angle so one could see everything.

Plucking out a tinted foundation that was also a crème, she started her count. "This. It performs as a moisturizer but gives one a bit of color. Even if a woman has a darker shade of skin it helps. Of course, it's fantastic if you're pale." She then placed another quite small vial in her hand. "Above the lip."

"That?" Harry stared at the tiny vial.

"You only need a small amount. Put it over your top lip. The lines disappear. Lip wrinkles are always a giveaway, you know?"

The two nodded.

"Then you need mascara." She picked up a half-sized tube. "And maybe the smallest amount of eyeliner. Optional." She put a pencil, soft point, in her hand. "Lastly, I'd pick an all-around blush. Anyone looks brighter with peach. You can't go wrong. Now, of course, if a woman wanted pink, she could select that. Same with lipstick. I wouldn't include lipstick for a basic makeup bag. I'd put in lip gloss. Again, you can't go wrong."

"And those items would work for most women?" Harry focused on the small lip vial.

"Would. They may not be a lady's favorites but if I didn't know her, had to put together a makeup kit, small, that's what I would choose and the best part is, it wouldn't cost you more than one hundred twenty dollars. Buy them on a day we have discounts, less money."

"Interesting." Cooper's eyebrows knitted together. "I expect you've seen a lot of different types, coloring, skin, dry or not. Stuff."

"Officer, I have, and I'm not saying this because I work here, but any woman can benefit from low-key basic makeup. Even men can use some tinted moisturizer and if they are very, very clever and learn, they can get away with mascara, too."

"No." Harry couldn't imagine Fair with a mascara brush, twirling his eyelashes.

"Oh yes. And so many men have long eyelashes. Looks hot."

"You mean gay guys?" Harry asked.

"No. Plain guys. Dark eyelashes bring out one's eyes. It always enhances a face. Do my eyelashes look fake or caked with mascara?"

Both women replied, "No."

Milly plucked out a big tube from a special cosmetic line. "This is it."

"I've gotta have that. And a vial of the lip wrinkle stuff, too," Harry declared.

Harry and Cooper paid for their purchases.

"I'm surprised at how few items one needs. What you selected to show us would fit into a small bag." Cooper felt the bag handed to her with the company's name printed on it, nice thick paper.

"Milly, here's my card. Should anyone come in here and buy a lot of stuff, put it in the small zipped bags you have here or buy stuff like you selected, no bags, please call me."

Looking up, curious, Milly murmured, "I will. If you know anyone who wants lots of product, send them to me."

Cooper grinned. "I will. It would help me if I knew anyone purchasing items in bulk. I'm working on a case where makeup might be important."

"Really?" Milly's voice rose a bit. "Makeup?"

Not wishing to divulge too much, Cooper said, and it was true, "A clever woman, one who knows makeup, can completely change her face."

"That's true." Milly nodded in the affirmative. "Look how different an actress can look from part to part. Those makeup artists are wizards." Examining the card she looked up. "I will call."

As Harry and Cooper left the store they looked at the other shops in the nice middle-class shopping center. "Do you want anything while we're here?" the blonde officer inquired.

"Yes, but I don't want to pay for it."

Closing the squad car door once seated, Harry looked at Cooper. "Nice girl."

"Yes. I bet if someone is a makeup artist for TV, film, or even big fundraising events, they can make good money."

"Probably. One would need to be diplomatic."

"You need that to cut hair." Cooper laughed as she started the engine.

"I bought that vial. I'm on the offense. Maybe I can stop those lip lines before they start."

Driving slowly through the back parking lot, eyes on the road, Cooper simply said, "You look fine. You look healthy, fit, don't worry about lip lines."

"You are kind."

"Are you afraid to grow old?" the officer asked her neighbor.

"Of course not. I just don't want to look old."

"Glad we could check out the makeup, and on my work hours, too." Cooper braked at the red stop sign.

"Everyone certainly pays attention." Harry laughed at the car behind Cooper and the driver turning left on the other side of the stop sign, kept checking his rearview mirror.

Cooper's phone rang, she picked it up, liking the old-fashioned police phone in her car, listened intently, then turned on her siren. "Hold on."

Harry did just that as they pushed through traffic, turned left onto one road, then turned right onto Route 250.

As they roared down Barracks Road, Cooper informed Harry, "People smashed the door into a house being remodeled and are or were stealing everything out of it. We'll be there in fifteen minutes, if that."

Cooper, accurate about the time, pulled into a gravel driveway where Sheriff Shaw's and two other cars were parked. Shifty Brennan and Mac, standing outside the house, were talking to Sheriff Shaw while inspecting the broken door.

Cooper joined them, leaving Harry in the squad car.

"We got here too late. They cleaned out the house," the sheriff told her.

Shifty interjected before Sheriff Shaw could continue, "I was driving by, saw three people carrying out lamps, chairs, stuff."

"Come on in." The sheriff led her inside. "Nothing much left except a twin bed frame upstairs. Mac stopped by when he saw us here. Turns out this was one of the houses that he and Bumpy worked on."

"No fists through walls?" Cooper scanned the living room. "Any focused damage anywhere?"

Sheriff Shaw shook his head. "No. The only damage we've found is the smashed door. The other thing is that Mac said the items in here were temporary. Stored here. They'd be used in the other renovations. I asked how temporary, and Mac estimated maybe a month before the next job was completed."

"And it was Shifty who called?" she asked.

"Yes. He said he was driving by and saw three people, women no less, loading up trucks at Dr. Anglin's renovated house. He thought it was strange. He stopped but didn't go into the house. He had no idea what was going on and if this was people stealing, he didn't want to get in the middle of it. Not a bad decision."

She walked to the kitchen. "No appliances. Who owns this?"

"One of Dr. Wilson Anglin's homes. I called him and he confirmed he was using it for temporary storage. He asked if he could replace the door today. I said he could, so I guess one of his team will install that before nightfall."

"Anything upstairs except that twin bed frame?"

He replied, "No. But Dr. Anglin said he still wanted to get a door up and locked. People sleep in empty buildings, especially now that it's getting colder."

She looked around. "Three women."

"Shifty said he couldn't identify them. Headscarves, COVID masks."

"Technically that's not really a mask."

He nodded. "Whoever is behind this isn't totally stupid. They knew a regular mask calls attention, negative attention, and it won't help if you're arrested. Most people will conclude you planned the theft which obviously they did."

"I'm sure Dr. Anglin has an inventory of items."

"He's already sent that to the office. He said nothing was costly, the bed frames were new, the chairs, small nightstands. Same with the lamps. He said they didn't have regular mattresses yet, just a sort of under mattress. I don't know what that means."

"Thinner than a mattress. Some people use them because it will raise the height of the mattress when you buy one. Also less expensive than buying a regular, thick mattress, I guess. Mattresses can be expensive."

"So I hear. Well, whoever did this walked away with new bed frames, twin, same number for the mattresses, one new small kitchen table and four kitchen chairs, as well as ten lamps."

"Doesn't sound like a haul that will make money."

He stood in the doorway to the kitchen. "It doesn't. So why steal these things?"

"Mac offer any ideas?" she asked him.

"No. But he, too, thought it was strange."

"I guess someone has been watching the house. All right, I'll get the team here to see if they can pick up fingerprints. Better go out and tell Shifty and Mac they can go. We'll update Dr. Anglin."

"Shifty might hear something at the store. He'll be all ears." Sheriff Shaw half smiled.

Once she satisfied herself that she examined each room, Cooper went out to the squad car where Harry patiently sat.

"Took a bit of time."

"That's okay. At least no murder," Harry responded.

"No. Mattresses, a kitchen table, and chairs and lamps stolen. Shifty said he saw three women and they hurried to their trucks, shut up the tailgates, and drove off while he watched. Not exactly like robbing a jewelry store." She shrugged. "Tell you, things are odd. If someone had broken into one of the big houses and taken all the silver, I could understand it, but bed frames, lamps?" She shrugged again.

"Maybe someone with a big family."

Cooper smiled. "That's a thought."

As his wife was at the robbed house, Fair sat with Paul in the tack room of the unused carriage house. One buckboard reposed in the large place. Mim Sanborne no longer used carriages. Then again, most people didn't unless they competed in driving contests or gave tours at historic sites. The tack room, heat turned on, quickly warmed, so the two men were comfortable. They chose this location, as no one would hear them. No one really came into the carriage house, although some rabbits had nests there, as well as a few birds who had become spoiled by the barn quietness and protection from the elements. Apart from house sparrows, Carolina wrens, as well as the odd traveling gopher in a stall, two huge ravens roosted in the eaves, having made a big nest.

Removing his jacket, Fair settled into an old director's chair. Paul did the same.

"I've never seen ravens in a barn nesting," Fair commented.

"Me, neither. No one comes in here. They have it all to themselves." Paul shifted his weight in the chair. "I didn't want to talk to Big Mim until I talked to you. Silver Silence. He's increasingly difficult."

"I'm sorry to hear that. He's got such terrific conformation. Those good old bloodlines." Fair smiled.

"He doesn't want anyone to bring him in from his pasture. He swings his butt around. And today he bit Kyle. That horse hates Kyle."

"Can you keep Kyle away from him? Doesn't make your job easier, but the stallion comes first."

"I"— a pause. "I don't trust Kyle. I want to get Mim to fire him. Wanted your opinion first."

"No theft. Worries like that? Any other horses dislike him?"

"He's not a thief. No tack is missing. No meds. As to the other horses, he brings the mares in, turns them out. Grooms them. I wouldn't say they particularly like him, but they don't dislike him. Silver Silence hates him. He takes an extra day off once a month to go to Maryland, where his father is failing. I don't like it but I agree to it." Paul then added, "Have never seen any of his family here."

"There's no point taking a chance that either the horse or the human gets hurt. And who knows how long it will take Silence to calm down. I'd recommend turning him out. Leaving his outside stall door open. Let Silence come and go."

"I will. Any thoughts about how I should present this to Big Mim? You've known her far longer than I have."

Fair smiled. "I grew up with her, Aunt Tally, so many people. You grow up here, you tend to stay. Or you leave with big dreams and sooner or later come back." His smile broadened. "Mim is reasonable. If she thinks this is the best thing for the horse, one for whom she has high hopes, she'll do it. Yes, she'll have to give Kyle good severance pay and probably a good recommendation, but she'll do it."

"Will you back me up if she has questions?"

"Of course I will, Paul. But she respects you. She's not going to doubt you. Granted, sometimes an animal will dislike a person or another animal. Then again, sometimes they have their reasons. I say, trust Silence. Get rid of Kyle. The sooner the better."

"I'll go up after work if she can see me. You're right, the sooner the better."

"I'll be on call. If she wants a second opinion, let me know."

"I will."

That evening, Harry and Fair caught up. The animals listened.

"Do horses attack humans?" Pirate asked.

"Very rarely," Tucker responded. *"Stallions sometimes, rarely one will go after a person in the field, try to get them in their front legs and drop down with them. Crush them."*

"Why?" Pirate wondered.

"As I said, it's rare, but some stallions are mean. Killers, really. If Silver Silence were that way, Dad would have said so. Maybe Silver is now some kind of misfit, I guess."

"Sometimes people don't like one another, other times animals don't like some people, and then again sometimes animals don't like one another," Pewter, overhearing, remarked. *"Like you, Bubblebutt."*

"You're trying to get me in trouble," Tucker wisely answered, not buying into a fight.

Meanwhile, Harry was now telling Fair about her Sephora adventure.

Mrs. Murphy thought makeup strange. *"Can't people just accept the way they are?"*

"Obviously not." Pewter puffed out her chest. *"Our humans are wonderful but they can't smell much, hearing so-so, slow, oh so slow. No fur. No claws, no fangs. What would they do without us? And then on top of that they waste time on their hair, change clothes every day. And think what they look like if they're going to a big fundraiser? Harry is in a gown. Can you imagine tottering around like that?"*

Tucker barked. *"I think she looks pretty."*

"She may look pretty but what can she do? They're helpless without us. Helpless." Pewter sniffed.

16

October 2, 2025

Thursday

"People are flipping houses. Even the ranchers are selling. Keeps me busy." Mac hoisted a fence board on his shoulder.

Harry, window rolled down in her old Ford F-150, said, "Pasture?"

"In the back. The small acreage places go the fastest. This place is twenty-five acres. Once you get past the power station on the corner, it's beautiful back here."

"Well, I'm glad I turned this way. Hardly ever go down this street. Looks like the house is empty. New plumbing, electricity? The big stuff. Fair amount of trucks parked here. Lots of work, I guess."

"Everyone wants double-paned windows, you name it but it does save on the heating bills. And this place has two fireplaces. It will sell fast. Look what's happening to the rentals. The place that was robbed will sell fast, I bet, when Dr. Anglin puts it on the market."

Harry felt the brush of wind, a bit chilly. "People turn these places into B and B's. Well, not this place. Someone could have horses. Be okay for that."

"It's good for that." He thought a moment. "I miss working with Bumpy. We worked well together. Never had to talk much. I knew what he was doing and he knew what I was doing. Makes no sense. His dying."

"Doesn't. If he were alive, what would he be doing on this house? I'd guess it was built in the early 1970s."

"Put those windows in tight as a tick. Then he'd press Dr. Anglin to buy one of those twenty-thousand-dollar generators for the bad weather. Easy to set up if you do everything at once. A buyer who knows anything about how weather affects our power would be happy. Bumpy would push. He had a sense of what people want."

"I'd love one of those. We have a small generator to keep the furnace running, the refrigerator. Not much else. And I swear the weather gets worse every year. One storm after another."

"Does. Well, let me get this set up. Big pile of fence boards in the back. I don't want the fence boards out in the weather. There's a run-in shed behind the house. Putting everything in there. Dr. Anglin will need to buy another one thousand boards to enclose more pasture. He probably won't want to hear that."

"It's a big order."

"He can swing it."

"What about the Dunkin House? Did you like working on that?"

"I did. We stripped some of the old wallpaper off. Sanded the floors. Basics. There's more to do though. I reckon we'll get back to it."

"How many of you guys work on these places?"

"About seven of us. We each have a specialty. When we're done there's the cleanup team, usually women. And sometimes Dr. Anglin will let someone bunk in. Keeps people out. Saves both parties money. He's got a real system. He needs someone in the Dunkin House."

"Well, good to run into you."

"Good to see you, too. Oh, hey, before I forget, did Miss Maki finish getting her big shed painted?"

"No. The side where Bumpy was pulled away isn't visible from the road, the farm road. So she's left it. For now."

"Tell her if she wants to finish it, I'll take a weekend day and do it. Just be done with it, you know?"

"I do. I'll tell her." Harry rolled up the window, drove out.

The two cats rode with her. Tucker and Pirate had stayed back at the farm. The old truck couldn't fit Pirate in.

"If I had money, I'd buy a new half-ton truck with an extended cab. Could fit Pirate in. Or maybe a true station wagon. Makes so much sense, a station wagon. SUVs, well, the prices are now through the roof," she grumbled to the cats.

"We'd like a station wagon." Pewter quickly put her two cents in, *"Easier to get in and out of and there is room for all of us if you put the seat down."*

"You can put the seat down in an SUV." Mrs. Murphy didn't see the difference.

"The ride's not the same. I'm sensitive." Pewter blinked, looking sensitive or so she thought. *"I like the station wagon ride. Doesn't sway. And I don't feel like a big jump up or being lifted up."*

"Tucker will still need to be lifted." Mrs. Murphy adored her dog friend.

"Who cares? She has a pot gut now. She's not jumping up on much. She struggles to get on the couch." Pewter relished this observation.

"Fortunately, we have claws." Mrs. Murphy wisely did not call attention to the fact that Pewter was fat.

"Pot gut. How big do you think Mac is? He's not as tall as Dad, but he's big. I bet he weighs three hundred pounds."

"I'm not good at guessing human weight. He has to be super-strong. But that's why he gets the construction work." Mrs. Murphy noticed how big Mac's arms were.

"Yeah." Pewter stared out the window. *"I'm hungry. I hope were going home."*

"Me, too."

They were on their way to the farm. Two cats, one human all eagerly dashing to the winterized porch and then into the kitchen.

"Boy, am I glad the porch is ready for the winter." Harry walked to the thermometer on the wall, pushing the heat up to seventy-two. She'd pulled it down to sixty-eight when leaving, thinking the temperature wouldn't drop. The house held heat, which was good, but wind could drive the indoor temperature down. Those old windows, from the date of construction, in the mid-1800s, leaked air. A stiff wind made them rattle.

After putting down crunchies for the cats and dogs, Harry picked up her cell, called Susan.

"Hello." Susan always recognized Harry's voice, plus her phone number appeared on Susan's phone.

"Is it cold there?"

"It never got out of the low sixties today. Now it's, by the thermometer, the one outside the kitchen window, it's fifty-two and falling."

"Same here. Drove into Crozet today to pick up odds and ends and decided to cruise around. Went north of town, turned right by the substation. Ran into Mac, you remember the big guy moving stuff out of the Dunkin House." She added, "Lots of work trucks. A few cars, so business is good."

"Yes."

"A rancher back there is being remodeled. Twenty-some acres. Mac said houses are turning over fairly quickly in the area. People are making short-term rentals out of some, others are being flipped as family homes. I guess I wasn't aware of all this. I mean, I knew the Dunkin House was special, but maybe the place is getting hot."

"Where else are people going to go? They can go east, even as far as Kent's Store, or they can come west and that's Crozet, or you can go over the mountain to Waynesboro."

"Got out the horse blankets, hung them on the indoor bottom half of the stall doors. They've been cleaned. Won't be long before they'll need them at night, anyway. Bringing them down the ladder from the hayloft took me longer than I thought. I figure we get the first frost mid-October. Think it will be a bit earlier this year. Susan, the time goes so fast."

"Yes, it does. I put away my summer items. Brought out my sweaters, scarves. Takes me forever. And I have to throw out some of what I've kept too long. I love the fall colors."

"Me, too. You're ahead of me. I've sorted some clothes. Anyway, I wanted to tell you I saw Mac. The house is in a nice location. If this keeps up, houses selling at these prices, will we be able to afford where we live?"

"I don't know but I bet we aren't the only people asking that."

As they were catching up, Cooper was driving down the farm road to her house, the trees swaying. She figured the wind had bumped up to thirty miles an hour, the gusts were erratic.

Her phone rang. Pulling in front of her house she answered it.

"Cooper."

"It's Dot. I've driven past the Hamilton Street address a couple of times when I'm in the area. No lights. No sign of habitation. I finally stopped, walked up to the rental office, it's a rental complex, quite nice. The sight of a uniform gets people's attention. Walked in and asked her if anyone lived in 14A. Her first response was 'Is there trouble?' Mine was 'I hope not.' So I asked, 'Is it rented?' She replied that it was until yesterday. The renter had paid up through December thirty-first, the end of her lease. Then left." Dot filled her in.

"Did you go into the apartment, or whatever it is?"

Dot replied, "They are two-story units sharing a common wall.

Yes, I asked to see it, and the agent unlocked the door. A sofa, a chair, and a small table. That was it. The appliances go with the unit."

"Did it seem clean, not like she left in a hurry?"

"Nothing there. Clean enough. I asked what the rent was, and the woman said two thousand two hundred per month."

"Our makeup lady had funds."

"So it seems."

"I asked the woman, not quite so taken aback now, did she know much about Miss Mason. She noted that I knew the name. Her reply was pleasant, superficial exchanges. No visitors. No noise. Oh, I checked upstairs. No bed."

"Odd."

"Then again, maybe this wasn't her main residence."

"Thanks, Dot. I checked with New York. As you said, nothing. Not even a speeding ticket." Cooper watched as the wind strengthened.

"No car. Only the rental. She seemed to own next to nothing."

"Right." Cooper was thinking along those lines, as well. "No ownership of anything except a sofa, a table, and one chair. No traces."

"I can't but think she may not be involved in criminal activity, but whatever she's involved in, she left evidence of nothing, except once carrying cartons of makeup bags."

"Something about those makeup bags is criminal. My neighbor and I went to Sephora yesterday. Nice products. Many well priced. So I asked the young lady behind the counter if she had to put together a small makeup bag with the basics, what would she use, how big would the bag be? She threw stuff together and while you couldn't fit it in the pocket of your jeans, all would go in a quite small makeup bag that would fit in a glove compartment or a purse."

"Can't jump to conclusions. Our job is to piece it together."

"Exactly. It's possible a small jar of crème could contain an illicit substance. Buy the jar, clean it out. It would be so much easier to transfer drugs."

"Yeah. Well, the bird has flown the coop."

"Dot, I know something is wrong, crooked. That makeup bag in the woman's car at the library, it's all we've got. Need to track down Kylie Mason."

"She's out there somewhere."

She was.

17

October 3, 2025

Friday

Walking across the back pasture, Harry inhaled that first tang of fall. The unmistakable smell lifted her spirits. She headed for the creek that divided her property from Cynthia Cooper's. Tucker and Pirate walked along with her.

The cats busied themselves in the barn, checking all the mouse holes. As the mice cleverly hid their entrances and exits, Harry had no idea where they were.

"Running fast." Harry looked down at the clear water.

As her land backed up to the first ridge before the steep climb of the Blue Ridge Mountains, the water clear and pure, had made this the perfect site for the early settlers, her mother's early ancestors.

"*The beavers are building bigger dams,*" Tucker remarked.

"*Do they ever stop working?*" Pirate wondered.

"*Sometimes,*" the corgi answered. "*They can sit in the sun like any of us. I don't mess with them. They have their place and I have mine.*"

Harry followed the stream down a small raised footbridge between her property and Cooper's. Built years ago, it occasionally needed rebuilding if the flooding proved powerful. Checking that out, she headed back toward the house, her dogs in tow. Reaching the closed-in porch, she stopped to study the clouds building up in the west then stepped into the kitchen, removing her light jacket.

"Could rain."

Hearing the pronouncement, Tucker replied, *"It will. I can smell it."*

Pirate seconded the forecast. *"Will get colder, too."*

After tidying up the kitchen, Harry looked at the big wall clock. "Well, you all, it's nine in the morning, people are at work. Let's make a run for it before the weather hits. I want to look at the Dunkin House. Just us. Need to think. I wish I hadn't said I'd be the Headless Horseman. Susan can talk me into anything."

"Oh, you want to do it." Tucker knew her mother very well.

"Come on." She grabbed a slightly heavier jacket, a thicker, fleece-lined denim, and walked out the door, holding it for Pirate.

Had it been ten degrees cooler, she would have worn a heavier work jacket, but this lined jacket would be fine.

Checking out the last mousehole, Pewter heard Harry come out. *"She has no idea."*

"Why should she? We've made our deal with the mice and we've kept it for years. They have, too."

"She's heading for the station wagon. That wagon will soon be as old as the truck." Pewter forgot to add the extra years of the truck, so it would always be older.

"Better for us." The tiger cat loped out of the big open doors, meowing for good measure so Harry wouldn't forget her.

"We're going with you," Pewter added to the chorus.

Harry smiled as her cats sped toward her. She opened the back for Pirate, who easily climbed in. She lifted Tucker up. The backseats were down. It was spacious. An old blanket covered that area, along with an old beach towel pushed to the side. This way the animals had a cozy bottom and could pull the blanket over if they wished. When it got colder, she'd put in a second, heavier blanket. They argued about it but it usually turned out. The cats would use Pirate for a heater. The sweet Irish Wolfhound liked to cuddle. Sometimes Mrs. Murphy would cuddle with Tucker so her feelings wouldn't get hurt.

"Everybody in?" Harry closed the back. She had to reach up to do it.

"All right." She got in, cranked the motor.

"*I'm going up front.*" Mrs. Murphy liked to drive.

Harry drove out of the farm, turned left, headed for town.

"*How were the mice?*" Tucker asked.

"*Okay,*" Mrs. Murphy answered from the front. "*They get all that grain the horses drop so they're happy.*"

"*They don't show themselves. It's a good arrangement. Killing mice is hard work. You wait forever, then one pops out. I've got better things to do with my time,*" Pewter remarked.

"*Like eat.*" Tucker couldn't refuse.

"*You weigh more than I do.*" Pewter turned her head away from the dog.

"*I'm bigger than you are.*" Tucker should have shut up. That fast, Pewter whapped Tucker's sensitive nose. A rumpus started, accelerated.

"Stop it."

"*Death to dogs!*"

"*Ha!*"

Pirate had the sense to duck his big head.

"All right." Harry pulled to the side of the road, got out, reached in for an enraged Pewter. "That's it."

She put the cat, who did not scratch her, in the front passenger seat.

Then she slid behind the wheel, checked her mirror, the back road was only lightly traveled, then off again for Crozet.

In fifteen minutes, she cruised down the street where the

Dunkin House sat. She drove to the end of the street, turned around, and stopped. Opening the window, the outside air cooler, she pressed in her mileage indicator. Looking around, she noted where she would park the trailer. She'd done that before with Fair, but she wanted a reminder. No houses back there, no traffic to worry over or driveways that might be blocked. Then she slowly cruised to the Dunkin House, a quarter of a mile. For Halloween, both sides of the road would probably be filled with parked cars, near the house. She rolled past the Victorian home to the street leading directly into Crozet. That, too, would be parked full if the fundraiser was a success. So she'd need to arrive a good hour before the house opened, or she wouldn't have a place to park the truck and trailer.

"All right." She looked in both directions, pulling out onto the north–south road. That took all of six minutes, as her speed was forty miles an hour. She braked at the four-way stop by the overhead railroad trestle, she then pulled out, heading straight, turning right at the library. She then turned left on the narrow road leading behind the school grounds. As she continued, a few modest homes lined the road once she passed the football field area then the baseball field. They weren't jammed together. Continuing on, she noted a renewed house, lights coming on inside. Then she turned right, again modest homes spaced far enough apart to provide privacy.

"Securing the school has made it attractive back here."

"You all did a good job on the old school," Tucker complimented her. As clouds rolled in, it grew dark. Most people were at work but a few homes had lights come on. She also noted another house spruced up.

"Whoever bought these and fixed them up, I bet they made a bit of money on their sale. Or rented them out and are doing well. There's so little to rent in Crozet." She talked to the animals, who looked out the windows. "And someone out here, maybe out here, has new beds and lamps."

Just beyond a house with a basketball hoop on a pole sat a Nissan Sentra, a driver behind the wheel. The car had no lights on, the engine wasn't running. Harry noted the automobile but paid no attention.

The driver was Kylie Mason. She was dead.

The sheriff's department didn't receive a call about the car until that evening, rain falling. A neighbor noted the parked car.

Cooper got there first.

Kylie, not slumped, sat in the driver's seat. Cooper knocked on the door although she knew the woman was dead. The door was unlocked. Opening it, she touched nothing. No marks on her. No signs of violence. A coat and a purse were on the passenger seat. Sheriff Shaw arrived shortly. Putting on surgical gloves, he opened the glove compartment, pulled out the registration.

"Rental. Richmond," he said.

Cooper had told him about Dot's findings when she came to work that morning. The two stood there in the rain as the sheriff returned the registration to the compartment. Then he took her purse, head bent over to keep out of the rain. Opening it he found a thin wallet with a credit card and cash. Five hundred dollars. He also found a small makeup bag, which he showed to Cooper. Unzipping it, they found blusher, mascara, eyeliner, lip gloss, and moisturizer. Nothing more except a small spray perfume, which looked like lipstick until you pulled the top off.

"No suitcase," Cooper remarked. "So she has to have a place somewhere for clothing if nothing else. Dot said all was gone from Hamilton Street except for a sofa."

"Three murders. Get in my car. We're getting soaked."

"I'm willing to bet when we get the medical examiner's report, cause of death will be chlorine."

Wiping his face with his handkerchief, he muttered, "We'll see."

"If it is, I don't know if that makes our job harder or easier. We know we're dealing with someone, or someones, who is ruthless, kills quickly for no apparent reason. When you think about it, it's effective, draws no attention, no noise, no blood. Effective," she repeated herself.

"What could Bumpy have in common with a woman, or two women?"

"Rehab?"

"Possibly. They met in rehab or they met out of rehab but recognized the struggle. I don't know, but I bet the media will have a field day. And people will be scared."

"Lots of calls citing this and that. I'm always amazed with how nosy people are, and I'm glad they are. Those tips can sometimes help."

"Right." He looked at her. "Aren't you cold? You're wet."

"A little bit. I'll turn on the heat when I get back in my car."

"I can do that now." He leaned forward, flicking on the heat.

As they waited for the ambulance and the forensic unit, they voiced their frustration. Except for the method of killing, they had nothing.

"There has to be money behind this." Cooper didn't think this was about sex or revenge.

"Right. Drugs? That's always a possibility, and with the most unlikely of people." He took a breath, glad for the heat himself. "But I don't think it is. I doubt Bumpy would have been selling drugs unless he was using them. By all indications he wasn't. All that effort, all the times in rehab, and he's killed painting a shed." Sheriff Shaw shook his head. "Something or someone seduced him into what, I don't know, but it can't have been good."

"Do you think he knew these women?"

"I don't know. It's only conjecture, but as they were killed in the same manner, well, we have to wait on this one, but let's say she was known to him, there has to be some uniting factor."

"Two makeup bags," she responded.

18

October 4, 2025

Saturday

"Same place." Harry, on top of the ladder, looked down at The Very Reverend Herb Jones. "But it's not as bad, at least not yet."

She climbed down while her cats and the three Lutheran cats at St. Luke's observed.

"Any idea of the cost?" Reverend Jones asked.

"Won't be under a thousand dollars, that's for sure and, really, we should take up a larger area of the roof than we did before. Put down new shingles, tight. This church was built right after the Revolutionary War. Those shingles have been up there that long. Good builders. The roof has also withstood violent storms, blizzards, a hurricane or two. If this is all the damage we've got, we're lucky." She loved being in charge of the church's buildings and grounds.

"Don't you go up there."

"I won't." She could, but it would upset him to see a woman up on that steep roof.

Sometimes it's not quite right to insist on gender equality with an older gentleman who is devoted to you, cares for your well-being. After all, he baptized her.

"I've checked all the rooms, flicked on the heat as a test. Everything seems to be okay. Those new water heaters we bought are working wonderfully well. I know why the Good Lord walked with his disciples. Who could afford a church even then?" He laughed.

She laughed with him. You could say anything to the Reverend Jones, bring any question from life or the scripture. He would sit with you, consider your trials, worries, plus celebrate your jubilations.

The two humans and cat posse walked back to his spacious office overlooking the two quads in the back of the church, at different levels. The lower one contained the symmetrical, beautifully maintained graveyard, the tombstones going back to the late 1770s. A large portion of the old families of Albemarle County slept therein.

"The barn swallows left. It's so quiet in the barn." Mrs. Murphy made conversation.

Lucy Fur, one of the church kitties, remarked, *"For us it's the mice coming back in. Nights are getting cooler. We police the mouse holes. Daddy doesn't know where they are."*

"We've got mice in the barn but none in the house." Pewter liked the shiny hall floor, feeling she could skate on it.

"None coming in from the ground. I suspect we've got some in the attic, but no one ever goes up there." Mrs. Murphy added to Pewter's information. *"Daddy goes around the house every early fall and checks where the house meets the ground. He's vigilant."*

"Mice and rats are a lot of work. Eat everything." Elocution, another of the Lutheran cats, responded. *"I think last year's drought pushed them into the house. Heat burned up so many crops. Those rodents can live off the droppings, especially corn, but there wasn't much. In they came."*

Cazanova shared observations of the large number of cowbirds this year, the raw feel to the air today, as she joined the humans in the beautiful office. She was an observant kitty.

Harry and Reverend Jones sat on the sofa overlooking the quads. His assistant, a high school friend of Harry's, brought them tea, little cakes.

"Rev, I'll get right on this. The biggest times for repairs are now. Everyone realizes the weather is closing in."

"You're right. How are things at the farm?"

"Pretty good. I was over at Cooper's putting in stargazer lilies. She loves your home place. Doing a lot outside."

"I thought it would be hard to part with, but it wasn't. Cooper's a treasure." He smiled broadly. "And given that I've lived in the pastor's quarters here since I came back from Vietnam, I have everything."

"Considering the house matches the stonework of the church, it's a historic site just like the church." Harry called out to BoomBoom, her high school friend. "Everything okay?"

"Yes, except one of my boxwoods has a virus," the beautiful blonde called back.

"I bet Big Mim would know what it is and what to do. She's a marvel with landscaping."

"Heard she fired Lawler." BoomBoom called Kyle by his last name.

"News travels fast," Harry remarked as Herb shrugged.

"Anything involving the Sanbornes travels fast." BoomBoom smiled.

"Reverend, sorry to get off the roof subject here." Harry returned to him.

"No. I hadn't heard about the firing."

"Her prize stallion hated him. Big Mim did the smartest thing before someone or the horse gets hurt." Harry loved horses. "He kicked Fair, not because Fair was doing anything, but Lawler stood outside the stall when Fair went in to draw blood."

"Anything can happen at any time." Reverend Jones stated the truth.

"How about the woman found dead in the car yesterday?" BoomBoom couldn't help it, she joined the conversation from her desk.

"Boom, come here so you don't have to shout." Herb motioned for her to sit.

Just then the phone rang. She answered it. "St. Luke's, may I help you?" A silence, then she said, "Of course, here he is now." She held her hand over the mouthpiece as Herb, now on his feet approached her. "Bella Taylor."

He took the phone. "Yes. That is so sad. Yes, Topsy will be in heaven." Silence. "Yes. Tomorrow is Sunday, so we would have to do this later in the week. Ask your mother." Silence. "Christina, how good to hear your voice. She's crying her eyes out." Silence. "I don't mind at all. Monday or Tuesday? Monday, then. After school. See you at four-thirty." He handed the phone back to BoomBoom. "Topsy, her turtle, has died."

Lucy Fur, on the back of the sofa, said, *"He has his sermon written for tomorrow. Now he has to write a second one."*

"A turtle. In Heaven?" Pewter twitched her tail. *"Does everyone get in?"*

Elocution licked her paw. *"If Daddy gives the service, yes."*

Sitting down, Herb picked up his tea. "This will be the first funeral for a turtle in my life." He beamed. "All things bright and beautiful. All creatures great and small. The Lord God made them all."

Harry smiled broadly. "Bella will never forget this."

"BoomBoom mentioned the woman found in the car, speaking of death. Plus the woman found in the library parking lot." Reverend Jones shook his head. "The one woman is identified, Kylie Mason. The other one, nothing. There must be someone somewhere wondering where they are."

Harry agreed, adding, "Perhaps they were women with troubled lives. Maybe absences weren't unusual."

"Like Bumpy," BoomBoom chimed in.

"I haven't heard of a service for Bumpy." The Reverend Jones shook his head. "Yes, it was a troubled life, but you'd think someone would organize something. Like his rehab friends."

"You'd hope so, but maybe he's not that important to anyone. Maybe he burned too many bridges." Harry got up to pour more for herself, then asked Rev. Jones, "More?"

"Believe I will."

"You two sit. This is my job." BoomBoom took Harry's teacup, picked up the reverend's.

Harry sat back down. "The library woman is Latina. Cooper asked around to see if anyone recognized her from photos she brought. No one did."

"Interesting," Reverend Jones said.

"She was killed like the library lady, and like Bumpy. That makes no sense."

The Reverend Jones said, "It makes sense to somebody." Then he took a deep breath. "All right, girls, give me some ideas for Topsy's funeral."

Lucy Fur replied, *"Don't stick your neck out."*

19

October 5, 2025

Sunday

"Good as Reverend Jones's sermon was I had to fight to stay awake," Ned confessed as he poured wine into the special glasses.

"Honey, you've been working too hard, plus the weather is changing." Susan sat down. "You might have missed the sermon, but you won't miss grace."

Harry, Fair, and Ned bowed their heads, while Susan offered a short grace. Then they passed around the dishes, homestyle. Tucker sat right at Harry's knee as Owen stuck by Susan. The cats were back home.

"What's going on in Richmond?" Harry asked.

"Both parties are already firing up for the '26 election. As our governors are elected during midterms, unlike most other gubernatorial races, so much attention focuses on candidates. I really believe it's all too early," Ned pronounced.

"I'll think about it next May." Fair smiled. "Plus, all this attention, who will get nominations, what about lieutenant governor? I just wish people would shut up and do their jobs."

"Never happen." Susan tasted the simple dish of carrots and peas, deciding she thought she'd done a good job, speaking of jobs.

Harry tasted her peas and carrots, too. "This is so fresh."

"Farmers' market," Susan announced.

"That's grown locally." Ned watched his weight, especially having a wife who was a good cook. "Everywhere."

"People need to buy local, whether it's food, flowers, seed. Even the products like alfalfa seed should be bought from your local farm dealer." Harry cut into the Beef Wellington.

"Yes, it is better to buy in the community," Ned responded. "But people think saving a few bucks is really saving. It isn't. They spend it on something else."

"Honey, we all do that." Susan laughed.

"Imagine," Harry said, "if law enforcement weren't local. Say you could summon an online sheriff. Never work." She paused. "Susan, this Beef Wellington is fabulous. I don't know how you do it. Beef Wellington is hard to make."

"You just have to take your time, and it helps to buy a great piece of meat. But back to local, some services have to be local. I really think buying local food is so important. It isn't a service, but you pick up vegetables, meats at the farmers' market, no chemicals, no preservatives. Of course, the food will taste fabulous if you cook it in time."

"I feel like we've gotten so disjointed." Fair changed the subject. "For instance, Kyle Lawler ripping Paul and me to shreds on his Facebook page. I'm certainly not responding. He was fired. Most people will put two and two together. But some will think I covered for Paul's inadequacy with stallions, especially Silver Silence. People can accuse you of anything."

"Sour grapes." Susan got up. "Forgot the bread."

Harry got up and followed her. "I'll take out the butter and butter dishes."

Once that was accomplished, the dogs following the women to the kitchen and back, the conversation continued.

"If Big Mim gets angry enough, he'll be sued for something." Harry passed the warm bread. "I doubt she'll bother. A few words from her means he'll never work in a good Thoroughbred barn again."

"Power." Susan simply nodded.

"I guess we all want it on some level." Ned worked in the midst of people greedy for it. "I like being able to get things done. I like having my work considered, but that fever, the fever to be governor, senator, president, cabinet member, God help me. If I show signs of it, slap me in the face."

"Yes, dear." Susan lightly touched his cheek as they laughed.

"Where's Cooper today? She wasn't in church," Ned asked.

"Working overtime. The three deaths have people worried," Harry answered. "Given the manner of each death, how are these people, only one unidentified, connected?"

"Has the medical examiner specified the manner of death of the latest victim?" Ned wondered. "I'm a little out of it. Even though we're not in session, the committee meetings, the party meetings, it's nonstop."

Harry sighed. "Chances are strong she died the same way. Cooper was the first officer on the scene. She saw nothing obvious."

"There has to be something," Susan posited. "How many drugs can you make money on if illegal? Whatever they were doing had to be illegal."

As Ned placed another slice of Beef Wellington on everyone's plate, Fair replied, "Being a vet, we have medicines people will steal, like ketamine. Drugs don't have to be cocaine, they can be substances doctors, vets have. Maybe this was some form of, shall we say, a legal drug operation? Something from doctors."

"OxyContin. Stuff like that?" Ned sat back down.

"Yes, and doctors are in on it, illegal prescriptions or legal prescriptions in excess. The victims drive the drugs wherever they are distributed. Pick it up from a doctor, drop it off somewhere. A doctor can't have an office crammed with people using too much ketamine, fentanyl, etc."

"That's an unhappy thought." Susan slipped a piece of beef to Owen.

"Me, too." Tucker pawed at Harry.

"Beggars." Harry gave her a delicious morsel.

"Illegal alcohol, but that's heavier, harder to cart around." Ned then had another thought. "Illegal immigrants. Cheap workers."

"Wouldn't we know, say, if Bumpy brought in workers? That's probably beyond his capabilities." Harry couldn't imagine Bumpy hiding such an activity.

"There must be ways to be brought here that are less obvious." Ned was thinking out loud.

Susan noted everyone was finished. "Dessert."

"Yes, but let's sit for a minute and let this sensational dinner settle." Harry didn't want to move.

Susan, finger tapping the table, listed things people would kill for. "Power, money, sex, social status. You think social status? Something that would cost you your place, if you were caught red-handed? The shame would be too great."

"Susan, there is no shame anymore. Women attend lawn sales with their boobs hanging out." Harry shrugged. Then turned to Fair. "Do men really like that?"

Fair looked at Ned, who replied, "You first." Fair took a breath. "I would be horrified if you appeared in public, well, you know."

"But you'd look at a woman in, in a state of undress."

"Yes," Fair honestly answered.

"Honey, you can't help it," Ned responded to his wife. "Would I think it proper? No. But, really, you can't help it."

"Even women can't help it," Fair supported his friend. "Think of that famous photograph of Sophia Loren staring at Jayne Mansfield's breasts."

Harry and Susan started laughing.

Susan sputtered, "It's true. They jump right out at you."

Harry looked down at her pleasing but not huge bosom. "They are not jumping out at you."

They all laughed again, then Harry said, "You know there is a bird called a booby."

Fair tapped his wife's head. "Honey, what's going on up there?" He tapped his head.

With that, they all laughed even harder, especially Harry.

20

October 5, 2025

Sunday Later

While their husbands watched the football game, Harry and Susan, with Tucker and Owen, drove to the Dunkin House in Susan's car.

As they cruised through Crozet, Susan noted, "Quiet in town."

"Football. You know a lot of women watch football now. We never did but some schools teach it. It is a bit complicated," Harry replied.

"Maybe it's the only way to be with their husbands. You can watch football or play golf." Susan half smiled.

"Since you've won the country club championship twice, everyone wants to go on the course with you."

"Except my husband. To be fair, he has never liked golf. He's been talking about pickleball. He says he's getting slow on the tennis court. I'll learn if he really wants to do it." She slowed the car. "I'll park here behind what looks like Mac's truck."

"It is his truck. Wonder what he's doing here?" Harry rarely forgot a vehicle.

The two women stepped out of the car, corgis in tow. The door to the Dunkin House was closed. They had intended to walk the grounds to determine where to hide Frankenstein, devils, scary people. Susan turned the doorknob. The door opened.

They heard shuffling upstairs as the dogs immediately put their noses down to investigate.

"People have been here," Owen said.

"Anyone home?" Harry called out.

"Who's there?" Mac called back.

"Harry Haristeen and Susan Tucker. We're sorry to disturb you. We came to walk the grounds, but thought someone might be inside."

Mac came down the steps, his tread heavy. "Does the boss know you're here?"

"No," Susan answered. "We should have called, but we didn't intend to come inside."

"He told me to come over. Shifty drove by and said he saw a flickering light last night. Someone has slept here, upstairs. There's burned wood in the fireplace in the biggest bedroom. Probably had a sleeping bag. We have more homeless people than we know, I guess. I think Dr. Anglin should have a person in every house he's renovating or has renovated sitting empty. There's always a room where you can stick people, even if the house is torn apart. Or maybe some building."

"You're right," Harry agreed with him. "Look at the stuff stolen out of the rancher. Shifty seemed to have walked in on that."

Mac smiled. "He's nosy. Then again, he notices stuff. That theft was the darndest thing. New beds, bottom mattresses, lamps, a kitchen table, and four chairs. Oh, some nightstands."

"I bet the cost added up." Harry didn't think anything new was cheap.

"Yeah. Shifty said they were two women and one man, he thought a man; anyway. Too much going on in Crozet that doesn't make sense. When are you all going to start fixing this place up for Halloween?"

Susan answered. "Probably start about a week before. We have chairs to bring in for the ballroom, a few chairs in each room if people get tired from walking. We'll have the ghosts upstairs. We have a fair amount to do."

"And now we'd better have someone sleep here," Harry added.

"We'll all be working on our costumes, the haunting," Susan replied.

"It should be a man. Just in case."

"Harry's right." Mac looked up as he heard the dogs upstairs, their claws clicking on the wood floor. "The place is clean. Dr. Anglin has a good cleaning team. Bumpy and I moved furniture, but the girls do the floors, windows, all that stuff."

Upstairs, the dogs had gone into the room with the burned logs, ashes mostly, in the fireplace.

"A woman." Tucker lifted her nose.

Owen double-checked the spot where Tucker had been sniffing. *"A little perfume. I don't smell another scent."*

"Tucker, Owen, come down here," Harry called.

"Don't worry about them. They can't hurt anything." Mac stepped to the foot of the stairs, blocking Harry from going upstairs if she had tried.

She hadn't intended to go upstairs but she noticed.

The dogs checked out the rooms and the hallway. *"Faint but there used to be people in here."* Owen was intent.

"Right. Rubber soles. Even though floors get swept and washed, that's a scent that can linger. Can mar the floor a bit. These are dark floors. The humans wouldn't notice."

"People maybe hiding out?" Owen said to his sister.

"You'd think they'd need to go out sometimes. Even if only at night." Tucker

sniffed some more. *"Well, except for whoever was here last night, and I think the night before, only one."*

The dogs dutifully trooped to the first floor, while Harry and Susan told Mac they would call Dr. Anglin and ask for specific times to go into the house.

"Thanks. If you give him a schedule, then I can check from time to time. A week is a long time."

"Well, thanks for letting us look again. We're going outside. Those bushes can hide ghouls, I hope."

The two walked out with the dogs. Mac was behind them. He locked the door.

The dogs followed Harry and Susan, stopping at a row of thick boxwoods.

"This could hide people," Susan noted. "Have to be careful of the boxwoods though. You know how slowly they grow. Damage will take a couple of years to heal."

"Susan, do you want, say, Frankenstein to jump out at people?"

"Sure, or maybe follow them quietly then scare them. And we'll have the ghosts on the second floor. A few screams here and there would be perfect."

"Luckily, I don't have to scream." Harry grinned.

"You'll really scare them."

"I can scare people." Tucker wanted to be part of the night.

"We could growl, but I don't think corgis scare anyone." Owen squashed his sister's hope.

"We could bare our fangs and growl." Tucker bared her fangs.

"We could try." Owen bared his fangs, too.

Harry noticed the two dogs. "What are you two doing?"

"Being scary," Tucker responded.

After another forty-five minutes, re-checking every bush, every possible hiding place or where to hang a witch on a broom right under the roof, the two left.

"All right. In you go." Harry picked each dog up. "Susan, before it slips my mind, remember to bring over the sliding ladder. If we're going to hang anything, we need a sturdy ladder. I figured round, big-headed round screws will do it if you want a witch."

"Come on, close the door. Getting colder again. I don't know why, but I am feeling the cold more than when I was thirty," Susan complained.

Harry shut the door. "You're only thirty-nine now."

"Ha."

"We're the same age, remember?"

They laughed, batted around ideas as they drove back to Susan's.

21

October 6, 2025

Monday

"This is one of those times when artificial insemination would help." Fair walked with Paul down to the barn.

"The problem, you know, is it can be easy to cheat." Paul felt tired.

Thoroughbreds must use a live cover to be accepted by the Jockey Club. Most all other breeds now accept artificial insemination. Collecting sperm from a stallion could prove risky but most of the time it could be safely done. Live cover can hurt the mare as well as the stallion. One well-aimed kick with her hind legs and she can break one of his legs. It rarely happens, but over the years when it did everyone remembered. The stallion could also savage the mare if he becomes uncontrollable.

There was nothing romantic about horse breeding.

"It never fails to amaze me how much time, effort, and thought goes into cheating." Fair quickly stepped in the barn. "Wind has been nonstop this fall. Seems like it."

"Gets me when it hits me in the face." Paul walked to Silver Silence's stall, where the horse stood quietly. "He's calming down."

"All it took was for Kyle to get out," Fair remarked. "If someone missed the window last year, Silence will be ready come January, February."

"Yeah." Then Paul grimaced. "That damn trash talk. Costing us."

"Only to people who don't know Thoroughbreds. You all have a stellar reputation. It's the person who's just made some money, cruising the internet, might affect one or two of them. And those poor souls always learn the hard way."

"I don't want horses to learn the hard way. I'm lucky Silence didn't usually hurt anyone or himself. The minute that son-of-a-bitch left the barn, my boy settled down."

"We can't prove it, but there would seem to be abuse. This didn't come out of nowhere."

"I should have picked up on it. My damn fault. I listened to Kyle. He handled the horses. He could groom them until they gleamed. He was mindful of each horse's different food needs. When Silence began acting up, I didn't put two and two together."

"Paul, thinking your employee was mishandling or abusing your stallion wouldn't be anyone's first guess. Wasn't mine. There are other stallions here. No problem with them."

"They aren't bringing in the money. Silence is. They have good bloodlines but are out of fashion. When I started in this business, stallions like A.P. Indy were the big moneymakers. Changes."

"That's why the great barns usually have someone old running them. You're not old, but Big Mim's getting up there. Knows her stuff. I remember when everyone was crazy for Mr. Prospector blood, Secretariat blood. Some crosses worked. Some didn't. I was still in vet school. There's fads in every profession." Fair paid attention to those fads, for they can damage animals.

"Yeah. There's still so much luck involved." Paul threw a lead rope over his shoulder.

The two walked out to the mares' big pasture. Paul put two fingers in his mouth and whistled. Six mares ran up to him. He walked back to the barn and they followed. He took the lead rope in case, but he didn't need it.

"Cracks me up. Everyone likes to check out everyone else's stall. What if someone is getting better food? There's a few pellets, mash in a bucket. Gotta check." Fair smiled.

As each mare finally walked into her stall, Paul closed the doors behind them. Then he clipped the lead shank on a dark bay mare, beautiful head, a bit long-backed. He walked her out into the main aisle.

"Stone bruise. Pretty sure. But after the mess, best to double-check."

Fair leaned over, picking up her left foreleg. He stepped over it, bent leg between his legs, gently pressing his thumbs on the frog of the foot.

"A little tender." Fair repeated the process then moved to the side of her foreleg, putting the hoof down. "Bruise. Got anyone to walk the field?"

"Me." Paul put the mare back in her stall, unclipping the lead shank. "I don't mind. Need a sunny day."

"We're due one."

They walked to the tack room. Paul sat. Fair remained standing.

"Busy?"

"No. It's been quiet." Fair then took a chair. "No foxhunting accidents. I'm appreciating the quiet. It won't last."

"It's the ice that gets you." Paul, like most people who kept horses, dreaded ice.

"Yes, it is. I think the ER fills with people falling on the ice, too."

"ER. Ran into Winston Anglin a couple of days ago. He bought more land, wants to build a new house. I think he's going to hire my wife to be the architect." He mentioned Tazio Chappers, whose career was in building. "He's also thinking about a high-end subdivision. Lots of t's to cross and i's to dot. If it gets through the county commission, big bucks."

"He did a good job fixing me up in the ER. People who are good at what they do often succeed in other ventures. I'm not one of them." Fair smiled.

"He's making money. Has been. Buying old houses, fixing them, renting them out or selling them. Tazio and I have talked about buying a place, fixing it up. I don't know if we can risk the money. And I just don't know how long Mim will stay in the horse business."

"Aunt Tally is over one hundred." Fair cited Big Mim's aunt. "Mim will go on forever. She'll never give up the horses."

"I hope not. Taz will take more risks than I will. I'll take them with horses but not investments. What if we buy one of those fixer-uppers and the mortgage rates spiral up? We'll be stuck or sell without making much. It's all out of my control."

"It is." Fair smiled. "I never knew worry to do a bit of good."

As the two men talked, Sheriff Shaw strode into Cynthia Cooper's small office. "Chlorine."

"Damn," she swore.

"Medical examiner got on it."

"Do you have your announcement ready? You're good at that."

"I try. We are making these chlorine deaths our first priority. Anyone with information contact us."

She leaned over the desk. "I do not have one idea. Not one. People have closed their swimming pools. I'll call pool services to see if there have been any chlorine purchases. Shouldn't be any now."

"Right. That's a start though. What sticks in my mind is, no struggle. Whoever is killing people is able to sneak up on them, hold their head tight, put the cloth over their mouth. Or they know the killer."

"I vote for that."

"Let's start by meeting with every hospital administrator in the area. Ask them to review their drug purchases. Stealing drugs from a hospital or hospitals can be big business." Sheriff Shaw thought about other medical offices, too. "Do they have chlorine in the hospital?"

"Our killer is smart enough not to use any of those drugs to kill their victims. We might want to question people in rehab. Those who took illegal drugs. They'll be frightened to give names. Don't blame them, but we can ask what did they take, what did they see? Drugs didn't kill these victims, but they could have led up to it."

Sheriff Shaw said, "It's a start. This may not be about the profit from illegal schemes, but maybe it will lead us to the true profit. I've thought about a business not paying their taxes. But there's nothing in the area that sets off those alarms. I think this is about something being sold."

"Prostitution," Cooper suggested.

"We didn't have any houses of ill repute," Rick Shaw said. "Yes, we have some women with a side hustle but no real houses of a lot of women."

"There used to be one down at the train station." Cooper volunteered that information.

"Years ago. Women now, I guess some men, use their apartment, or there's a rented room in a decent neighborhood that people can use."

"Drugs are probably more realistic. Easier," Cooper said. "But sex sells."

"Especially in a college town. I'll keep that in the back of my mind. Most prostitution now is freelancers, forgive the pun."

She grinned at him. "Yes, Boss. Back to chlorine."

22

October 7, 2025

Tuesday

"Why did I ever start this?" Harry looked at matchbooks, rubber bands, small penknives, so much stuff that was in her catchall drawer in the kitchen.

"You were looking for quarters," Tucker reminded her.

Her corgi understood more human speech than vice versa.

Harry looked down at those big brown eyes. "Too bad you can't count pennies. I throw everything in here. Dumb. I am dumb."

A pile of coins, some quarters, covered part of the countertop. She pulled a soup bowl out of the cupboard and picked up pennies, nickels, the quarters, and a few big fifty-cent pieces, dropping them in with a clatter.

"If I pushed that over she'd have a heart attack." Pewter was sitting on the counter. *"She has no idea how restrained I am."*

"No Harry, no tuna." Mrs. Murphy knew Pewter well.

Pewter patted the bowl to hear Harry fuss.

"Don't you dare." The woman pointed a finger at the cat, who slapped her finger.

"Fishies." The gray cat tapped the bowl again.

Harry opened the cupboard door, plucked out the fishies bag, put some on the floor. She took out greenies for the dogs, too. Then she returned to the crammed catchall drawer, unaware of being expertly manipulated.

Forty-five minutes later a garbage bag was now full of the unnecessary notes, broken pencils, tired rubber bands, odd folded pieces of paper on which were written notes.

"Progress." Harry then wiped out the bottom of the drawer, placing the penknives, a few ballpoint pens, an old address book, a rolled-up measuring tape back into the cleaned drawer.

"More fishies," Pewter meowed.

Harry complied. Odds and ends still covered the countertop. She grabbed the paper coin rolls, in different colors for the different denominations, and sat down at the table. She kept coin rolls from the bank for her annual penny count.

"I knew I'd use these eventually."

Sitting there dividing up pennies, nickels, quarters, and fifty-cent pieces, she heard a car come down the long drive.

"Cooper." Tucker recognized the tire sound, as did the other animals.

To humans, most tires sound the same. The animals could identify tires a quarter of a mile away. If they didn't recognize the signature sound, the two dogs barked louder.

As the porch door opened, Tucker hurried to greet the tall blonde as Harry opened the kitchen door.

Cooper bent over to pet the sturdy dog. Pirate received a pet as well, an easier reach.

"Fishies," Pewter repeated herself.

Mrs. Murphy advised her, *"You'll need to wait."*

"I'm starving," the gray cat wailed.

"Ha." Tucker sauntered past the fat cat, who smacked her rump.

The races were on.

"Cooper, sit down before they run you over."

"Think I will."

"Can I get you anything?" Harry offered.

"No thanks. Let me help you count out the coins." She reached for the rolls. "I need to clean out drawers, too."

"Pulled up local news on my phone. The chlorine death of Maxon—"

"Mason."

"Was all over. You're not surprised."

"No. Rick," Coop called her boss by his first name, "checked her license. She was only twenty-nine. She looked a little older, and when we ran checks it turned out she was Guatemalan. She looked white. We can't find next of kin."

"No Masons." Harry stopped herself. "Takes time. Maybe she left home under a dark cloud. Maybe a false card."

"It's a legitimate New York State driver's license. So far, no trace of anything other than her New York address, Rochester."

"This is getting creepy."

"I don't know about that, but it's a big fog right now. Nothing in the car. Before, when she was stopped, she had those cartons of makeup bags, as you know."

"They had to be stolen or illegal." Harry was positive.

"No one reported a theft of makeup bags. No one reported Kylie Mason missing. No prison records. No one reported a woman missing who matched the description of the woman found at the library, either."

"Maybe it will take a while for their families to realize a daughter, a sister is missing. When people end relationships it can take years," Harry said.

"True. Seventy-eight dollars and fifty-three cents." Cooper stacked the rolls on the table.

"Fishies," Pewter persisted.

23

October 8, 2025

Wednesday

"The leak is five loose shingles." Harvey Stalton climbed down the ladder.

Harry, at the bottom, asked, "Easy to fix?"

"Not so bad." He put his hands in his overall pockets. "To be safe, I'd remove a three-foot square of shingles. Patch the hole. Then replace them with new shingles."

"Do you think the damage has traveled? I can see what's leaking down inside but maybe water has gone horizontally."

"That's why I thought to remove a three-foot square. It's more money, but if there is more leaking, this should take care of it."

"Yes. I'm fine with it. But I have to ask Reverend Jones first, and he'll have to go to the board, the treasurer."

"Harry, that will take too long. If we get a hard storm, I promise you there will be more damage."

"I know." She sighed. "How long will it take you to get the slate shingles?"

"Two days. I'll drive over to the slate quarry. There are cut squares for patios, shingles for roofs. Slate comes in different sizes. These shingles are the true late 1700s kind. I can match them."

"Once you're up there, how long till you can finish?"

"I'll bring Frank. We can patch that in a day, but let's figure in possible unseen problems. Now, you know, the replaced shingles will not be a one hundred percent match in color. But no one is going to come back here to see it."

"Oh, Harvey, someone on the board will. Never underestimate people's desire to find fault. Might be a little fault, but there has to be a fault. Tell you what, go ahead. I'll take care of the board. What's your estimate?"

"Twenty-two hundred."

She took a deep breath. "Onward."

He pulled the long ladder back, sliding it together so it would fit on the roof of his truck. He carried it to the truck, bent over a minute; a coin fell out of his pocket. He didn't notice, as he was balancing the ladder on his shoulder.

As Harvey slid the ladder onto the truck's roof, Harry picked up the bright coin. He affixed the ladder to one side, started to walk to the other side.

She held the coin in her hand. "Fell out of your pocket. A gold Bolivar. Where'd you get this?" She dropped it into his palm.

"Pretty, isn't it? Picked it up over at Front Street. Put a new roof on a remodel. Found it on the back step. No one was living in there. Finders keepers."

She was tempted to mention the Bolivar that Carolyn found. Something told her to shut up.

"Are you getting a lot of work?"

He smiled. "I am. Crozet's becoming a destination. Lots of houses selling."

"Good for all of us, I hope. When can you start?"

"Friday. I start another full roofing job next Tuesday. You won't believe this. They want a full copper roof."

"That will cost as much as the house." She laughed.

"Damn close. New people."

"I would think so," Harry replied. "I'll see you Friday."

As Harvey drove off, Harry called Cooper.

"Busy?"

"Parking lot. A Range Rover rammed into a BMW X5."

Harry teased, knowing the cost, relatively, of the cars. "Expensive store?"

"Harris Teeter." Cooper named the supermarket close to Crozet. "What's up?"

"I just saw another Bolivar." Cooper noted Harry's information while the angry drivers of the two cars discussed their problem. "Let me get back to you on this."

"Sure."

Harry then went in to Reverend Jones, telling him of her decision.

"Our treasurer will be unhappy."

"He'd be more unhappy if I waited until the monthly board meeting. One bad rain and the problem would be compounded and more expensive. Slate is expensive. Harvey has just enough time. He has a big roofing job that starts Tuesday."

Herb tapped his fingers on his desk as the cats lifted their heads.

"He's thinking," Cazanova announced.

"Maintenance gets you," the kindly pastor said. "Car. House. Land. Your stove. It's always the maintenance."

"Yes, it is, and St. Luke's has been well maintained for over two centuries."

Herb stood up. "Show me, in case Greg," he named the treasurer, "wants to see."

The two walked outside, followed by the cats.

Harry pointed upward. "You can see the loose shingles. Not many, but we talked about horizontal leaks. So that's why instead of simply replacing the five shingles, he'll do a three-foot square, the five loose shingles being in the middle of the square."

"Hmm. For two thousand two hundred dollars."

"Roofing is never cheap, plus we have to buy slate."

"I know." The Reverend Jones exhaled.

"Don't forget to take Greg upstairs to show him the leak inside."

"I won't." He turned to head back to his office.

"*Me first.*" Lucy Fur sprinted ahead, the other two chasing her.

The humans laughed, as the cats were having fun.

Once everyone was inside, Harry sat on the arm of the sofa. "I haven't brought bad news but it isn't wonderful, either." She paused. "Do you know much about foreign coins?"

"No." His eyebrows rose.

"In the last week, two goldish Bolivars from Venezuela were found on two different properties. One on the ground. One on a doorstep. Two different places."

"Seems odd, but could be a coin collector. A sloppy one." He grinned. "What little I know of currency is that the value fluctuates. It's kind of a game."

"Thought you might know. Is there anyone in the congregation who collects coins?"

BoomBoom, from her desk, called out, "Dr. Carmelo. The only reason I know that is he once showed me paper money from 1901 and then an old one-dollar piece. He was putting it in his safety deposit box and I happened to be in the bank. I think coin collectors are kind of like stamp collectors."

"Thanks, Boom." Harry would pass that on to Cooper. "Before I forget, Rev, your sermon for the turtle was wonderful."

The reverend blushed. "I had no idea so many people would show up."

Driving home, Harry passed Kyle Lawler and his wife traveling in a brand-new Ford three-quarter-ton truck.

She said to herself, "How much severance pay did Mim give him?"

She opened the door to a rapturous greeting except for a fretting Tucker.

"Why didn't you take me?"

"She needed a break," Pewter sassed.

As the two animals were getting wound up, Fair came home. Harry told him about Kyle's new Ford.

"She couldn't have paid him that much. A King Ranch Ford would cost almost eighty thousand dollars. Maybe more."

"I thought so." Then she told him about the roofing, plus the Bolivar. "It's a coincidence I guess. Or maybe not. A bag of coins would be worth something."

"You'd think so." He kissed her on the cheek. "A mystery."

Harry replied, "The mystery is chlorine."

"Oh, Honey, I'd rather think about coins than murder."

"People kill for money." Harry looked somber. "I'm blabbing on. Let's forget it for now. Sit down. I made shepherd's pie earlier. I'll heat it up."

He sat down as suggested. "I'd kill for your shepherd's pie."

"You don't have to do that." She put the pie in the oven. "But killing seems to be in the air."

24

October 9, 2025

Thursday

The rich smell of leather filled Big Mim's large tack room. Fair and Paul walked along the bridles hung neatly in rows. Late afternoon sun drenched the paned western windows. The large stable, built in 1821, reflected the early days of Monroe's presidency. People made money and spent it, witness the barn.

"See." Paul pointed to the row of saddles and bridles. "Nothing missing."

"All English leather and English steel. The best. He knew that."

"Well, I can't see that he stole anything."

"Nothing in the drawers?" The very tall vet noted the desk almost as old as the stable.

"Look." Paul pulled out a drawer. "The kitty is still here."

Neatly folded bills rested on a French change tray, while the coins filled a large coffee mug.

"I'm sure you counted the money."

"Of course I did. One hundred twenty dollars, paper money.

Eight dollars in change. Always surprises me how change adds up."

"Harry finally rolled ours up. But you'd think lifting the bills would be easy, attractive, especially if angry."

"All here. Every penny."

"Chores done?" Fair asked.

"Yes. We're losing light. Brought everyone in," the shorter, lean man replied.

"Silver Silence?"

"Came in like a baby."

"Take a couple of minutes with me. Get in the truck," Fair requested.

"Let me call the boss first." Paul dialed from the old landline in the stable, wisely kept in place.

He asked if Mim would mind if he left early with Fair. She was fine with it.

Sliding into the passenger seat, Paul looked around enviously. "Looks brand-new."

"Eight years old. I'd better keep it looking brand-new. I can't afford a new one. For one thing, I had the back rebuilt so I can stand in it. Need to lock it. Better organize the meds, the ultrasound, stuff. Lots of stuff."

"I think of anyone starting out in medicine on their own, veterinarians, dentists, physical therapists. The equipment cost must be staggering."

"X-ray machine. Ultrasound." He turned down the long, winding driveway toward town. "But you know, someone stealing from a vet would need a specialized fence. They're out there, but not in the numbers of people who steal human drugs."

"Ketamine."

"They'll lift what they can. At least with ketamine most people have an idea of dosage. They're smart enough to cut a horse pill. Other vet drugs, they don't know what they've stolen. They don't think about how much a human can absorb. So people die. Drugs are an epidemic."

"I don't see it ending." Paul thought the seat comfortable.

"I don't, either. If anything, more death. So many young people."

"As you know, I travel with some basic drugs, Banamine, the usual. Not one was touched."

"That doesn't mean Kyle's not getting drugs and selling them. He's stealing something, I swear." Fair reduced speed through Crozet now heading north to White Hall.

They passed Pinnell's brick building, where the stunning leatherworks were created, kept going north.

Passing Smallwood, a stable, Fair slowed. "Just past here, look right. The place is set back."

"Never knew where he lived." Paul strained to see. "Damn. One big truck."

"Told you. He doesn't have that kind of money. And his wife works at the BP station. Where'd he get that kind of money or that kind of credit?"

"How'd you know he lives here? I mean, I knew his address, but I never saw it. This is kind of a veiled area."

"Harry's been driving around looking at renovations. There's a big farm behind this with nice living quarters. Being renovated. She notices everything, but I actually saw the truck, she didn't. I took the chance he'd be home, since he was fired."

"One big truck," Paul repeated himself.

Fair continued all the way to White Hall, turned around at the convenience store, headed back.

"Right. Mim no doubt gave him decent severance pay."

"Not enough to buy that. How would he get financing without a job? I don't know what she gave him. She is really smart that way."

"She's smart every way." Fair greatly admired the older woman.

"I can't think of any way Kyle would get that much money. Other than drugs. Country waters."

"Cigarettes. Driving them up north. Same with 'shine. He goes to Maryland once a month, he says to his folks. Maybe there's something there." Paul stared out the window at the rolling countryside, a lower ridge behind it part of the Blue Ridge Mountains. "He put in a good day's work at the farm, but he never did more than he had to. To me that's lazy."

"Lot of people like that."

Fair slowed, as the road was getting twisty. "Next year I'll probably look for a partner. And I worry I'll only find Kyle types."

"You need someone who will step up."

"I'm lucky enough to need a partner. The work is piling up. So many people coming to the area. They fall in love with the beauty. Horses come next."

"That and swimming pools." Paul laughed.

"Don't mention it. Chlorine."

Paul's face sobered. "Now, that's crazy stuff. Kyle driving a new Ford is crazy, but dead people? Chlorine. Totally nuts."

"I think so, too." Fair added, "I worry about Harry. She thinks she can solve things. She hasn't gotten far with this chlorine stuff."

"Good. It's not safe." Paul also worried about Harry.

"Yes." Fair sighed. "She has courage, but she needs to let law enforcement do its job."

"I'd be scared if Tazio were as bold as Harry. She's bold enough. Fortunately, she doesn't get obsessed with crime."

"We hit the school traffic." Fair was stuck behind a stopped yellow school bus.

"Hey, at least those in the back haven't flashed or mooned you." Paul laughed, a nice deep laugh.

Fair laughed, too. "You never know what kids will do. Forgot to tell you, before I came to you, I was at Pepperpot Farm. New people. Very nice. Pepper, the lady, called me because both of her horses have swollen eyes. Ran tests. Allergies. I explained to her that horses, like people, can get spring or fall allergies. The eyes are a bit swollen, weepy, but no danger to vision. It will pass. I counseled her not to even think about allergy medicine."

"Doesn't last long," Paul noted. "Look, that kid has a bear knapsack. Clever."

"Cute." Fair now followed the bus, a line of traffic behind him, getting longer.

Another stop. A mother waited on foot, other mothers with her, as the bus doors opened. The children running to their mothers. A modern brick house fifty yards down a path had an older woman standing outside the door.

"I don't know any of these people," said Paul.

25

October 10, 2025

Friday

"So there's no real value? It's not gold. I wouldn't know the difference, which is obvious." Cooper smiled.

Dr. Carmelo, retired, smiled back. "The old ½ centavos, brass, can be shined up. The only gold Venezuela coins are late nineteenth, early twentieth century. Something like five Venezuelans. People who dabble in currency usually don't use much from Central or South America."

"Why?"

"Volatility. Now, people who collect coins who bank on workmanship could have antique Bolivars. Say one from 1840. The detail is precise. Venezuelan coins old or modern have interesting designs."

"Do you collect them?"

Dr. Carmelo shook his head. "My interest is fifth century B.C. Athens, Sparta, Corinth. I have a decent collection from Tiberian

Rome but my ancient Greek collection is extensive. We're all a little weird, collectors. We'll have lunch, talk amongst ourselves."

"So this coin has no great value?"

"No. You said there was another one?"

"The same. The man who found it kept it. This coin was found near the site of Bumpy's murder."

"Bumpy. We all knew Bumpy."

"We don't know if it belonged to him."

"As far as I know, Officer, there aren't many Venezuelans in Crozet. I know of no one."

"I don't, either. I've taken up too much of your time. The sheriff, the department, is on this. A coin is a long shot, but given the recent political focus on Venezuela, the coins were an oddity. You've been helpful."

He rose to walk her to the door. "Given the use of chlorine, it's possible the killer has some medical involvement. Your average guy probably wouldn't think of chlorine."

She thought of that driving back to HQ. She and Sheriff Shaw, tired and frustrated, had talked to people who owned pool supply businesses and those who dug pools. Nothing.

As to someone in medicine, wouldn't even a school nurse know about chlorine? Cooper exhaled, frustrated. She still had a lot of work to do.

Sheriff Shaw's voice rang out over the squad car phone. "Coop, meet me behind the post office. Hit and run."

The ambulance was there by the time Cooper arrived. The body, on a stretcher, was being lifted in. Officers in yellow reflective vests redirected traffic.

Cooper looked at the bloodied deceased.

Sheriff Shaw said, "Another Latina woman. No papers. Nothing in her coat pockets. Young."

"Yes. Her face is intact, a small help."

They stood behind the post office, a narrow convenience road curving around it. Whoever hit the woman had escaped using that curving road. The tire tracks where the woman was hit moved off in that direction then disappeared.

"Deliberate, I think. She was walking, hit hard from behind."

"Who found her?" Cooper asked.

Rick Shaw replied, "The postal clerks heard her scream. By the time they ran out, they didn't see the vehicle but they heard it speeding away. One of the girls," he called them girls, as they, too, were young, "tried to help. Took her pulse. She was gone. Shifty Brennan, also at the post office, came out. They all tried to see if they could get her heart beating without pushing on her chest, as she was so badly hit. I sent them all back in."

"Right." Cooper inhaled deeply.

"Shifty said she sometimes came into the store accompanied by an older lady, who would have her carry groceries in a little cart. She'd tell the young woman what to pick. He knew nothing about either one, but he recognized the young woman. Shook him up."

Cooper looked at her boss.

"Get a statement." Rick looked up and down the street. "People who drive cars into other people or crowds are sick. Sick."

"Seems to be more of them." Cooper agreed with this statement.

The dead woman was currently being zipped into a body bag. She didn't stand a chance.

"The other unidentified victim was found across the street in the library parking lot." Rick shook his head, confused, frustrated.

"Another young woman." The tall deputy ran her fingers through her blonde hair. "At least we've identified the Mason woman." She stopped. "Or think we have. We've found no relatives."

"The only murder victim we can identify is Bumpy. We know him, who he worked with and for. We know the people he disappointed, we know who counseled him. We know how often he wound up in the ER. We have no idea who he provoked."

"If Bumpy, the library victim, and Kylie Mason weren't all killed the same way, I wouldn't connect them." Cooper leaned against Sheriff Shaw's car. "And here is a woman killed by a car. She's young. No I.D. It could be a coincidence, I don't think it is."

"We've got a lot of digging to do. Even if we found a pack of cigarettes on each of them, it would be a help." He rubbed his throat. The slanting rays of late afternoon were blocked by trees on the west side of the two-lane road, the deep glow could be seen when looking toward the west.

"Speaking of cigarettes." He punched a pack out of his pocket.

"No, thanks. I thought you had quit again."

He lit one up, took a grateful drag. "I did. Relaxes me."

"Does it make you understand addiction?" Her eyebrows raised.

"Up to a point, it does. Yes." He half closed his eyes for a moment. "Smoking a cigarette won't cost me my marriage, my friends, or my job."

"No, but it might cost you your life."

"Now you sound like my wife."

"You don't listen to her. You won't listen to me."

He half smiled. "You're both right, but this little habit makes my life more bearable."

"I believe you. I believe that's also what's behind ketamine, fentanyl, fill in the blank. Or a stiff drink when you get home at night. Nicotine worked for me, but I had to stop. Do I miss it every day? Yes. And the pressure is building up with four murders. Boss, it's right under our noses. It's right here in Crozet."

He forcefully blew out the smoke. "We've gone over illegal activities, moneymakers."

"It's under our noses." She repeated herself.

"If this keeps up, I'll need all the tobacco in Virginia."

"Don't say that." She inhaled the odor of the tobacco smoke. "Here's my bet. If I figure it out, you'll stop smoking."

He eyed her, held out his right hand. "Deal."

Two Hours Later

Having worked late, Coop parked at Brennan gas station. Pushing open the store's door, she looked for Shifty.

"Alex, where's Shifty?" Coop asked the middle-aged woman behind the counter.

"In the back."

"Thanks." Reaching the door to the back storage room, Coop knocked. "Shifty, it's Deputy Cooper."

Clipboard in hand, he was counting beer cartons. "Hell of a day. Thought I answered all the sheriff's questions."

"You did. I'm double-checking. I want to get that bastard. Sorry."

He put the clipboard on top of a case of Heinekens. "I feel the same way. Come on into my office. Better place than here."

She followed him to his small, surprisingly tidy office.

Sitting across from him, she asked, "You didn't see the car or truck?"

"No. I heard it. Throaty eight-cylinder engine. Squeaking tires. I'd say the vehicle was a big truck, true eight cylinder, probably early 2000s, like 2003."

"If anyone could identify by sound, it's you."

"Cars, trucks, now SUVs, all I know. If I heard a Ferrari, a Testarossa, I could tell you. But there are a lot of older trucks around here. People hang on. You can't buy stuff like that anymore. For one thing, you have to be able to drive a stick shift." His voice was flat.

"Anything you can think of will help."

His face paled as he remembered. "That woman didn't stand a chance. She was hit from behind and she was walking right on the edge of the road. You saw the tire tracks."

"Yes. Can you think of anyone who had a grudge against the woman?"

"I'd say some nutcase boyfriend she'd dumped. Something personal. From the looks of it, there was nothing to steal," Shifty offered.

Coop sighed. "Have you had a lot of strangers at the station recently?"

She pulled out her notebook.

He shrugged. "No more than usual. Of course, now that you can pump your own gas, I don't notice who is at the pump unless I know the car. I'm in here most of the time. The victim, as I told the sheriff, had been in here a few times with an older woman. She must live here somewhere."

Cooper scribbled. "Do you speak Spanish?"

"Not a word."

She smiled. "Shifty, I am sorry to bother you. I know that was a shock. But if you think of anything, call me." She slid her card across the desk. "Thanks."

"All these murders. It's getting spooky. I'm starting to look over my shoulder."

She stood up. "Never hurts to be careful."

26

October 11, 2025

Saturday

"Why do I let you talk me into these things?" Susan flicked on her windshield wipers as it began lightly raining.

"Because you need excitement in your life." Harry grinned.

"Oh, please."

"Susan, you visit your mother and grandmother. You are a delightful wife to our district delegate to the House of Delegates, and you garden. You need something out of your routine."

"Every time I give in to you I land in trouble or some kind of mess."

"You always get out of it. May I remind you, you, yes you, talked me into being the Headless Horseman for your Halloween fundraiser."

A silence followed this. "I am grateful. But it's not the same."

"I think it is. I want to cruise around Crozet as a passenger so I can concentrate on houses, people, and then we can drive to St. Luke's."

"Do you need a prayer?" Susan pulled over to the side of the road. "I hate it when someone rides my ass."

"Me, too. That and people going slow cause just as many accidents as speeding."

Owen, silently looking out the window, watched everything from the back right side of the car. Tucker was at the left window. Pirate was too big for Susan's vehicle.

Susan then drove along the narrow macadam road behind the post office building to the back. She stopped, then turned right.

"Good. No one back here to push me to go faster."

"Now that we're here, go slower. Go around the curve. Right behind the post office building is where the woman was hit. The vehicle got out this way, according to Cooper."

They carefully looked, noticing the color on the deciduous trees starting to turn.

Harry commented, "There's no place to hide. The few houses back here aren't secluded enough. Keep going."

Susan crawled along at twenty miles an hour. "The driver knew this road."

"A Crozet person?" Harry wondered.

"Well, someone who knew their way around Crozet."

"Then what Cooper said about the victim, I'd guess she did not know her way around Crozet."

Susan nodded. "I've thought of that, too. Ninety-nine percent of people have a few dollars on them, their driver's license, perhaps a credit card. Yet another unknown person."

"Unknown to us. Oh, you're back at the good road. Turn there, then take a right into Wayland's Crossing." Harry's nose was almost pressed up against the window. "The development keeps growing. Doubt she was from here. You have to have a bit of money to live here."

Susan echoed Harry's concern. "The new people contact Ned quite a bit. They live in spiffy neighborhoods and want to keep them that way. If she did live here she'd have had some money on her."

"Turn left. Nice horses in that pasture." Harry admired the sleek animals.

"We'll come up behind the orchard." Susan again slowed as the rain was picking up. "Damn."

"Damn is right. There won't be anyone walking around. But we can look at remodeling or a lot of cars in a driveway or a yard."

"What do a lot of cars tell you?" Susan asked.

"If work is being done on the house or if a lot of people live there, maybe even graduate students at UVA." Harry took a breath.

"Okay. There's nothing on this road but pastures."

"Yeah. Let's go to St. Luke's, with this rain we can't see anything."

They passed a two-story traditional Virginia farmhouse. A few work trucks and regular sedans were parked up to the garage built to match the house. One man exited by a side door, hurried to an Altima. He looked furtive.

"No work clothes," Harry noticed.

"Could be a county inspector," Susan replied.

Another decently dressed man darted out to a car as the rain increased.

"Ever notice how few female construction workers there are?" Harry listened to the rain on the windshield and car's hood.

"Pay's good, but the work is not really inviting to women," Susan answered. "I'll be glad to get out of this rain."

They talked about the Seeing Eye Rescue group as Harry involuntarily shivered.

Susan turned on the heat.

"Thanks. By the way, that leak at St. Luke's is fixed." Harry leaned toward the heat vent. "This is what I get for not bringing an umbrella in the car."

"The weather report predicted a light rain. Not this. We didn't see young women, say a bit drier than you and I, when we could see."

"The rain took care of that. I racked my brain to think of other similarities the murder victims share."

"Except for Bumpy, they were young."

"And two of them had the little makeup bags."

"Right. That seems more unique to me than their youth or nationality. But other than that, Harry, there's nothing."

Flopping back in the seat, Harry shook her head. "Susan, something is right in front of us. We can't see it. Is something being smuggled in, say something small, from another country?"

"Doesn't explain Bumpy, but his death could be unrelated."

"Chlorine, Susan, chlorine. The last woman was a hit and run. I'm telling you, the answer is under our noses."

Tucker said, *"If we could smell it, we would know."*

"We haven't sniffed the dead people," Owen remarked.

"Bumpy. Paint plus sweat."

"Tucker, let the humans figure it out."

"My human gets in messes. She's too curious. By the time she or the others figure this out, it will be too late."

27

October 12, 2025

Sunday

The light looked softer, the crisp smell of fall hovered in the air. People stayed to talk after Reverend Jones's service.

Finally in the car with Susan and Ned, the three discussed the sermon per usual. Ned dropped her off at home. Fair was at Big Mim's.

Before Harry stepped out of the car, Susan asked, "What's going on over there?"

"I don't know. Silver Silence has been troublesome. Fair said he settled down once Kyle left, but early this morning he was ferocious again. He was out in the pasture, the five-board-fence pasture. Paul will start bringing him in when the true frosts hit."

"If our personalities can change, so can an animal's." Ned thought mammals were more alike than different.

"I agree." Harry watched as Tucker zoomed out, while Pirate barked inside.

"Love this." Susan smiled, looking at the burgeoning color in the leaves.

"Is. We get to live such wonderful lives out in the country, with our pets, watching wild animals. I couldn't live in the city. I'd die."

"I would, too," Susan agreed.

"Well, let me get in the kitchen, give everyone treats. Actually, if you would like to come in, I can make you breakfast. I bought bacon yesterday. I know you like bacon."

"Thanks. I promised my husband steak for breakfast. We're on a high-protein diet."

"You two keep up with food ideas. I stick to the stuff my mother and grandmother used to make. Thanks again for the ride. Good sermon."

"He's always good," Susan agreed.

"If you have tidbits left, I'll take them for the cats and dogs. Little bites. Little steak tidbits."

"I'll save some for you," Susan promised.

Opening the kitchen door, Harry was greeted with one wagging tail that was so big and forceful, she had to slide by Pirate.

"I've been thinking about a special tuna casserole," Pewter announced.

"Where'd you hear that word casserole?*"* Tucker was surprised.

"Yesterday when Mom was watching the morning news. They have a brief food section. That's my favorite." Pewter remembered everything connected to food.

People think animals don't have good memories, but they do. As for Fatty, food was an enlivening memory.

Opening drawers, Harry yanked out odds and ends. Offering bacon to her two dear friends had made her hungry. She slapped the frying pan on the stove, pulled out the bacon, separating the fragrant meat, then pulled three brown eggs from her egg keeper on the side of the refrigerator door.

Soon all was sizzling.

"Think we'll get some?" Pewter wanted it now.

"We'll get a little, but she'll pour the grease on our kibble." Tucker couldn't wait, being as impatient as Pewter, thanks to the glorious odor.

Pirate, ever the gentleman, sat, eyes fixed on the stove, but waiting. Mrs. Murphy sat next to him.

As Tucker predicted, after Harry filled her plate with eggs and bacon, she poured grease into each animal's bowl. Enough to give the kibble special flavor.

As everyone was eating, Harry, notebook by her right hand, was making notes as she used her left hand for the fork.

Scribbling in her notebook she listed Aramaic, distances between Rome, Alexandria, Bethlehem. She added another column, including more eggs, flat noodles, Irish butter, then she laid down the pencil and concentrated on her food. For whatever reason, she was hungry.

Her cell rang. She picked it up, saw Cooper's name.

"What are you doing?"

Cooper replied, "Putting away my summer clothing. Bringing out the fall and winter. My closet is a mess. Half the clothes are on the bed. Hearing that you and Susan organized your fall clothing, I knew it was time for me to do it."

"Come on over. I'll make you breakfast."

"Thanks, Harry, but I just ate my McCann's oatmeal this morning."

"Well, come over, we can both have tea. As for your clothes, organize them by color. Easier to see all the reds in one place, the beige in another. Anyway, who is going to look in your closet but you?"

"You have a point. See you in a minute."

By the time the animals cleaned out their bowls, Coop walked through the kitchen door.

"Happy Sunday." Harry beamed as she put the teapot on.

The two sat down, chattering away about what was happening around them.

"Are you starting your tractor every day?" Harry asked.

"Once a week. And I put the snowplow on the front, with Lucas's help." She named a neighbor. "My tractor has been a godsend, even at twenty-five horsepower."

"That's all you need. The snowplow fits the tractor. It's the right size. That big old one hundred fifty horsepower that we have is a monster, but great for haying. The sixty horsepower is perfect for the snowplow. We've got so much more to plow than you do. I can't believe we're talking about snow." Harry got up to get more hot water. "Are you sure you don't want some bacon? I have four pieces left."

"I'll have two if you'll take two."

Harry put the bacon on a small plate in front of her. Both women devoured the bacon in record time.

"I'll want what's left," Pewter meowed.

Harry glanced down at her plate, clean. She rose, opened a cabinet, and put down a small handful of crunchies on the plate for both cats, repeating the process for the dogs.

"I'm surprised your cats and dogs aren't huge."

"Coop, they run it off, as I do. Back to snow. Won't see any until maybe late November. The weather is all screwed up." She savored her tea. "While I'm talking about screwed up, let me tell you what Susan and I did yesterday."

She described the weather, the drive, the one house possibly being worked on, even St. Luke's roof.

"Did you notice a lot of cars at any of these in-the-back houses?" the deputy asked.

"A few. Why?"

"We know there are drugs in Crozet. We have an idea who sells the low-end stuff. People stop by these houses. Can we catch them? So far, no, but nailing someone for marijuana, not illegal in 2025, small beer, is a start. Maybe the cars will lead us to our killer or killers. Anyway, it's a thought."

"People can sell drinks with some marijuana in them, or

things that look like jellybeans," Harry noted. "Speaking of small beer."

"Is weed a gateway drug?" Cooper paused. "For some people it is. How do you know if you're that person? Especially when you're a kid. It's like that first time you get drunk. Will you do it again and again or did the misery the next day teach you you'd better learn to drink or not drink at all. The real problem for me is people loaded on whatever getting behind the wheel of a car."

"Do you think whoever killed that woman behind the post office was drunk?" Harry asked. "A front fender would be dented, maybe bloodied?"

"As this was premeditated, I expect that vehicle is in a specialized shop somewhere." Cooper was frustrated.

"So organized crime?"

"Harry, if you pay someone thousands of dollars in cash to repair your truck, most places will do it and not ask questions, especially if you bring it in at night and no one knows but whoever is there that you can trust, say like the owner."

"Money is king. Our entire society is focused on the almighty dollar."

Cooper shifted in her seat. "I think it always was."

28

October 13, 2025

Monday

"This will be easier for me." Fair stood on the stepladder as Paul handed him a little black square.

"Okay," the trainer agreed, as Fair was a good six inches taller.

The vet fiddled up there, putting the box in one position then another. "Is this better?"

Paul walked to the four corners of Silver Silence's stall. "There. Now tip it down a bit. Got it."

Fair then put medium-length thin black nails around the cameras.

The tap, tap, tap echoed through the barn.

"My turn." Paul touched Fair's leg.

"Why?"

"Because I can reach the crossbeam and I can hide the wire. We need to put it into the next stall, high, then come out and plug it in the outlet."

Fair stepped down, left the stall to check the center aisle outlet. "It's not hidden."

Paul, carefully stapling the wire, replied, "We'll have to string this farther. Someone would have to be looking for a camera. I don't think he's that smart."

Fair watched his friend painstakingly staple then push the wire into the next stall, where it dangled. He walked into the stall, picked up the wire.

Paul took it out of his hand, running the black wire just below the board under the stall bars. It was a kind of windowsill.

Then Paul dropped the plug over and Fair plugged it in.

"Paul, he's smart enough to steal Silver's semen."

"If I can get a picture, then Mim will have proof and she can see for herself. I never thought of him collecting the stuff in Silver's stall. We have the breeding shed. Let's hope this works."

"You really need two people in a breeding shed," Fair stated. "You can do it alone, but it's more dangerous. Kyle, worthless dick that he is," Fair would not speak that way in front of a woman, "was smart enough to use the stall. If he backs the horse in, he stands a chance, but if he comes back, I think he'll bring someone. Silver will now try to kick him through the wall."

"Wish he would. If he does, I'll get a picture for sure of him getting semen. I never thought of this until you mentioned crossbreeding. He sure can't collect the stuff outside."

"A Thoroughbred can almost always improve a non-Thoroughbred breed. You can't charge as much, obviously."

"Like what kind of fee?"

"This is a proven horse. Let's say a warmblood breeder wants to cross. They are AI. I bet Kyle can get at least ten thousand dollars," Fair answered.

"No wonder he has a new Ford dually. He's done this more than once." Paul shook his head. "Maybe Silver Silence will kick him and break his back."

"It would be justice. He has to have manhandled the horse to get the reaction he now gets, but Kyle will plead innocence, he'll claim Big Mim keeps a dangerous horse. It would be a real circus." Fair had seen and testified in enough equine cases to know when people are involved there is no justice.

Trust the horse.

"Think we've got it." Paul folded his ladder.

"Call me in the morning. Tell me what you see," Fair said.

29

October 14, 2025

Tuesday

Horse people tend to get up early, especially vets.

Fair's phone rang, an organ chord. "Yes."

"Got it. It's him." Paul sounded triumphant.

"Give the footage to the sheriff. By the time you call Rick Shaw, Mim will be with her lawyers. Kyle wasn't hurt, so she's in the clear to nail him."

"Okay." Paul called the sheriff's office. He couldn't get through to Sheriff Shaw, who was on the phone with Cosmer Auto Repair.

Sheriff Shaw put Cooper on it. She drove out to Kyle Lawler's address. Gone. No truck. She called Paul, who was furious. He called Fair, also furious.

"Damn, I hope the cops catch him." Paul cursed some more.

"Me, too. At least Silver Silence is safe. He'll come back to his old self. I hope so, anyway." Fair was making a morning pot of tea for Harry.

When she came into the kitchen, he gave her the whole story.

"He'll get caught sooner or later," Harry predicted. "And he'll have to sell that truck or hide it somewhere."

"You know, Honey, there is too much going on in Crozet right now."

Later, Sunset

"Sunset means the bats come out, other birds go to their nests. The night creatures start looking for food. Everything feels different." Harry spoke to Mrs. Murphy, Pewter, Tucker, and Pirate, happy in her old station wagon.

"Good time to hunt," Pewter added. *"We cats have the eyes for it."*

"The one with the great eyes is the barn owl." Tucker didn't disagree but didn't praise the cat's abilities.

"She can be right over my head and I barely hear her," Pirate confessed.

Harry had a hunch whoever had been in the house when she and Susan surprised Mac might come back.

Harry turned onto Dunkin House Street. She glided by, drove to the end of the road, where she would park the trailer come Halloween. She cut the motor.

The house, clear view from the front as well as one side, intrigued Harry. Lifting her binoculars up, she focused on the second story.

"If only I could see the whole back of the house."

Parking where she was, if someone walked or parked in front of the house, they wouldn't notice her.

She scanned what she could of the grounds, then swept back to the front door. Apart from a few bats, nothing. She, the cats, and the dogs sat for fifteen minutes.

"Getting cold." She switched on the motor as twilight deepened, quickly cutting the lights, hoping no one had seen them.

"We've got this old blanket." Tucker snuggled in it.

"You're hogging most of it," Pewter complained.

"*No, I'm not*." Tucker did move a bit.

Harry cracked her window, listening intently.

She slowly rolled down the road, lights off, stopping about fifty yards from the house, the front of the old station wagon facing out. If she needed to, she could pull right out. There wasn't much traffic, as there wasn't much back here.

Again, she picked up her binoculars.

She backed up a bit to get a broader view of the long backyard. Tensing, she leaned forward. A low flicker danced in a window toward the back. She thought she saw a figure walk near a window. She strained to see. Then she did see a figure, she couldn't determine if it was a man or a woman, facing the window, then the light went out.

"Damn whoever blew the light out."

She sat, noticing a figure running across the back lawn. She wasn't close enough to determine anything, but a person did leave the house by the back door. Tempted though she was to get out of her car and try that back door, she did not. Harry didn't know what she was up against. Was this a squatter? Were there others up there?

She looked at the chimney. No smoke. Whoever was in there had not built a fire.

Something told her not to tell anyone about this. Not to call Dr. Anglin. Not to tell Susan. Maybe later she could tell Susan, but not yet. Mac knew someone had been in the house. Surely he drove by periodically and checked or even went in. Then again, whoever stayed there knew his schedule. Somone who didn't need a bed. But when she and Susan had stopped by unexpectedly, not thinking anyone would be there, they hadn't gone upstairs. Maybe there was a bed up there now, a table, who knew what? If whoever was using this place had a bedroll, they could carry it or stash it if they didn't want to carry it. The house was big enough to hide a sleeping bag.

"Something is going on."

"You don't need to know," Tucker counseled her.

Harry drove away, not turning on her lights until she reached the intersection.

"What if Mac knows who is there?" she said out loud.

"Her curiosity." Mrs. Murphy shrugged. *"She'll kill herself trying to find out."*

"There's enough dead people already." Tucker dropped her head on her paws.

30

October 15, 2025

Wednesday

The sun broke over the horizon, sending long red slanting rays across Harry's eastern pastures. The frost glittered with color while the western pastures, yet untouched, remained silver. This was the first frost of fall; light, but a frost nonetheless.

The stall doors to the outside remained open. The horses chased one another, enlivened by the chill. When hard frosts arrived, Harry would close them in for the night, shutting the Dutch doors to the outside. By then, they'd each be wearing a light blanket, the heavier ones to come as the season deepened.

Tucker and Pirate sat by her feet, little puffs of air coming out of their mouths.

"*They like to play tag,*" Pirate noted.

Tucker, now leaning on Harry, one paw on her warm, old country boots, remarked, "*They play a fast game. When I was a puppy, I liked tag. Then I learned to play fetch. I like that better.*"

"All right. Back to it." Harry, enjoying watching her horses, spoke to the dogs.

Walking in the stable's back doors, sliding one stall door open, she inhaled the lush scent of horse, leather, hay, sweet feed. She checked each stall. Every bucket was empty. They could never get enough of their sweet feed.

She returned to the big back doors, fully opening them.

"No point closing them. Good to get fresh air wafting through as long as we can. Don't know why I closed them last night." She looked at her dogs. "All this uproar preys on my mind. I need to focus on what I can do."

She walked into the tack room, her little office, flicked on the stove.

"Good." Pewter burrowed in a tidy pile of saddle pads and propped her head up.

The fleece pads weren't tidy for long.

Mrs. Murphy sat on the desk. The cats evidenced no desire to go outside this morning.

Harry kicked off her boots, pulled one of the director's chairs in front of the stove, propping her feet up on a small box filled with brushes, combs, small towels, leather conditioner.

"Feels good. I need to get the holes in my boots repaired."

"You need a new pair of boots," Pewter advised. *"These won't keep out the cold anymore."*

"What about work boots with special lining?" Tucker thought they'd smell inviting.

"Good idea," Mrs. Murphy agreed.

Harry luxuriated in a few moments to herself with her feet warming. She dozed off.

"Coop," Tucker barked, waking Harry from her fifteen-minute nap.

Harry got up, padded across the floor, opened the door. "Come in."

"Cozy in here." Cooper pulled up another director's chair, to sit beside the one in front of the stove.

Harry slid over another boot polish box, placing it in front of Cooper. She then sat down, propping up her now warmed feet.

"Worked late last night so Rick said I could come in at noon," Cooper informed her.

Harry had to bite her tongue. She wanted to tell her friend about a person or persons in the Dunkin House, but she wanted to investigate more before she opened her mouth.

"Fair told me Kyle and his wife have flown the coop. Thanks to him my husband's ribs are cracked." Harry wiggled her toes.

"I'm sure Big Mim will retaliate legally," the deputy said.

"Yeah. But whatever he did was hard on the horse. I hate people who abuse animals."

"Me, too. Came over to tell you Kyle's big truck showed up in Leesburg. Parked on a side street in downtown. Totally cleaned out. He's probably across the river."

"Have you ever heard of people ditching trucks?" Harry's eyebrows shot upward.

"Yes. Kyle made decent money." Cooper added, "But given the cost of the truck, it's possible he had another side hustle. Again, would have to be quite a bit. Fair explained the semen price would not be a Thoroughbred price. No artificial inseminations. So Kyle probably rented the truck."

Harry put her hands together in a steeple. "Think you're right. Ideas?"

"Yes, actually." Cooper smiled. "Immigrants are getting deported. So far we're okay, but you know some of our farm workers have to be illegal. It's so time-consuming and expensive to get work papers."

"The best is a green card," Harry said.

"Yes, it is, but let's say I'm an employer. Would I go through all that if I thought the worker would leave?"

Harry quickly replied, "Make him sign a time contract."

"That's a start." Cooper shifted her weight. "There's so much an employer can't know. What if it's a bad harvest? You've got money tied up in employees."

Harry sat up straighter. "It's possible. But Crozet seems an unlikely stopping place."

"But it's not impossible." Cooper was firm about that. "Albemarle County is well placed. You can easily get up and down the East Coast. Illegal immigration could make a very clever person huge sums of money."

"Enough to kill someone who threatened it?" Harry asked.

"I think about that, then I think about the discrepancies among our victims. Or for that matter, making money selling Silver Silence's sperm."

Harry said, "In his prime, I think A.P. Indy's stud fee was three hundred thousand dollars."

Cooper, deadpan, replied, "Yes, but that's a Thoroughbred. A human will give it away for free."

They both exploded into laughter.

31

October 16, 2025

Thursday

A light wind from the west promised a cooldown. At forty degrees in the morning, it seemed cool enough. Harry completed her chores, checked the thermometer on the outside of the barn. It had risen to forty-six degrees.

In the tack room, stove on, she checked The Weather Channel. Sure enough, a cold front was coming, bringing consistent morning frosts.

Mrs. Murphy sat on one side of the computer, Pewter on the other. They enjoyed the images, in this case pictures of weather in Maine, some snow there, then a bounce to Manhattan. If only the weather people had cats with them. Would make for more reliable weather predictions.

"*It's coming.*" Mrs. Murphy patted the screen, which made Harry smile.

"*As long as it doesn't snow.*" Pewter never liked her feet cold or wet.

"When it does, it keeps your blue jay in his nest." Mrs. Murphy wasn't overly fond of the bird but would tolerate him.

"Why doesn't he freeze to death?"

"Because they build good nests. Sometimes they'll nest in a tree cavity, but usually they build a twiggy nest out of the wind. That and their feathers keep them warm." Mrs. Murphy added, *"They're smart."*

"Mom should stop feeding him. I don't know exactly where his nest is, but it's somewhere in the big tree by the window over the kitchen sink. I think it's high up." Pewter thought Harry was a softie, which she was.

"She likes everybody, the birds, the possum, the deer, the beavers. She likes to watch animals." Mrs. Murphy saw a dog food ad. *"Would you look at that."*

"The last thing Bubblebutt needs is more food." Pewter giggled.

As if on cue, Tucker pushed through the door. *"I'm here."*

"What a thrill," Pewter remarked.

Knowing Pirate was on the other side of the door, Harry rose, opened the door, and the giant dog came in, kissed her hand, and plopped down.

"It's getting colder," Tucker announced. *"We were back at where the black walnuts start. A wind came up. Made me glad I have fur. Winter is around the corner."*

The four talked about the coming cold as Harry bounced between weather channels. She turned the sound off, picked up the old office phone.

"Susan."

"I'm watching the weather, too. Know you are."

"We'll put on an extra layer. How long do you think we'll be outside? A half hour?"

"I'd figure forty-five minutes to be safe. The porta-potty fellow won't take long. He'll know the best place to put them. Need to get our order in now. Wilson Anglin might take longer. He has to show us how to turn on the heat, stuff like that. I doubt he gets to visit his investments much. One of the reasons he got robbed, I bet. But this house is so unique, he really knows it."

"I was thinking of cleanup. I hope we can return the next day.

The dump will be closed, but if we get our workers to bag trash, I'll put it in the back of the truck. Even with the trailer connection, should be enough room."

Susan exhaled. "A lot of stuff to think about and do."

"You've got the music. We've got the people for witches and ghouls. We still need a lot of dancers."

"I'm working on it."

"I know you are. How about I pick you up at one? We need light. It gets dark now early. Twilight lasts until maybe six. I kind of enjoy noting the light."

"Okay. One, do you need anything?" Susan asked.

"We should probably take pictures. You have the drawings with the room dimensions but pictures will help."

"Okay. I'll bring my old Nikon. I can't take pictures on my phone. I need a real camera."

As the porta-potties truck drove off, the two friends stood by the west side of the Dunkin House, thirty yards from the house. The dogs and cats sat with them, although Pewter wanted out of the wind.

"The porta-potties won't distract from the house." Susan, gloves on, put her hands in her pockets.

"No, they are a bit far from the house, but as people park or walk up they'll see them. Be smart to go first." Harry's feet felt warm with her cashmere socks and old redwing work boots.

She needed new work boots, but until the chill air got in the holes in these, she'd hold out. Her cashmere socks helped ward off the cold.

Harry stuck to the basics. No $350 Winton work boots for her.

"Let's go inside," Pewter complained.

"That wind is picking up." Susan flipped up her coat collar. "Let's go inside. I have the front door key."

"When did you get that?"

"Tuesday. Drove to the Anglin's house in Ivy Farms. Beautiful place," Susan enthused. "The landscaping at their house makes a difference. Makes a difference here, too. Nothing like mature bushes, big trees. Amen." She trotted to the front door, slipped in the key, opened it, closed it.

Ivy Farms was close enough to Crozet, but not truly in Crozet.

"It's as cold inside as out," Pewter moaned.

"No heat's on. But you're out of the wind," Tucker explained.

"I don't care," the gray cat meowed.

"We're stuck." Mrs. Murphy didn't much like it, either.

The front door opened and Wilson Anglin stepped in, unbuttoned his coat. "Girls, come on into the old kitchen. Will heat up in a minute." He had pulled up behind them as Susan opened the door.

They followed him in, the impressive wood-burning stove intact, as good as new, a large fireplace across from the entryway. All the old kitchens had a door opening out. Many from the eighteenth, early nineteenth century also had an outdoor kitchen for the hot, humid months.

He bent down, put a starter log on the raised iron grate in the fireplace, lit it, then made a teepee out of slender fatwood, crossing dried logs over that.

"That didn't take long," Harry said admiringly.

"When you're a poor kid in medical school, you learn every trick in the book." He smiled. "There were four of us. We pooled the expenses, had a chore wheel. It worked, and we still keep in touch with one another."

"Did everyone wind up in the ER?" Harry, ever curious, asked.

"Move your butt." Pewter wedged next to Tucker in front of the fire, while Mrs. Murphy sensibly laid on Pirate, snuggling in his dense fur.

"Pain in my ass." Tucker curled her upper lip but she did make room.

"No," Wilson replied. "Artic specialized in esophageal cancer, what killed General Grant. Ronnie stuck with cardiology, always a sure bet, and Bronwyn also focused on cancer, but lungs."

"You picked ER." Susan stated this, didn't ask.

"I did. It's for adrenaline junkies. I like the pressure, but I also wanted to deal with problems then go home. My buddies have patients. They have relationships with them. I really don't. Granted, I know people like your husband." He looked at Harry. "But it's not the same as a patient calling at three A.M. My wife appreciates my choice."

"I never thought of that," Harry honestly replied.

"By the way, I heard about what happened at Big Mim's. No wonder Fair was kicked."

"Dr. Anglin, it's not anything a vet or a horseman would think of. Stealing stud fees." Harry slightly grimaced.

"No." He shook his head.

Susan began walking them through the downstairs rooms, explaining the plan. Pewter left, returning to the kitchen. The humans might be dumb enough to dig through cold rooms, but she wasn't going to do it. Mrs. Murphy, on the other hand, kept up. She and the dogs listened intently, plus used their scenting abilities.

The house was empty, supposedly, but the animals smelled people.

"Do you think someone is living here?" Pirate wondered.

"I do," Tucker shrewdly answered. *"Like putting down a sleeping bag then leaving. Someone not wanting anyone to know. We saw someone leave when Mom parked here. They must clean every day. No sign of people."*

"We won't allow anyone upstairs, but as I've mentioned we'll have some ghosts up there walking by the windows to scare people outside." Susan warmed to her subject, explaining the plans for upstairs, downstairs, and outside.

"Everyone will be in some kind of costume." Harry enjoyed Susan's enthusiasm.

"Come on. Let's go back to the kitchen. I have a few questions. We might as well be warm." Wilson headed in that direction.

Once in the kitchen, they unzipped their coats, removed their gloves.

"What took you so long?" Pewter asked.

"Susan had to explain everything," Mrs. Murphy told her.

"What about Mother?" the gray cat wondered.

"She didn't say much," Pirate answered.

"That's a miracle." Pewter flicked her tail in merriment.

Susan went over the porta-potties.

"Sounds okay. When will they be picked up?" Wilson held his hands out to the fire.

"They swear the next day." Susan handed him a copy of the contract, as she had signed for two. "And here. This is our insurance contract for this specific event."

"How'd you get this done?" His dark big eyebrows raised.

"Well, I learned about specific events from horse shows. I used to compete. Not so much now, but every foxhunting club, trail riding club, carried a special policy. If you have an event for, say, fifty people you have to be cleared by the insurance, plus you pay more."

"We'll all die from paperwork." He shook his head.

"If you tell people that in the ER, it will give them hope that their bodies aren't too much in trouble, only their bank accounts." Harry smiled.

"I'll remember that. It's true." He sighed. Looked back at the papers. "I'll read them more carefully at home. Actually, I'll give them to my wife. She's a wiz."

They chatted some more.

"We picked around 1870 for our period costumes. Clothing for both sexes was so beautiful then, especially the military uniforms." Susan was again enthusiastic.

"Will anyone be, say, a baron from England?"

"Our dancers get to choose. That, and the music will be beautiful. The ballroom will be the last stop before leaving the house," Susan explained. "We're hoping our visitors will dance."

"I hope so, too. Will you have any of the Seeing Eye dogs here?" He asked good questions.

"No, it's too much. We'll have pictures in the foyer of some of our graduates. I am praying we'll make money." Susan meant that.

"It's unique. I'm sure you'll make a penny or two." He was encouraging. "You might even start an annual event."

"Miracles do happen. Before I forget, Harry will be the Headless Horseman." Susan gave Harry a light poke.

"Not on the dance floor, I hope." He laughed.

They talked more, then Susan remembered the cold. "Wilson, I'll turn the heat on the day before. This is a big old house. Will take a day to get the chill out. So two days on your heating bill; we will pay it, of course. Same with electricity."

"No you won't. That will be my small contribution."

"Thank you. Thank you so much." Susan reached for his hand, squeezed it.

"Doc, I have a question. Nothing to do with Halloween. Do you have special hiring protocols like to identify illegal immigrants?"

"Where'd that come from?" He leaned slightly toward her.

"We've had this bizarre rash of murders. It seems two of the victims may have been illegal immigrants. I just wondered."

He shook his head. "No." Then he added, "If a child or woman appears abused we have a protocol, but so far not for immigrants. I expect that is coming. My job is to put people back together. I don't care where they come from."

"If you got a patient, chlorine held to their mouth, could you save them?" Harry wondered.

"No. Only if the killer's hand slipped and the victim got a deep breath of air. They'd be injured, but they might live. Lungs are peculiar. The semipermeable membrane is unique. When people don't take smoke from fires seriously, they are literally playing with fire."

"You've probably seen everything."

"I think I have, then something surprises me."

"If I'd had any sense, I would have brought drinks," Susan chided herself.

"The light's gone. Time to go home. Let's douse this fire." Wilson took the bucket standing in the kitchen, filled it partway with water, and then carefully poured some on the fire.

One should always have a bucket near a fireplace.

Then Harry took the brass fire rake by the fireplace and raked the coals. As two glowed, he poured on more water.

They all finished up and left, Pewter leading the charge to Harry's wagon.

Harry opened the back door for the cats and Tucker, closed it after them, then opened the back hatch for Pirate. She had an odd feeling that they were being watched.

Pewter curled her lip but kept the peace.

As Harry drove home, Tucker told Pewter about the human scent.

"Fresh?"

"Somewhat," the corgi declared.

Pirate chimed in, *"We think we've smelled it before. A hint. Can't say for sure."*

"Where?" The gray cat was all ears.

"When we found Bumpy." Tucker's eyebrows lifted in concern. *"I can't say for sure, but the odor is close."*

"That's not good." The gray cat hoped they were wrong.

32

October 22, 2025

Wednesday

Six days had passed, no uproar, no solution to the crimes. Fall settled in. The willows dropped their yellow leaves, often the first to bloom in the spring, the first to surrender to fall. The redbuds, almost maroon, stood out, as did the sugar maples, flaming red. Oaks varied from the crinkled brown to electric orange. The height of color was about a week away.

Harry, on her oldest tractor, drove the manure spreader over the back fields. Each stall had been completely stripped down, left bare. She'd fill them with a mix of shavings before sunset. Once a week she performed this chore. Each day she mucked stalls, but once a week she took it down to packed dirt over EquiGrids, interlocking sections, squares within. The horses couldn't dig up their stalls by pawing.

Initially, twenty years ago, she'd rehabilitated the old lovely barn. She had each stall dug down two feet. She then put in layers of stone starting with number five stone and finishing with essentially stone dust. She then put a thin layer of dirt over this, sort of a cushion. It was time-consuming and expensive. Once done, she never had to level the spots where a horse created holes.

Thorough, thinking long-range, Harry was a good farmer. She was also very observant.

As she puttered along slowly, the manure spreader grinding up shavings, straw, and manure, she noticed how solid the beaver dams were and how their entrances provided safety. She always put out bird boxes and squirrel boxes.

The inhabitants had readied them for the winter. Squirrels especially liked bits of old soft towels. The birds, some, used yarn she set out. Whether in a tree trunk or one of her boxes, the nests all faced south or east, since most of the weather rolled in from the northwest. Occasionally a squall would come up from the Gulf or a nor'easter would surprise everyone, often with heavy snow.

Content, she had overseeded the back acres with a redbud clover and orchard grass mix. The thin layers of manure shavings would be so helpful protecting the seed, ever more expensive. The rain and subsequent snow would ensure strong spring blooms.

The changing seasons were tricky. A hard frost could be followed by a sixty-degree day. Those bounces diminished in November. On other occasions, a snow hit in late October. The sunlight softened, shortened. The summering birds had all left. The invigorating fall fragrance energized Harry.

Tucker sat in her lap as Pirate paced beside the tractor. The cats stayed in the barn.

Harry passed the sunflower field. She'd had a good crop this year. Apart from the usefulness of the seeds, she loved the color, loved seeing them turn their heads to follow the sun.

It hadn't rained for a few days, and as she turned to head back to the barn, she noticed a rooster tail of dust heading away. She picked up speed, making it to the barn just as Cooper pulled in.

"Hi, neighbor."

"Hey." Harry cut the motor, climbed down.

"On my way home. Wanted to tell you Kyle Lawler's been arrested."

"Great." Harry clapped her hands once, which got the dogs' attention, as well as the cats', who emerged from the barn. "Come on in, sit down and tell me."

Once at the table, Harry put a glass of bourbon and branch, two big ice cubes, in front of Cooper. She grabbed a co-cola for herself, then put a few special crunchies in each pet's bowls.

"I needed this." Cooper tasted the Woodford Reserve, her favorite.

Although not a heavy drinker, she liked a sip after work.

"Crackers? Cookies? Carrots?"

"That's a combination." The attractive officer grinned. "No, I'm good. Kyle was in Damascus, Maryland, trying to sell Silver Silence's goods."

"There's horse people there. Warmbloods. Hunt horses. But how could he think word wouldn't get out? We may not know one another but we know about one another."

"He's not entirely an idiot. He told the sheriff there he'd make a deal, reveal what he knows about the illegal immigrants for a deal. He knows he'll be shipped back here."

Harry sat still for a minute. "We're on the right track. When Susan and I were at the Dunkin House last week, I asked Wilson Anglin if there was a protocol in the ER regarding identifying illegal immigrants. He said not so much, but there was one for abuse. I knew something was weird with Lawler."

"It's entirely possible he had the same idea and knows nothing. He's a liar." Cooper took another sip as she listened to the animals eat their crunchies.

"When does the department get Kyle back?" Harry asked.

"Lawyer wrangling. He's hired a sharp Maryland fellow. This guy is trying to keep him there, saying he won't get a fair trial here. And he's also saying selling stallion sperm is a small crime."

"Not if you own the stallion it isn't." Harry rattled the ice cubes in her soda.

"That's all we know for now. But bringing in people across the border is a national problem. Maryland has its share. If this is an issue here, who is to say some of the people passing through don't wind up in Maryland?" Cooper paused. "He's using drama. Asked to be put in solitary confinement for his safety."

Harry plucked out an ice cube to chew it. "Oh sure, a breeder will kill him."

Cooper watched her friend. "You know that's bad for your teeth."

"Do you worry for yourself?" Harry asked, as she so cared for Cooper.

"You know when I'm afraid? When I'm sent out on a domestic violence call. That's when you get shot."

"I don't think I could do it. Go into a house where usually the wife or woman had been thumped. He has a gun, or she does. I'd be terrified."

"It's my job. I've even had a kid hold a gun on me as I arrested his mother. Fortunately, there was another officer. Well, let me get home. Thanks for the pick-me-up. You know your bourbon."

"Most Southerners do." Harry smiled.

"Oh, before I forget, I'm the officer at the Halloween fundraiser. Rick's worried about the traffic."

"We've got our costumes. Susan has been amazing. We start decorating Friday. I think it will be exciting. I'll have my flintlock on my belt. Have a plastic pumpkin. I'll scare the bejesus out of everyone."

Little did she know.

33

October 23, 2025

Thursday

Kneeling down at a thick boxwood by the side of the Dunkin House, Harry tied an obtrusive red string. She stood up then knelt down, untied it, moved it a bit higher, tried it again.

"That should do it."

Susan, at the far corner of the house, also tied a string around another boxwood. "These boxwoods are big."

"Old." Harry walked over, the three dogs with her. "How many outside bad guys do we need?"

"Two here, one at the back door, and maybe one on the other side of the house. I've thought about someone at the front door, but better off saving that scare for inside."

"How many ghosts do we have upstairs? Remind me."

Susan brushed hair out of her eyes. "We've got two, so one empty window."

"Doesn't mean one of the ghosts can't cover two rooms. Or we find a third ghost. Probably scarier if you don't know exactly where they are."

"I have to think about it."

The two stood, a light breeze creating a refreshing high-fifties day. Enjoy it while you can.

"Dr. Anglin said we can go in tomorrow and every day thereafter. The real work is inside. Let's have another look."

Susan reached for the key in her coat pocket.

"We never did go upstairs. If we see those rooms, maybe we'll get more ideas."

Susan turned the key in the old doorknob, the door opened with a slight creak. "Let's not oil it."

Harry laughed. "Okay. There will probably be enough noise. People won't hear the creak. But why not?"

They stepped inside. The three dogs followed.

"I hate a cold house." Harry felt the chill immediately. "If we turn the heat on two days before, the house will be warm."

"That's what we decided." Susan started up the stairs.

Harry had not told her of seeing a light, someone leaving by the back. Usually she told Susan everything, but she wasn't sure what this meant. And she didn't want to worry Susan. Interested to go upstairs, she climbed behind her friend.

Susan stopped on the landing. "This is where I want Shifty."

"Who is going to build the guillotine?"

"Ned said he'd do it. He can be handy. Said he has it figured out. There won't be a real blade, of course. Do you think we should put a chair here so Shifty can sit down from time to time? He'll be on his feet a long time. Shifty told me he's going through his old pharmaceutical collection. His grandfather owned the pharmacy. Shifty kept everything. He said even the prescriptions are fun."

"What's he going to do with them?" Harry asked.

"Put them up on the main hallway. It's either that or shrunken heads."

"Susan, that's gross."

Susan grinned. "Is, but there is one shrunken head in town."

"I don't want to hear about it." Harry's lower lip protruded.

"Isn't it that you absorb the power of the enemy?"

"Susan, I don't know. I don't want to know."

"Come on." Susan continued climbing the stairs.

"It's nice and light up here. Colder than downstairs." Harry was glad she had worn her old but still warm cashmere sweater.

Tucker zipped into the first bedroom. *"Nothing."*

Owen and Pirate checked the room out. *"Nothing."*

The two women walked into the middle room, the one where Harry had seen a flicker. She went over to the fireplace.

Susan followed. "Someone's been here."

"No bed. No chair. But if you rested in front of the fireplace, even just rolled in a blanket you could stay warm," Harry offered.

"Do you think Dr. Anglin knows?" Susan's eyebrows rose.

"Mac checks the house. He told him probably. I don't want to say anything." Harry knelt down to inspect the logs, which were half-burned.

"Whyever not?"

"If some homeless person is sneaking in here at night, I don't want to make their life worse."

Susan thought about that. "It's trespassing."

"It is, but there are worse crimes. Look at it this way, there's nothing to steal, so if someone comes here at night, builds a fire, stays warm, so what?"

"You'd think someone would notice the smoke," Susan sensibly said.

"Yes, but this street is mostly empty, off the main drag. I don't know, but whoever is sleeping here knows hard wood is better than soft. Probably started the fire with newspapers or even fatback." She took out her penknife and swirled around the cold remnants. "Whoever has been here carries the wood upstairs. Like I said, I'm staying out of it."

"Why doesn't Mac report this? If you've seen it, he has. Even if Mac doesn't check out the house every day he'd find this eventually."

"I don't know. Maybe he knows the person and is covering for him or her."

"What do you think?" Tucker asked her brother.

"A human for sure."

"A woman, I think. What I really smell is the scent of a candle. Like vanilla. It's faint," the intrepid dog said.

Owen, sniffing again, deep inhales, remarked, *"Yes. I think it's a woman, too. Male scent is stronger, not bad but muskier. This is light."*

"Last time I was here, I smelled a hint of cologne," Tucker declared.

"An empty house as the weather turns would be a draw." Owen was right.

"Owen," Susan called.

"Tucker, come on," Harry called, too.

The two, brother and sister, trotted out, joining the humans in the third room.

"Well, more ashes," Harry told her corgi, then looked at Susan. "Why am I telling her?"

"Force of habit." Susan knelt down. "It's possible there have been a few people up here, maybe even at the same time."

"Susan, you'd think someone would see them coming and going, although if anyone exits the back way, you can get into the woods quickly. The next question is, then where do you go? But if someone is careful, they could be undetected, I think."

"Odd jobs? Sitting on a bench somewhere? I don't know, but if there were lots of vagrants, we'd see them."

"True."

The two then clattered down to the kitchen the back stairway.

Harry opened the rear door. "Secluded."

Susan stepped out with her. "See what you mean. Maybe it's people back on drugs."

The two looked at each other. "Well, whoever it is won't be here as we decorate. At least I think not. They don't know when we're coming. If a person was asleep, they'd have a devil of a time getting out unobserved."

"Harry, surely they won't be here."

"I don't think so. The question is, will they return when we leave? Maybe the way to address it is, after the fundraiser suggest to Dr. Anglin that he has someone sleep here, watch the place. Our reasoning can be that so many people have now seen it. It's the truth, we just aren't saying what we've seen now. And if we did, we'd put Mac on the spot. He has to know."

Susan thought a long time. "I get your point."

"And if he is on it, we aren't saying what we've seen, only what we surmise after the fundraiser. I don't want to get on the bad side of Mac, or to get Mac in trouble."

"Right."

As the two discussed this in the old huge kitchen, dogs sitting, Cooper took a phone call, in her office.

"Dr. Anglin."

"Deputy Cooper, I couldn't get Sheriff Shaw, so thought I'd inform you. The stolen beds, chairs, and lamps were located at a secondhand store in Staunton. I put out an email to secondhand stores after the theft. Worked. Anyway, I'll send one of my men to pick them up. I'm not pressing charges. Won't help anything."

"Did the store owner describe the people who sold the items to him?"

"He couldn't remember. He's lying. Who knows how many stolen goods he sells."

"I'll tell the sheriff. Glad you found the items."

"Going to put them back in that remodel, better locks. I'll be using them soon enough."

Cooper hung up the phone. One mystery solved, more or less.

34

October 24, 2025

Friday

A crew of volunteers spread out in the Dunkin House. Susan had a list for every room.

In the hallways she wanted small orange and black lights fastened to the place where the wall meets the ceiling.

Her husband, on a stepladder, accomplished this while Susan fed him the lights.

On the floor, hands and knees, Paul fastened tiny white lights so people could find their way. Bright lights would distract from the scariness.

Tazio had taken time off to hang small speakers in various rooms except for the ballroom. Screams, grumblings, and threats would be played over the speakers, a few quite bloodcurdling.

Susan wanted to concentrate on everything electronic. She especially didn't want people tripping over wires. Tomorrow she planned to move odd pieces of furniture in the rooms, as well as affix faces peering into the house from the outside.

Today was lots of crawling around.

Harry's cats stayed home. Pewter evidenced a penchant for wires. She'd steal them or pull them up the minute someone's back was turned.

The dogs, on the other hand, were there bringing tools to Harry and Susan. Pirate could carry a workman's belt while Tucker carried a rag and Owen carried a Phillips screwdriver.

"Owen, bring me your toy." Susan requested the screwdriver, which he promptly gave her.

"Honey, what are you doing with a Phillips screwdriver?" Ned asked from the ladder.

"Just have a few places where I want more security. If I use this, I won't make as big a mess as I do if I use a regular screw. And I will carefully fill in the small holes after this fundraiser is over. All we need is a snag in the wires, someone gets their foot caught, and down it all comes, accompanied by screams from the speakers. But let's start high first." She handed him a few Phillips screws then the tool. "Make a few places extra secure. Then I'll get down here with Paul."

Not entirely convinced, her husband nonetheless said, "Good."

Harry, upstairs, arranged a few chairs for the ghosts. She'd also taken the upstairs because she wanted to again check the fireplace, plus the back stairway. Once again, someone or someones had slept here last night. They swept clean the room before she again swept it. The sleeping bag had left a few little marks. What little dust there was signified that, but the ashes, swept back by whoever had slept there, provided more evidence.

Harry carefully went down the back stairwell using her bright flashlight. She returned to the upstairs before reaching the kitchen. No point looking nosey, not that it would have surprised anyone who knew her.

Faint footprints from somewhat muddy shoes marked the steps. Small footprints. She returned to her upstairs chores more convinced than ever that the Dunkin House was serving as someone's temporary home.

Hands on her hips, her gaze covered the middle bedroom.

A heavy footfall brought her out into the hall.

"Mac, are you checking us out?"

"I am." He smiled. "You've got people on their hands and knees, some on ladders. Bet this house hasn't seen so much activity since the last Dunkin lived here."

"What can I do for you?"

"Me? Nothing. I wanted to see what you're doing up here. It's a little chilly. Boss said you could turn the heat on the day before the fundraiser. You'll need it. Supposed to have a temperature drop."

"We're having ghosts and goblins up here. So I brought a chair for each room in case they get tired of spooking at the windows and need to sit."

"If there's a fire in the fireplace, that will create odd light. Tell you what, I'll bring three screens. Boss has all kinds of stuff stored in his different houses. You bring the wood, a starter log makes it easy. Will be warmer up here, but I bet the reflection from the fireplace will add to the spookiness."

"Mac, thank you."

He walked over, looked at the fireplace. Said nothing about the remains of charred logs. Harry didn't say anything either.

He told her about the beds, tables, lamps being located at a secondhand store in Staunton.

"Doesn't that beat all?" He smiled.

"Someone needed quick money. Wouldn't be much, but if you're broke, I guess it helped. Any idea who stole the stuff?"

"No." He shook his head. "But if you'd like beds up here, I'll bring them. I don't think Dr. Anglin would care. He has stuff all over. I'd leave them here. Ghosts might need a lie-down."

"I suppose a mattress can make a big difference."

"Harry, the stuff is close by. I'll get the beds right now and you can show me where you want them. Twin beds."

"Thank you, Mac. What an offer. I think close to the fireplace would be best."

"See you in about an hour."

As he thumped down the stairs, Harry knew he knew what was going on in the house. The beds would be better than sleeping bags, and if Dr. Anglin came in to make sure all was well after the fundraiser, Mac had a good explanation.

She went downstairs and told Susan of Mac's generosity.

"That is a nice idea. If someone winds up living here to protect the place until it's sold, it's perfect."

"Right." Harry wanted to tell her what she had seen now that she felt this was known to Mac, but didn't want anyone to overhear. She'd get to it later.

Back up the stairs.

Tucker came up. Harry heard her claws on the hardwood floors.

"You're a busy girl."

"I have to supervise," the corgi replied in all seriousness. *"But I'd rather be with you."*

Looking into those lovely eyes, Harry bent over to pet her beloved dog. Standing up again, she realized they needed small tables by the windows.

Going back down the stairs, she asked Susan, who was still feeding Ned wire, "What about three small tables upstairs with three old plates? That way our people can put their candles on the tables if they need to take a break."

"I'll see if anyone has anything. They can bring it tomorrow. We're almost done with the lights. Tomorrow will be more work. We've got to put in all those chairs for the ballroom. Make sure the orchestra area is clean, unobstructed."

"When will the music fellow set up?"

"The day before. He's got waltzes, polkas, whatever people danced to from 1870 to, say, the 1940s. Won't be spooky if it's rock and roll, or maybe I should say emotional. Music from the World Wars stirs emotion."

"Do you think young people know any of those songs? Like 'The White Cliffs of Dover'?"

"Harry, I hope so, but everyone knows waltzes."

"Finished." Ned came down from the ladder.

Harry walked to the kitchen, put her hand on the doorknob to see if she could open the door quietly. She could. She closed it as Tazio put up the last speaker in the corner of the ceiling.

"If it gets too cold, our outside monsters can warm up in the kitchen for a bit. My weather apps aren't in agreement about the temperature."

"Mine, neither." Tazio folded up the stepladder. "We've done the groundwork. Do you have your costume?"

"Most of it. What about you?"

Tazio smiled. "I'm dressing as a Vanderbilt from the turn of the century. Vast amounts of fake pearls. Will have my hair done up. The question is, can women walk, much less dance, in those girdles? Can I dance in a girdle?"

"Bet you can. Plus, it won't have to be tied that tight. You're in great shape. To change the subject, since we haven't talked in a while, do you have any ideas about the women killed? I'm thinking since no one can identify them, no papers, well, I'm thinking they've been brought into this country illegally."

Tazio leaned against the old stove. "That's an idea. A sorrowful one."

"It is. Just crossed my mind, as those murders were deliberate. You'd think someone somewhere would be missing them."

"Maybe that someone is in terrible turmoil. If someone came along and promised to get you into the United States and get you a job, maybe your family would think that was a better life than wherever you'd lived. We have no idea what people face."

"That I know," Harry agreed as Tucker and Pirate each leaned on one of her legs.

"Why don't you call Father Barnstable at the Catholic church. Has he had new parishioners?"

"What a good idea. I would never have thought of it."

Tazio laughed. "You're not Roman Catholic. I am."

"Thanks. Will we see you tomorrow?"

"Yes. I'm going to help set up the ballroom. That will be something."

"If for no other reason than the two bars are there."

"How did you and Susan get the liquor donated?"

"Took up a collection from the men, first. As you know, at foxhunting socials the men provide the liquor. A few tend bar. We'll have to pay for bartenders, but our men friends wrote checks," Harry replied.

"You'll make money," Tazio predicted.

"I hope so. Thanks for your work, and thanks for the suggestion."

Once home, Harry called Reverend Jones, asking him to call the good father. She only knew Father Barnstable in passing.

Reverend Jones happily agreed to do it.

She couldn't help herself. As it got dark, she put the cats and dogs in the station wagon.

Fair rolled down his window. "Where are you going?"

"Get in the car with me. I'll tell you. Can you wait a little bit on supper?"

"Sure." He hopped into the old wagon, greeted with tail wags and purrs. On the way back to the Dunkin House, she told him what she had observed.

"You waited this long to tell me?"

"I'm practicing discipline. I don't want to jump to conclusions."

"All right, Honey." He brushed her cheek with his hand. He knew what keeping her mouth shut cost her.

Once she turned onto Dunkin House Street she cut the lights, drove to the end.

She turned off the motor.

"I'll turn it back on if we get cold. I didn't see any cars parked on this street. There are some on the main road, on the side. That's it."

She turned on the motor, kept the lights off, and crept closer, then stopped and cut the motor again. They could see the front of the house and the side. As it was dark, they squinted.

"There is a flicker," he whispered.

"I've been driving back here off and on since I first noticed it. Not every night, but I know someone is in there."

"Smoke." He looked up at the chimney. "Even though it's dark, you can see it. I guess whoever sleeps here is consistent."

"Maybe. I've checked the fireplaces up there, and two have been used. It could be that someone else comes in later. And I saw a figure leave by the back door. I couldn't tell you anything about whoever that was. But I don't think they were old. They moved without a hitch."

"Wonder how they get there? Walk?"

"I don't know. But I doubt they will be there as we keep working. Then again, we leave at sundown. I don't know what to think, but with everything that's gone on, I have to wonder. You know what I mean?"

He nodded. "I do. Perhaps it's best to keep away at night."

"I was thinking maybe we could put up cameras," she remarked.

"Worked in Silver Silence's stall." He then said, "But that was an entirely different issue. Even if you see who or how many these people are, what can we do about it?"

"Give the information to Dr. Anglin. But I think Mac knows."

"Honey, I'd stay out of it. If Mac isn't telling his boss, it's odd."

"Maybe Wilson doesn't care."

Fair cleared his throat. "I doubt that. Stay out of it."

"Okay."

"*Think she will?*" Pewter asked Mrs. Murphy.

"*I don't know. Once her curiosity gets aroused, she can't behave.*"

35

October 25, 2025

Saturday

Twenty people showed up Saturday to decorate. Five took over the ballroom. Shifty put framed prescriptions on the hallway from the front door to the kitchen as well as other oddities he had saved from the original pharmacy.

Babs Forsythe, who would be a witch on the fundraiser night, carried a large stuffed raven, which she affixed to the newel post at the bottom of the stairway to the second floor.

"How about you hold it and I'll wire it in?" The Reverend Jones volunteered.

"Oh, thank you. This bird is bigger and heavier than I imagined."

"Where did you get it?" He carefully hid a wire under the newel itself.

"Amy Simmons. She's an Audubon person in New York. Anyway, I love opera and her friend, Audrey, is a soprano. One thing led to another, I talked about Edgar Allan Poe and this big bird appeared in the mail. Scared me when I opened the cardboard box."

"I don't wonder. You've read Edgar Allan Poe?"

"Did we have a choice?" Babs laughed. "Things were different when we went to school."

"I hope they still do. Given that he was a student at the University of Virginia, we should read him."

"True. As I recall, you're a reader." She smiled at the pastor.

Babs herself was a Methodist, but everyone knew The Very Reverend Jones.

"Reading got me through Vietnam. Poe had a hard life. He probably suffered from some mental illness. On his deathbed he said, 'Lord, help my poor soul.' "

"You know, Reverend, that may apply to all of us."

Harry came down from upstairs. "What's this? How great."

"Babs is full of surprises." The reverend smiled.

"I'm studying spells and curses for Halloween."

"Was going to call you later. I did speak to Father Barnstable. He says he has not had an influx of new people."

"Thank you."

"How's it going upstairs?"

"My dogs find it fascinating." Harry grinned. "Good smells. Maybe there are already ghosts and goblins." She then added, "Put up small nightstands so they have a place to set their candles when tired. Have a chair in each room, and Mac brought up a twin bed for each room."

"That's full service." Babs laughed.

"Seems so. These beds were new, stolen, found again in Staunton at a secondhand store, brought back."

"Harry, that's a lot of activity for beds," Babs rejoined.

"It is, but"—she shrugged—"crazy times, I think."

"True." Herb stepped back. "The raven commands from this newel post."

"Hey," Harry called as Tazio joined them, carrying a large assortment of flowers.

"What are you going to do with them?" Babs wondered.

"Put them in the middle of the ballroom for now. They'll die and look forlorn. I'll put them in the living room on Halloween."

"That's a good idea," Harry enthused.

"Was just at Wilson Anglin's, showing him and his wife rough ideas for their new home. He said he's stop by one of the days before Halloween. You and Susan were smart to decorate over the weekend."

"All Susan's idea."

"Mom." A bark came from upstairs.

"Those two have been investigating everything upstairs. They want to be ghosts." Harry looked up then saw her corgi come down the stairs followed by Pirate.

"You two sit down. You'll get in the way."

"We're helping," Pirate barked.

Tucker looked up, beheld the raven, and barked.

"Babs, your bird is a success. Scared my dog."

"I am not scared. I was warning everyone," Tucker defended herself.

"All right, let me get back up there." Harry started, then stopped. "Herb, Paul and Shifty are going to build the guillotine today. As I recall you know a lot about the French Revolution."

"A turning point in history. What can I do?"

"We haven't found a big basket for the head to fall into. Can you think of where to look?" Harry answered.

"I've got a woven laundry basket at home. That could do it," Babs offered.

"They did use baskets for the heads." Herb stroked the raven's chest.

"Who has the body?" Babs asked.

"Susan has borrowed one from the UVA drama department. The head is detachable, so Shifty has to rig up how to drop the blade. It's not really a blade, but it has to drop and then people will hear the head hit the basket."

"That will send chills up their spines." Herb grimaced.

"It will, but Susan and I talked. We could have had a hanged man, then someone with their head in the stove. Over the many years there have been suicides and murders of that nature here. She said at the turn of the century one of the brothers who owned the big lumber company, still going strong, killed his wife by making it look like she stuck her head in the oven with the gas on."

"Clever," Babs replied.

"Up to a point. He didn't get away with it. Babs, thanks for the raven, Reverend Jones, you always help no matter what. I'm going upstairs again. Think it's all settled, except for the curtains. They haven't arrived yet. Will be more frightening if a curtain is pulled to the side then a face appears."

"Scares me just hearing about it." The Reverend Jones smiled indulgently.

Harry entered the bedroom at the top of the stairs, the rooms were identical. The twin bed sat in front of the fireplace crossways, to get the most heat. She placed a small nightstand by the window and a chair there, too.

"The question is, do I hang thin white curtains then heavier ones? Looks better. But hanging curtains is a lot of work."

"You can still smell the fire, the logs burned down." Pirate sniffed the fireplace.

After looking at the old valances, Harry once again carefully stepped downstairs, going to the back door.

Tazio was in the kitchen with Paul. "This old stove is fabulous."

"They look better than the new ones." Harry carefully opened the back door then closed it, checking the temperature. "Do we want people to come in the back door?" She called Susan to the kitchen. "Susan, what about the back door?"

"We have to keep it unlocked. Some people might want to

leave, and if they do, a monster will scare them. And the monsters might need to come in for a break."

"You're right. Just checking." Harry added, "Maybe people will leave this way to avoid the crowd at the front door. There will be lots of people. I just know it."

Susan beamed. "You're being so helpful."

"I am. Look how much work we've all gotten done today. And I was thinking, is there anyone who we can get to be the Joker? He's a terror just to look at." Harry made a face.

"Let me think on it. There might be someone."

"We'd better wrap it up. Losing light. We really don't have that many lamps, and the colored bulbs overhead don't throw off much light."

"Right."

"Susan, I've got old curtains I've stored away. I want to put them upstairs. If we both do it, with two ladders, won't take long, but I want a gauzy white curtain with a heavier one over it. Add to the effect."

"What time?" Susan was for it.

"How about after church? We don't need other people, we've gotten so much done today. With just the two of us we'll work faster," Harry replied.

"We might need more workers in the ballroom."

"We can make that decision tomorrow. The important thing is, we've got the music, the speakers, the chairs, and a bar at each end of the ballroom. A lot has been accomplished. People need something to look forward to, to lift their spirits. It's been an unsettling time."

"Has."

"I'll pick you up at two."

"All right."

36

October 26, 2025

Sunday

Hanging three sets of two curtains took longer than Harry or Susan thought it would. Finally finished, they went outside, got into Susan's car. All three dogs rode with them.

Susan turned on the motor. They drove out, going home the back way, passing Chiles Orchard.

"Whoever is sleeping at the Dunkin House knows our schedule. They'll be there tonight, no doubt. It will be dark soon," Harry predicted.

"Whoever it is takes their stuff with them," Susan mentioned.

"They're smart enough to leave very little trace. I told Fair, and Mac has to know."

They drove in silence, then Harry said, "Turn left. Go on the street behind the schoolhouse."

As the light faded, although still glowing in the west, they passed few cars.

"It's quiet back here. Eventually it will be developed." Susan rolled along at thirty-five miles an hour.

"There's the house where the beds, tables, lamps were stolen. Cars are parked in the driveway."

Susan laughed. "Maybe more people came back to steal beds."

"Maybe these are drug parties. Why would this many cars be here tonight?"

"Could be guys watching football together."

"Susan, I don't see any flickering lights, TV lights. Something is going on."

"I'm not going to stop and peek in the window."

"I would."

"No, you won't."

"Listen to her, Mom," Tucker barked.

"Well, something is going on."

"If it's drugs, Harry, you don't know the condition those people are in. If it's beer and football, you don't know either, although it's probably better."

"Okay." Harry sounded a bit crestfallen. "But something is going on. It may well not be legal."

"That's not your business. Tell Cooper."

"I will. You know, they still have no I.D. for two of the dead women. The woman whose driver's license said Kylie Mason can't be found. The New York driver's license is valid, but no Mason is at the stated address in Rochester. She also left her apartment in Richmond. Whatever is going on, there is no paper trail. Three lost people," Harry responded.

"Whatever they were doing has to be highly profitable," Susan wisely noted.

"Bringing drugs across the border is profitable. Those cartels are worth more than some big businesses. In fact, illegal drugs is probably the biggest business in the world."

"I wouldn't doubt it. If people want something, they're going to get it. No amount of laws, police, agents, you name it, can really stop them."

"But if this was about drugs, wouldn't we know? Wouldn't some of our people be dead from fentanyl, or we'd see them losing jobs?"

Susan looked in her rearview mirror. "Someone is following us."

"From the party house?" Harry became alert.

"I don't know. But I noticed it earlier when we passed the orchard. Thought someone would pass me."

"This is a twisty road. You can't really speed up."

"No. I'll pull into the Greenwood Post Office lot. See what he does."

She pulled into the lot, half circled, and faced out. Susan figured if she had to get away, she wouldn't have to back out.

The car, a big SUV, pulled right up to her, shined the lights in their faces, then backed out.

"New Kia SUV. I got the first part of the license plates: 971, then he backed out."

"Harry, that's a warning."

"For what?"

"I don't know, but we're getting close to something." Exasperated, Susan said, "Look, let's get through this fundraiser. And let Cooper and Sheriff Shaw do their jobs. Please."

"The fundraiser first. But I think this has to do with the chlorine murders. We are close."

"Then let's back off. Please, Harry. I so want my Seeing Eye Rescue mission to get money. I truly care about the blind."

Harry nodded, but at that moment she felt blind, metaphorically speaking. Blind, frustrated, and a touch frightened.

37

October 27, 2025

Monday

"Come along," Harry encouraged her four animal friends as they walked by the creek between her farm and Cooper's.

"*I am walking.*" Pewter puffed.

"*Slowpoke.*" Tucker jabbed at her.

"Look at that." Harry stopped, for the beaver dam seemed to have doubled in size since she last followed the creek.

"*Everyone is getting ready for winter,*" Pirate surmised.

"*They have two smaller dams. This one really has grown,*" Mrs. Murphy noted. "*Maybe someone wanted high ceilings.*"

They chatted as Harry reached the den, heard a tail slap the water before she got there. When she stood opposite it on the creek bed, ripples of water flowed toward her, hitting the shore.

The beavers knew all the animals on the farm, including the wild ones. They recognized Harry. They didn't feel like putting up with Tucker's barking, so they retreated to their homes.

"All right. Let's double-check the fence line back here. Come on."

She walked the fence line of this pasture, farthest from the barn, holding each post and seeing if she could move it. Fortunately, she couldn't. Her idea behind this is, were there any loose posts, best to secure them before the winter. No one could fix anything with hard frosts. Maybe someone with a big ditchwitch could, but a shovel and pickax proved useless with hard frosts. A loose fence post needed to be made tight.

"Everything is good," Tucker announced.

"Good enough to sit on." Mrs. Murphy enjoyed sitting quietly on a fence post, observing everyone and everything.

"Good." Harry headed back toward the barn, looking over the harvested sunflower field.

She'd had a decent crop this year. Harvesting the seeds took time, but she enjoyed it. She'd allow the big heads to dry then cut the plant, cut the head off then brush out the seeds. Hard work, but peaceful. Maybe there was a mechanical way to do this, but she liked the way she got into a rhythm while working. Riding also gave her a rhythm. If weather permitted, she'd ride for an hour each morning. Given all the work at the Dunkin House, she was behind on this pleasure.

Stepping into the barn, she looked up at Simon, the opossum, who was looking down. He quickly withdrew, although he liked Harry. She often left sweet treats for him at the top of the ladder. She'd put treats out for the barn owl, too.

Walking into her tack room, she hung her ball cap on a hook by the door then turned on the propane stove.

Shedding her coat, she sat down, pulled out a notebook.

"Okay. You have to help me remember."

"We will," came the chorus.

"Monday. Make calls for overhead ballroom decorations." She looked up from her moleskin notepad. "We, well, Susan, not me, decided to hang the fall garlands and the party lights on Wednesday. I said that was too late, everyone will be obsessing with their costumes. But she said this stuff took ladders, four people at the least, so do it Wednesday. She's probably right. Okay, the booze plus sodas. We can't put that in early. Has to wait until Friday morning."

"*Why?*" Pirate asked.

"*Because some people might break in and steal the liquor, or at least a couple of bottles,*" Tucker replied.

"*Like they are alcoholics?*" Pirate wondered.

"*Some people can hide it better than other people, but other people are heavy drinkers. They aren't alcoholics, but they really want that drink especially at a party. Since some people are sleeping upstairs, and both Mom and Susan know this, this is smart. Will take time though.*"

"*And ice,*" Mrs. Murphy added.

Harry dialed a number from the landline phone on her desk. Given vagaries of the weather, having a landline even with cellphones was not a bad idea.

"Susan, who can we get to deliver and carry the booze?"

"Ned said he and a couple of his tennis buddies would do it. This is a big help. Glad you were thinking of it, too. Say, did you tell Fair about the car following us?"

"I did."

"I told Ned and he said don't go out alone. Well, we weren't alone. I also told Ned about the person or persons upstairs. I know we need to keep our cards close to our chest, but he's not going to blab."

"Fair, neither. If whoever is up there at night were a thief, we'd know by now, I think. And also, I think that person will bunk somewhere else on Thursday night or Friday. There will be too much going on, last-minute comings and goings."

"They have to know," Susan said authoritatively. "They've done us no harm."

"Well, they, or whoever it is, is either homeless or hiding from someone."

"It's the latter that worries me."

Harry sat up straighter in the chair. "That worries me, too. Homeless, not so much. Why do you hide? You've wronged someone or someone is out to get you. You owe money. You know something that could jeopardize others. It's not reassuring."

"No. Maybe we'll find out who is up there and maybe not. I won't be back at the house until Tuesday. My Monday is always jammed, but we have enough time for the little things, plus the ballroom finishes."

"Fair promised that he and Paul could hide a little tiny speaker under the raven's large breast."

"Why?"

"Every now and then one of the guys can pick up a microphone and croak out, 'Nevermore.'" Harry laughed.

"Actually, that's pretty good."

They caught up on whatever had transpired in a day then said goodbye.

Harry slapped her hands on her knees. "All right. Time to check the water buckets. It's Monday. Scrub time."

Thanks to chores, organizing the feed delivery, throwing down hay, should anyone want a nibble tonight, the day flew by. Harry did the major feeding in the morning, but always put down a flake of hay for nighttime. If humans want a nibble sometimes after sunset, she reasoned maybe horses do, too. At any rate, she had healthy, happy horses.

Finally back in the house, she fed the cats and dogs, sat down for a much-needed cup of strong tea.

"Cooper," Tucker and Pirate barked.

Cooper waved at the kitchen door as Harry motioned for her to come in.

"I just sat down. Bushed. Would you like a cup of tea? Anything?"

Cooper walked over to the stove. "The teapot is still hot. I'll pour myself a cup and join you."

Harry beamed at her. "It's wonderful when someone knows your house."

"This is good. What is it about Mondays that wear you out?" Cooper sighed.

"I don't know, but I don't think it will ever change." Harry looked down at Pewter's soulful eyes. "You had your supper."

"True, but a treat would be nice." Pewter attempted to look fetching.

Harry got up, passed out treats, then put cookies in the middle of the table.

"What a wonderful idea. Did you bake these?"

"Cooper, can't take credit. Susan gave me a tin yesterday when we went to hang curtains."

"Bless Susan Tucker. I've been thinking about you two getting followed. I'm glad you told me. Actually, I've been thinking about a lot of things, like the Mason woman. The first thing I did was contact New York, since Mason's license was from New York State and would not run out for four more years. A valid license. No speeding tickets. I had the original address on the license. Tracked it down. Her landlord rented her apartment out after it was empty for the appropriate time. She disappeared. Dies here."

"Maybe the dead woman wasn't Kylie Mason."

"Exactly." Cooper finished her tea, rose, turned the pot back on, and waited for it to heat up, since the water in it was still warmish.

"You know what? I'll have another cup, too."

"Treats." Pewter could always try.

"Maybe the real Kylie Mason was dead and someone lifted her license." Harry's mind was whirring.

"Another unclaimed body. So let's think this over. If she were, say, killed in an automobile accident, someone must have been there, someone with a criminal mind, shall we say, and lifted her license before an ambulance or law enforcement reached the scene. Possible."

"But unlikely."

"I think so, too. Look, whatever we are dealing with is making someone or someones a lot of money. No one is selling fake art, no one is stealing cryptocurrency, which may work and be legit and may crash. That leaves us drugs or . . . what?"

Harry thought, then softly replied, "Sex."

"Exactly. So how did someone get this license? We may never know, but if, say, a person in extremis is admitted to a hospital, to an emergency room, and dies on the stretcher, well, a nurse could take the license. A valid license has value."

"I see. And a nurse or doctor could sell it."

"They could, but that individual could also use it. Would have to be a woman," Cooper added to that.

The tea water boiled, Cooper poured them each a cup, dropped in new teabags, and sat down.

"You're saying this is well planned."

"I am. If what's selling is sex, I think we'd eventually know here. I'm trying to think about work, where you can hide profit, taxes. If it's one woman or, say, a graduate student bringing guys home, I can't prove she's selling sex. If she's in a house with other women, I can. A lone operator pockets all the cash."

"I think those days may be gone. For college students, anyway."

"What we've kept our eyes on is a few men renting a room, calling friends I guess or texting with a code and other men show up. An orgy. I doubt that's what we're dealing with, but there are decadent things like this, that happen more than people realize." She took a sip and a breath. "A famous man comes to the university to speak. He expects a beautiful woman to sleep with. Someone has to provide that woman, who is not part of the university. And I guarantee you, someone does."

"A woman as part of the speaker's payment." Harry shook her head.

"Well, people see a great speakers' list for a university, think highly of the institution. Some of those men are used to getting whatever they want. And someone in our area, someone at every university town, will provide the women. Never underestimate corruption nor the intelligence of the corrupt."

Harry sighed. "I guess not. I'm not that smart."

"You're honest. You'd not think of it. My job takes me down some disquieting roads. And the other thing about my job is, I know most people will lie to me."

"Really?"

"Sure. Might be a white lie, but they'll lie."

"That's depressing."

"It can be, but I tell myself that this has been going on for millennia."

"You're right. I don't think the human animal is getting any better."

They drank their tea in silence.

Harry put her cup down. "What if this is bringing in sex workers? Luring women from other countries, countries with little hope and far too much violence. They get here and they're trapped."

"That's where I'm heading. Listen to me, don't go cruising by houses with lots of cars parked outside, houses that aren't family dwellings. You and Susan worried someone yesterday."

"We cruised by a remodeling job, and the driveway was full on a Sunday night."

"Keep away from that type of thing. I think we're on the right track. How to spring the trap, I don't know."

"Maybe someone will make a mistake." Harry's eyebrows knitted together.

"I think three someones have. I don't know what to make of Bumpy."

"Cooper, I read stuff, stuff pops up on my phone or I pick up a newspaper. There are still a few. And some women who are sex workers declare they are in control of their destiny. They make a lot of money. Supply and demand. Do you believe that?"

"I don't know," Cooper honestly answered. "But I do know a

woman abused by her husband is not in control of her destiny, and I believe women brought here under false pretenses and then made to have sex with anyone who purchases a ticket, so to say, they're not in control of their destiny."

"Sometimes there are so many issues to think about, my head aches." Harry half smiled. "Like assisted death. Stuff. Some people are absolutely sure they're right. I think I know what's right and wrong, but there are exceptions. I don't truly know that I can judge. But lying to women, trapping them, I have no doubt. That's illegal, but more, it's a sin."

"I agree."

"Maybe someone will slip up."

"Harry, that's more frightening than your monsters at the upcoming fundraiser." Cooper paused. "Whoever slips up is a monster."

38

October 30, 2025

Thursday

"Susan, you were so smart to get people to come in yesterday. All those details, the last-minute stuff."

"Getting the bars in took more time than I thought. But our husbands and Paul somehow got them through the door."

"Heavy." Susan looked up at a bright red and yellow garland, sugar maple leaves and yellow oak leaves entwined together, black ribbon wrapping around to keep the colorful leaves in place. "Higher." She then turned to Harry. "I couldn't be happier than that men are bigger and stronger. I don't want to lift that stuff."

Harry laughed. "Me, neither. I swear, Fair is so strong, he could lift a house off its foundation."

"Babs, let's put fresh flowers on the bars. The dead ones can go in other rooms. The ballroom should be beautiful."

"Okay," Babs answered Susan.

"Most of the costumes will be imaginative, but a few people

may want to look scary, and I think as we get closer to our allotted time, our outside monsters should come in and dance."

"That would be lovely." Harry figured the outside horrors had a tougher job than anyone, as they had to stay warm. "Bet they will have fun jumping out at people."

"And they can look inside the windows and stir up a scream. Did I tell you that Lucas said he'd be the Joker?"

"No kidding? Did he say anything about Aunt Tally?" Harry loved the centenarian.

"She's too frail to attend. She's upset, of course. Aunt Tally never wants to miss a party."

Harry smiled. "She is the party." Her face reflected sorrow for a moment. "She's getting toward the end. My hope is she can make it to Christmas and Big Mim can throw a party for her aunt. Little Mim and Blair will still be there, along with their daughter. They'll leave for Ocala right after the New Year."

Little Mim was Big Mim's daughter and her husband, a former model, was Blair. Horses united the family. Given their vivid personalities, there was usually room for rabid disagreement. But not at Christmas.

"That's my prayer, too. Okay, do we need tiny lights in the garlands?"

"No," Harry quickly responded. "There's enough light in here. Soft. Will make everyone look good."

Susan rubbed her chin. "I take your point. And there will be sturdy lamps on the bar. Can't make change without light."

"How much are you paying the bartenders?" Harry knew a good bartender could help make a good party.

"Two hundred fifty dollars each. That's a fair price, and I gladly will pay it since both men agreed to bring the ice. Saves us another heavy job. And they each have a friend who will tend with them, help out. I'll give them a big tip, and I know many of our guests will tip, too."

"Are you nervous? I am."

"Mom, you're hardly ever nervous," Tucker, at her feet, remarked.

"I am. All the work, the effort, and the incredible help we've gotten from everyone. I don't know if I told you, but at this point I'm on overload. My brain is porous. But every person who we asked to put up our poster, at the beginning of the month, everyone agreed. And I think the ads in the local paper, the Crozet paper, helped, plus we're on *The Daily Progress* website." Susan named the Charlottesville paper.

"You did tell me." Harry looked around. "Chairs against the wall. A little table here and there. Can't think of anything else. This floor shines."

"We'll go over it again before the doors open. Easier to dance on a smooth floor. I can imagine what balls were like when the Dunkin House was in its glory."

"This will be the best one." Harry looked over to see Dr. Wilson Anglin striding in with two brown packages in each arm.

"Dr. Anglin, what do you think?" Susan asked.

"I wouldn't have believed it. Here. After the fundraiser there will be odd chores to do or maybe you'll wait until the next morning, already November. November." He paused. "Well, ladies, here. These are for all of you after the door is closed."

Susan pulled a bottle of champagne out of the first bag. "Dr. Anglin. After all you've done. This is too much."

He smiled broadly. "You know, it's been something to watch this somewhat derelict house come back to life. Take the bottles home. Bring them tomorrow and put them in a cooler in your car or someplace safe. Champagne is never safe."

"Too good." Harry didn't drink, but she'd sip champagne.

"Thank you. Thank you so much."

"Crozet has never seen anything like this. By the way, those old prescriptions on the wall are something. And the bottles on the shelves."

"Shifty," Susan informed him.

"That's right. His grandfather owned the pharmacy. Bet the

Dunkins bought their drugs there. So much of the old stuff contained heroine and cocaine. That stuff still works today. Which you know. Why anyone would take a chance on street drugs, I will never know. It's a death sentence. Forgive me. No downbeat subjects. I want to walk around a bit. I'll start upstairs."

Harry, dogs with her, accompanied him, thinking fast as she did. "We'll have the guillotine on the landing, and up here." She stepped onto the hallway. "We have ghosts, spooks, goblins. We've now got one for each room. Had a last-minute volunteer. Lucas's girlfriend. So many people have pitched in."

He looked around the first room. "Those curtains are actually nice. And I see Mac brought a bed and a little table."

"Yes, thank you again. If anyone becomes tired of standing, they'll have a minute to rest."

Dr. Anglin looked at the fireplace, five logs stacked far enough away in the corner. "Who's been using the fireplace?"

"I have. I wanted to see if the fireplace drew. Don't want smoke coming down. Turns out it's in good working order."

He studied the ashes, bits of log. "One less thing for me to do. And turning the heat on today was wise. Still a bit coolish, but will be comfortable in an hour or so. Harry, don't forget to have a bucket of water by each fireplace."

"Yes, sir."

Tucker and Pirate studied the doctor.

He checked each bedroom.

"I've got wrought-iron candleholders and candles. Figured I'd put them up here before I go. There's still stuff to do downstairs. We're almost there." Harry smiled.

"I can see that."

"Dr. Anglin, I'm heading back to the ballroom. A big job, the ballroom. Thanks again for lending us the beds and little tables."

"Easy to do. I ask myself, why would anyone steal twin beds?"

"If someone owned a bawdy house, might be a good idea," she blurted out. "But instead, they wound up in Staunton."

He looked again at the fireplace. "I'm sure in its heyday, Staunton had houses of ill repute. Mac's been up here, right? He didn't pawn off the delivery onto another one of my crew?"

"He's been here. He's helped us."

"Good. Well, good luck tomorrow." Headed for the back stairs. "You never know, I might fool you. Maybe I'll come as Batman. But I bet someone else will do that." He paused at the top of the back stairs and again said, "I might fool you."

"I have no doubt." Harry smiled at him.

39

October 31, 2025

Friday

The sun's bottom rim touched the Blue Ridge Mountains. The day had been cool but even with the waning sunlight, it felt cooler. Harry was at the Dunkin House for any last-minute problems, needs. She'd leave in an hour, go home, load up Shortro, her horse, change into her Headless Horseman costume, and come back, parking at the end of the street, where Fair and Paul had parked one of Mim's horse trailers so there would be space, no one else would park back there.

The fundraiser would open at six-thirty P.M. and close at nine. While that wasn't a long time, it would be enough, especially since Halloween as the night wears on can get rowdy. Best to avoid that, especially for the children.

The stairway to the second floor was now roped off. The landing had dim light.

The big stuffed raven sat on the newel post. "Quoth the raven,

'Nevermore,'" a touch added to the atmosphere. Thanks to Paul. Fair would walk by and pull out the little microphone, too. Plinths were placed at the ballroom corners. One had a fake severed hand, another simply an order for Robespierre to be guillotined. Susan and the group were clever, using historical truths plus literary frights. Poe never let them down. His room, on the West Range, now visible through a glass front door, remained as he was thought to have left it in December 1826, because his guardian wouldn't pay the cost.

The kitchen's old oven had the door open, but no victim with their head inside. Harry was still thinking a dummy could be used to spin a murder tale. Susan chose not to use suicide as a horror display, even though murder would be eventually discovered, well, there was enough going on.

The dancers, in good costumes, each wearing a mask, a few quite elaborate, sat on the chairs lined against the wall. Soon enough, the disc jockey would begin the music, and as the ballroom was the last stop on the tour, people could dance for as short or long as they wished.

Harry, wearing a black turtleneck, black jeans, thought if nothing else, the imagination and work that went into the fundraiser was worth the $20 at the door.

Susan, now coming through the ballroom, called out to her, "Ready?"

"I will be. Need anything else?"

"Think we're good."

Two bars commandeered each end of the ballroom. One could buy drinks. The liquor had been provided by the local liquor store, all the state paperwork filled out, a real pain.

Shifty displayed bottles of old drugs, like heroin, lined against a hallway wall, with explanations as to their effects, complete with doctors' orders. Shifty surprised everyone, as no one had known he had an interest in old medicines. He said it was because new ones didn't really work. As people began to come in, read the stuff in the hallway and on the shelves, they were quite surprised at what one once could purchase.

"I'm glad Shifty didn't put the poisons in here." Harry started counting the people in the ballroom.

"Everyone notices where I told him to put them. It's wonderful how many people wanted to give. Everyone understands dogs help blind people. It's not a subject where people take sides."

"Thank God. I thought you were going to be a witch."

"I was, then I decided I wanted to be draped in a gorgeous gown from 1890. The drama department at UVA was great. What do you think?"

"Stunning. You should dress like that all the time."

"You know, Harry, I often think I'd be happier in an earlier time. I guess many people feel that way, but emphasis on proper dress, which stayed with us until the 1960s, did I get that right?" Susan paused. "Now anything goes. I'd be so happy if things like the 'now shoes' didn't pop up on my phone."

Harry nodded, then said, "Babs Forsythe looks appropriately scary. If the lines are slow, she'll walk along and cast spells." Harry waved to Babs. "And how about all the people in costumes? I never expected this many," Harry remarked.

"You remember when we thought the dancing teachers would come if we allowed them to put their studio cards on the table? They got most of their students to participate. The dancing ought to be marvelous. Graceful. I'll be checking this and that, but once everything is running smoothly, I'm coming back here to dance." Susan looked at the special watch pinned to her bodice. "You know, I love these old watches. Time for you to go before too many people see you."

"I'll be headless. They won't know it's me," Harry teased.

A child screamed.

Susan grinned. "We're in business."

Harry replied, "I'll go out the back door."

"I'll probably hear you before I see you." Susan kissed her on the cheek, began to make her rounds.

Harry, outside, inhaled the air. Breathing the dropping cool air was invigorating. She looked upstairs. Candles were carried, so someone was by the windows. At one window, a ghoul displayed himself. Effective. Harry walked around to the front, found Cooper leaning against her squad car parked on the curb, near the main entrance.

"Look at this line." Cooper smiled.

"Fabulous. They'll be glad to get inside, because it's going to get cold. That mercury is on a slide."

The officer nodded. "That's why I've got this coat and my gloves. Well, it's October thirty-first."

"'Night on Bald Mountain.' Remember that animated feature and the music?" Harry inquired.

"Saw it when I was in junior high. You know, one of those times when *Fantasia* was re-released. Made me think about how evil can be glamorous."

"Coop, you never fail to surprise me. Would never have thought of it. Well, let's hope evil is somewhat glamorous tonight."

Susan walked through the house, chatted with each spook, murderer, the Joker. On her way back to the ballroom, she stopped at the foot of the wide stairway. On the landing stood the guillotine, with a dressed-up Shifty as the guillotiner. He had a dummy in the contraption. Would drop the blade, cackling as he did so. The dummy's head was already cut off and the blade made it tumble into the basket. Shifty would hold up the head and crow, "Long live the Revolution."

He was frightening. You believed he believed. No blood, but red yarn had been attached to the head, so it sort of looked like decapitation.

Susan walked into the ballroom. The music was wonderful, waltzes, mazurkas, just made people want to dance. The DJ, who was paid, pulled it all together.

She leaned against the wall, being unobtrusive, watching people enjoy themselves. Those coming into the room, the last stop before leaving, she first watched when a gentleman in costume tapped a lady on the shoulder, she said, "Yes." They all were having the best times in the entire event. Susan breathed a sigh of relief. Happiness was infective.

"Madam, may I have this dance?" A fellow in the uniform of a British regiment from the end of the nineteenth century took Susan's hand, led her on the floor. They moved to the music.

Susan said, "You have to be one of the instructors."

"I am."

"Thank you. My husband likes to dance. We rarely get to it. He's our representative, as you probably know."

"Bring him to the studio. Allow me to give you two a free lesson. It will be good for him to forget politics with a lovely lady in his arms."

"Oh, honey, now I know why you're successful."

Cooper listened to the screams inside, laughed. She waved to one of the ghouls in the window, who dipped his or her candlelight. Frankenstein jumped out of the bushes. Cooper emitted the obligatory scream.

Sheriff Shaw slowly drove up, stopped, put down his passenger window as Cooper came over. "The traffic is steady. They are parked all the way to the firehouse. You know, when Susan asked for permission to use the golf carts, I thought she was being overly hopeful. Good thing she did. It would be a long, cold walk for some people and hard on the little kids. Everything okay?"

"Oh yes. I'm out here listening to the screams. I can hear the music, too. It's faint, but Susan and her group have thought of everything."

"All right, I'll be on the slow cruise. You never know what an event like this will attract."

"Funny. I was just thinking what if our killer is in there? Who would know?"

"That's a thought. Well, it's someone who knows Crozet. Okay, you know how to reach me." He closed the window, grateful for the automatic windows, then slowly cruised down the street, turned around, and headed back out to the main drag. He didn't really think the killer would be in the haunted house.

Pulling a tight lumberjack hat over her hair, the cap black, Harry darkened her face so she wouldn't reflect light. Looking in the mirror, she figured this was the best she could do without true theater makeup.

"How do I look?" she asked the cats, who lounged in the trailer. They liked the tack room with saddle pads and blankets.

Mrs. Murphy replied, *"Not yourself."*

Harry's britches were black, and that had taken some time to find as most britches are shades of beige, mustard, or white. But she found a pair, pulled on her black boots, butcher's boots, so no tops. She wiggled her toes.

Then she carefully pulled the old black cashmere sweater down so the waistband was covered. It would be cold. She needed layers.

Sitting down in the tack-room chair, she held the black coat, cut so the flaps reached halfway down her thighs. She wanted a coat from the times of "The Legend of Sleepy Hollow," but she feared if she rented one from UVA's theater department, she might harm it or they'd complain about the horse scent. She found a good stand-in.

"You know, there's no way I can pull this up over my head, put two eyeholes in it. No way. The tight cap and the darkened face will have to hide me. Then, too, I don't know if I could see if I had only two eyeholes. This is more complicated than I thought."

"They'll be too scared to notice," Mrs. Murphy suggested.

"You aren't going to take us out in that cold, are you?" Pewter had wanted to stay on the farm, in the kitchen.

The sun had set already, the night's darkness enveloped everything, which was the point. The cats could see perfectly well. Harry, not so much, but she was vigilant.

"All right. Showtime." She smiled as Fair helped her into her coat.

"You'll be the star of the show," he said, and Paul agreed.

She'd organized the trailer tack room. Her pumpkin was in there, as was her flintlock pistol, which was loaded. She thought firing it in the air would scare people, along with tossing the pumpkin. The smooth grip, the twin barrels, the gun was a work of art. Those old rifles with engraving, which she much admired, should be given a show at a big art museum. She had a quick thought that she'd write the Virginia Museum of History & Culture, but figured the last thing they'd want to hear from was a farm girl from Crozet. She straightened her shoulders, thinking, yes, but this farm girl went to Smith.

She walked out, closed the door, Fair led Shortro out of his stall. He was tacked up except for his bridle. He was an angel horse. You can't put a price on a horse like that, and she would never part with him. Most of her horses were sensible. A few of the Thoroughbred mares had moments. Never lasted long.

Shortro readily walked out on the trailer ramp. Harry closed the sidebar for him, then followed out. Paul lifted the ramp with a grunt. He swore the older he got, the heavier that damn thing was.

Checking and rechecking, she opened the passenger door as two determined dogs sat there.

"I don't know about you two. Then again, you could be the Hounds of Hell. Tucker, I'm not sure you qualify."

"I do. I do. I want to go."

"All right."

"You look scary," Pirate told her.

"Why did I let Susan talk me into this?" Harry said to her dogs.

"You want to do it." Tucker knew her human well.

"Honey." Fair kissed his wife. "Our own Headless Horseman."

"Thank you two for doing this. Paul, I expect Tazio is in the ballroom."

"Girl can't resist a dance." He grinned. "Hey, we won't get to dance. Too bad."

"We'll make it up, sometime."

As she was adjusting the flintlock in her belt, plus trying to figure out exactly how to handle the pumpkin, the crowd in the Dunkin House evidenced no desire to leave. The ballroom was packed. Most of the children had left earlier with their parents, but those without children, having had a few drinks, were eager to dance, talk, listen to Shifty holler, "Long live the Revolution!" As well as "Nevermore," since Babs showed her husband the microphone.

Susan, checking the time, walked out of the ballroom, where she had been twirling and whirling, to the bottom of the stairs.

"Shifty, leave the head there. Come on down and have a few dances before we close up." Then she walked out into the hall. "Folks, we soon must close but why don't you all squeeze in a dance or two?" Spying Babs, still casting spells, she motioned to the witch. "Come on, girl. You've done a great job."

"You know, I think I will. You'd be surprised at some of the spells people suggested. Revenge is a big one, as is wooing someone. I had no idea Crozet was so, uh, so emotional."

"I'll remember that."

Then Susan walked up to the second floor. "Ghosts, goblins, put out your candles. Come on down for a dance."

"Woo woo." One of the ghouls giggled. "What do you think? We're up there. We see people walking around the house, but we don't know what's going on inside."

"Been a smash. A total smash. All right, hurry up. I'll go outside and get our monsters out of the bushes around the house, they're probably half-frozen by now."

She walked outside, instantly feeling the temperature drop, waved to Cooper, walked around the house, nicely landscaped. "Mike, come out. Good work. Come on." Behind the big English boxwood. "Come on, Craig. You've been great. I could hear kids scream even inside."

"Thank God." The two men readily left their positions as Susan reached everyone outside. There were only four, but they had been scary and they were cold.

She hurried over to Cooper. "Come on in if you like."

"Thanks, Susan, but I'm on duty. Best I stay here. A few of the folks have indulged at the bar. Watching them drive a golf cart is, well, let's say I'd hope not to be walking toward them."

"Oh dear." Susan's face registered surprise. "I never thought of that. If they tump over, they won't have far to fall."

They both laughed, especially since Susan used the old Southern expression "tump over." It meant a big tip, perhaps some sound effects.

Both Susan and Cooper peered down the road.

"Coop, she is about ready. I'm going to push people out. Will take ten minutes with help from the staff. Do you mind calling Harry on your cellphone? Tell her I'm ready for her. Most of the people will be filing out, so she can come as Washington Irving tells us. What a great story. Known the world over."

"I'll call her now. You have to be happy. This is a wild success."

She beamed. "Thank you. I hoped we could pull it off. I'm going in for a last dance."

Susan went in the back door as people filed out the front door. The music drew her to the ballroom, so inviting. What a pity homes were no longer built for dancing, large entertainments. What's better than a ballroom?

A gentleman, perfect white tie and tails, approached her, bowed low. "May I have this dance, Madam?"

"Indeed."

He was a good dancer, and as they glided on the perfect flooring, other men cut in. Most of the people there knew she was the driving force behind this and she truly was the belle of the ball.

"Ned." She recognized her husband's costume as he tapped her current partner on the shoulder.

"I have to stand in line to dance with my wife." He squeezed her tighter.

"Remember that."

"Sir, I wish the honor of dancing with this lady."

Ned reluctantly relinquished his wife. On and on the dancing continued, the music filling the room. Even though people were being encouraged to leave, no one wanted to abandon the wonderful ballroom.

A gentleman wearing a silk brocade waistcoat, fancy, with a sea green fitted long coat, dancing shoes with big buckles, swept her up, slowly dancing her toward the back door.

"I can't leave just yet."

"But you will." He had a gun under his coat which pressed into her waist. "Keep dancing. Keep smiling."

As he managed to get her out of the ballroom then out of the back door, Harry was galloping up the street, attended by Tucker and Pirate, neither one appearing particularly ferocious.

"Beware!" Harry shouted as she pitched the pumpkin.

People screamed, but they loved it.

Susan screamed. Her scream was lost on everyone but the two dogs. Her partner jammed the gun hard.

"Shut up."

"Pirate, Aunt Susan's in trouble." Tucker, those fabulous dog ears, shot alongside the house toward the back, Pirate, now in tow, ran alongside his friend. The big dog wasn't sure what was up.

"Hey! Hey!" Harry hollered.

Her fear was these two dogs would damage something.

"Come on, Mom." Tucker barked as loudly as she could. Cooper, alert as always, saw the dogs charge off, then Harry. She ran after them.

Harry beheld her dearest friend being dragged, coerced into moving farther away from the house.

"Leave her," she screamed at the man.

He paid her no mind. By now Cooper knew something was radically wrong.

Galloping toward her friend, her abductor pulled his gun, firing at Harry. The bullet whizzed by. That fast, Pirate, stretched to the limit, reached the man, who was preparing to fire again, hitting the fellow with one hundred fifty pounds of Irish wolfhound.

Down he went. Cooper ran as fast as she could. Tucker immediately hurried to Susan while Pirate, true to his hunting heritage, had the man by the throat. The fellow kept trying to hit the dog with his gun. He tried to turn it to fire properly.

"Susan, are you all right?" The frenzied corgi licked Susan's face for she had fallen on the ground, was getting up to run toward the humans.

Despite the huge animal at his throat, the man managed to turn his gun toward Susan, not the dog, but Susan. Harry, flintlock in hand, pulled back one trigger and fired. It hit him in the shoulder.

"Next, your head, you bastard." Harry's anger, a pure rage, pushed her to want to kill him.

At the last moment, Cooper, finally close, shouted. "Don't Harry, I've got him. Call off Pirate."

"Pirate, leave him. Good boy."

The dog immediately obeyed, but he didn't move away from the man. If that fellow took another step, Pirate would be on him again.

Harry, flinging herself off of Shortro, who stood quietly, rushed to Susan with outstretched arms.

"Are you all right?"

Susan hugged her best friend. "Yes. Yes. Thank God you and your dogs were charging the house."

"I heard you," Tucker told them.

Cooper was upon the abductor. "Stand up." She bent over to pick up a fancy Glock while Pirate stood next to the man.

Tucking the gun into her belt, Cooper motioned with her service weapon for him to get up and walk to the squad car.

People observed this, those who were late coming out thought this was part of the fundraiser. It was becoming apparent that it was not.

Harry, Shortro's reins in her left hand, the flintlock in her right, slowly walked with Susan toward the squad car.

Cooper pushed him into the rear seat as she reached for her phone. He opened the door, almost got out, but she quickly shot him in the leg.

His screams were the best of the night.

By now, Shifty, Babs, and others realized they should tend to their people, who were leaving. Susan's core group, all intelligent, knew something terrible had happened so thought: keep calm, always keep calm.

Fair and Paul, hearing shots, drove up, trailer behind. No time to unhitch.

"Fair, Paul." Harry looked at them. "Make sure Susan is okay."

"I am. I am," Susan said, then gasped. "He wanted to kill me. I swear that was his intent."

Cooper yanked off the assailant's elaborate mask, he was still moaning, flopped in the backseat, blood oozing from his leg.

"Doctor Anglin." Fair spoke his name with astonishment. "What in the—"

He couldn't finish his sentence.

Cooper had also reached Sheriff Shaw, who'd quickly showed up. "We need to get him to the ER, and then we need to get him right away into the jail. No way can he stay in the hospital. He knows it too well."

The shot man sat in the rear of the squad car, his head dropped back on the seat.

Sheriff Shaw drove ahead of her, sirens blaring.

As Cooper drove off, those standing there couldn't believe what they had seen.

Paul, finally under some control, quietly said, "I think we've found the killer."

"But why?" Susan now felt sore in her ribs where he had prodded her hard.

"I have no idea, but I expect we'll find out." Harry had never been so glad to see her husband or Paul in her life. She was lucky Wilson Anglin couldn't get off a good shot. She, Susan, Shortro, or one of the dogs would probably have been hit.

As everybody, feeling the cold, calming down, looked at one another, Susan couldn't help herself. "We'll never top this fundraiser."

40

November 1, 2025

Saturday

Indian summer bathed still-green pastures in a golden light, the temperature was maybe sixty-two degrees. A light breeze added to the physical delight of the afternoon. Harry, Susan, Ned, and Cooper, each wearing a sweater or light jacket, sat under the huge tree by the screened-in door. Fair had the firepit going. Everyone relaxed in a comfortable outdoor chair. They had had enough to eat. Harry had cooked a celebratory lunch for Susan's survival, plus the success of the Seeing Eye Rescue fundraiser.

"After expenses, we cleared close to thirty thousand dollars. Granted, a few people, like Big Mim, wrote us big checks, but we had over two hundred and fifty people at the door that we know about."

Fair asked Susan, "Did people cheat?"

She smiled. "No, but the two at the door became so overwhelmed, they lost an accurate count."

"There wasn't a slow moment. The people were steady." Ned then added, "At least in the ballroom, and that was the last stop. For some I think they snuck in and danced all night. But darling, what a success. You came up with the perfect idea, a great time of year and the decorations, spooks, Shifty as a guillotine operator, no one would have thought of all that but you."

"Having a real killer at the party," Cooper teased Susan, "was the crowning achievement."

"Who would have known?" Susan's hand flew to her chest.

"You missed it all, staying in the trailer." Tucker happily tormented Pewter.

"So what?" The gray cat tossed her head.

"Shortro gave us his version this morning. I'm sorry I missed it." Mrs. Murphy had listened to Harry's wonderful horse during morning chores.

"We stayed warm. We have better sense." Pewter was having none of it.

Pirate, as usual, listened but said little. What was the point of trying?

"It was under our noses all the time. I knew it. I knew it but I couldn't see it." Harry put her glass in the cupholder in the chair's arm. "It's hard to believe, and yet it makes perfect sense."

"You mean because Wilson could physically check everyone?" Fair asked. "Weed out anyone with disease?"

"No, although I guess that was important," Harry replied. "But the money he and whoever else, I doubt we know who all yet, were making. He was buying houses, buying land, he was raking in the dough. I assumed, as did we all, that he made a good salary as a doctor."

"He did," Susan chimed in. "And restoring homes is a moneymaker usually. We just misjudged the amount of money. Then again, who would ask?"

"He was in a good position to bring in illegal immigrants. He saw so much at the hospital. He knew women who were especially vulnerable. He knew people were getting into the country," Ned spoke up.

"But sex trafficking, Ned? That's a step beyond bringing in people illegally." Fair spoke a little louder.

"People. Women." Harry sat up straighter in the chair. "Everyone thinks of agricultural workers or men working horses. Right? But the money in prostitution has to be astronomical. Especially if you don't pay the girls. They are captives. So he got them out of Venezuela, and Guatemala, smuggled them here. Do you know how?"

Cooper, as the question was addressed to her, shook her head. "Florida's coastline. Any place with a coastline would be obvious. Someone is still down there in Venezuela telling young women he or she could get them out, get them to America, help them find a job. They'd live well. I could have gotten more out of him if other ER doctors hadn't come in."

"Venezuela is hardly the only place with these problems. The globe is full of crime, currently, warfare on one level or another. It always has been. A pretty girl, well, what's her way out?" Ned wondered.

"Anywhere. Anytime." Harry nodded. "So these young women, smuggled across our border or disembarking at a protected cove are put in cars, trucks, whatever, and brought up here."

Fair was thinking. "Kyle might well have driven girls up here. If he asked to be put in solitary, it makes sense. And it makes sense that some law enforcement people were in on it."

"I hate to think that, Fair, but it's more than possible." Cooper exhaled.

"You know, you don't see what you don't want to see, or what is so foreign to you."

Harry came back. "No, but it makes sense. And it makes sense that none of the victims had I.D.s. They didn't have I.D.s, period. They had no way out. No money of their own. Probably didn't know much English. What did they have? A bag of makeup?"

"They had to look good," Susan agreed. "The victims here somehow got out and were running away. Eventually that will all be clear to us."

"The Mason woman brought the cosmetics. May have been an enforcer. She knew so much about their operation. Somehow she got in the way. I doubt Wilson will ever own up to these killings." Cooper had been thinking she was not a prostitute.

"An enforcer maybe, someone in on the game. She wasn't one of the girls. Maybe she wanted more money." Ned got up to stretch his legs for a minute.

"Ruthless bunch. Killing came easy, I guess." Harry then said, "What about Bumpy? I keep thinking of him. He was our first victim."

"He wasn't making a lot of money. He was doing the remodeling. He fell in love and was planning to free one of the girls. But Mac had fallen in love with her, too. When he learned we caught Wilson Anglin, he turned himself in, with his record he knew he couldn't get away or take the women with him. And he did it to save his girlfriend. That's who was sleeping at the Dunkin House. She and her sister. What rattled the doctor was you two and the Bolivars. The first Bolivar had fallen out of Mac's pocket, according to Mac. He said his girlfriend gave it to him as a token. Bumpy was in love with her, too, but Mac believes she loves only him."

Harry sat up straighter. "Did Mac kill Bumpy?"

"Yes. He confessed. But there are traffickers out there who now are in jeopardy. Mac knows they'll try and kill him. So he's got a hot lawyer. And he's talking. He killed whoever Dr. Anglin told him to kill, but he swears he didn't run down the young woman behind the post office. He avoided killing when he could, but he was paid a lot."

"What about the woman he loves?"

"He has pleaded with us not to arrest her and her sister for prostitution. Not to send them back. We wouldn't arrest them.

They were captives. They'll be safe here until Anglin's and Mac's trials are over. They'll need to find good lawyers, because at that time they may well be sent back. They'd be killed, I'd think. Those people sweet-talking young women in Venezuela are still there. Safe. By the way, all the remodeling houses are empty. And the work has also stopped."

"Susan, who would have thought of Dr. Anglin? Now it fits but he was clever. No doubt a new group of girls replaced the older ones, as the older ones moved on. If anyone got pregnant he could take care of it. Same with STDs. Wherever men are in large number, have some money and feel entitled to sex, that's where the best-looking girls would eventually wind up. Big city. Big money." Harry couldn't imagine how hopeless those women felt.

Ned added, "For men especially, it's a kind of contract. You pay. She performs. No strings attached."

"I feel sorriest for the woman hit behind the post office, and the young woman at the library. They had to be trying to escape. Never had a chance. What a blighted life." Harry's eyes registered her surroundings. "Any idea who did that?"

"Mac gave us names. We're looking for them and will bring them in. Mac is telling us everything he knows. He has asked if his girlfriend and her sister can visit him. The sheriff says yes. He is allowing the women to see Mac. Makes him talk more."

Susan said, "Mac helped his girlfriend and her sister escape. He hid them at the Dunkin House. Dr. Anglin didn't know they were gone. As Mac kept tabs on the girls, they were safe."

"Is Dr. Anglin talking?" Harry looked down at Tucker, on her back, stomach exposed.

Pewter was sliding up to the corgi.

"No," Cooper answered. "Prosecution is determined to get him, really get him."

A silence followed this as Pewter smacked Tucker in the face. *"Death to dogs."*

Instead of chasing Pewter, Tucker let out a pitiful yowl, hurried over to Harry.

"Pewter, you can be hateful, mean. Come here, baby." Harry picked up the dog, putting her in her lap.

"I could throw up," Pewter spit.

"Please don't." Mrs. Murphy gave the gray cat a stern look.

"I'd gag. I wouldn't really throw up," the fat cat confessed.

"Here's an odd thought," Susan said. "Wilson will hire good lawyers. Should they get him out, he'll be killed."

Fair replied, "Even in jail he might be killed. Happens. A rich criminal pays off an incarcerated person, or pays money to their families."

"No one is safe." Harry's eyes widened.

"No, too much at stake," Cooper agreed. "This is a big network in our county and the counties where the women are found. A good doctor was critical to them. Not now."

Harry felt terrible. "Using women's bodies."

"It seems so extreme." Susan's voice rose a notch higher.

"When you're making millions, you can justify anything." Cooper knew that to be true. "Prostitution is a highly profitable business. There are girls for every budget. Think about it. Kind of like car models." Cooper hit the nail on the head. "She's both a service and a commodity. You don't have to go out and try to woo someone into bed. Spend money at a bar and leave empty-handed, literally. Here you pay your price, get what you want, and then leave. Maybe you'll become a repeat customer. People that run this business are smart. They have been since B.C. And some customers fall in love with a girl. She takes care of his body. Makes him happy. That's what happened to Mac and Bumpy. What women would have them, given their ruined lives?"

Harry felt a pang for the two men, then asked, "Anyone need anything else? Ned, sit down. You're making me nervous pacing."

"Sorry, I am nervous. What could have happened to my wife, my life, really, if it hadn't been for you, Tucker, and Pirate? Susan is the best part of my life."

Susan stood up, hugged and kissed him. "Sit down, Sugar. I'm right here. He didn't get me, thanks to Harry and Cooper, the dogs. I'm a lucky woman."

"Oh, don't praise the dogs," Pewter meowed loudly. *"There will be no living with them."*

They finally changed the subject to comforters. Harry was determined to buy a new winter comforter. This did not prove a fascinating subject except to the animals, who were hoping there would be a new comforter.

A truck was coming down the long driveway.

Harry stood up. "Maki. Oh, good. We can tell her everything."

"Honey, I bet she already knows." Fair smiled.

"Then she's coming here to see if we're safe."

Maki pulled up, Haley and Jeb disembarking. Jeb didn't disembark as much as fly out.

"Come on. Food and drink." Harry hurried over.

"Here." Carolyn had opened the door on the passenger side, handing Harry a leash attached to a half-grown Staffordshire Bull Terrier.

"And?"

"Found her wandering on the road. Close to you," Maki announced.

The other dogs came up, were nice to the frightened youngster.

"It's okay." Tucker sniffed noses. *"Everyone is good except for the gray cat."*

Fortunately, Pewter did not hear this.

Harry walked the puppy to the group. The dog was the color of pewter. "Cooper, someone wants to meet you."

The dog went right for Cooper, licked the tall woman's hand. *"I like you,"* the nameless animal said.

Cooper petted her as her tail thumped a bit.

"Your dog found you." Harry beamed.

"Well . . ."

"Leave her with me in the mornings. You need a companion."

The animal looked at Cooper with soulful eyes.

"Well." A long pause. "Gris. She's gray."

Love at last.

ACKNOWLEDGMENTS

Catherine Hanlon, MD, an emergency room physician, former Air Force Flight Surgeon and beloved friend, put up with my bedeviling her about emergency room protocols and events.

We have no idea. They see every sickness, wound, breakdown imaginable. Some you can't imagine. They also see the addicted, the homeless, the lonely. They must take these people in. It's the law. So when weather or times are bad such unfortunates flood emergency rooms.

Another group of people, events not as dramatic but who at times are overwhelmed by the homeless, the addicted, the lonely, are librarians.

You and I pay for this. If we do not successfully address these problems they will worsen and so will your taxes. Our elected officials, many of whom desperately scan the horizon to find someone upon whom to blame for these problems, are no help.

Dr. Hanlon opened my eyes to the magnitude of this. We can fix it if we want to but that's another issue.

Carolyn Maki, another dear friend and former polo teammate, provided historical details about her house, barn, outbuildings, pastures. Her home has been in the family for generations. It is perfect.

Her sweet lab, Haley, passed away while I was writing this book.

That was a good long life. Jeb, the Jack Russell, then a puppy, is now full grown, a devil dog. Carolyn found another Jack Russell to keep Jeb company, Macy. As of this writing Maki's house is still standing. Two Jack Russells!

I'm sure I have forgotten people. I hope they'll forgive me.

Rita Mae Brown and **Sneaky Pie Brown**, a tiger cat rescued from the local SPCA, have collaborated on twenty-eight Mrs. Murphy mysteries, and they are involved in many local events to raise money for animal shelters. Rita Mae also writes the "Sister" Jane Arnold Outfoxed series, the Runnymede series, and the Mags Rogers series, and has authored the memoir *Animal Magnetism*. She and Sneaky Pie live with many other rescued animals.

ABOUT THE TYPE

This book was set in Joanna, a typeface designed in 1930 by Eric Gill (1882–1940). Named for his daughter, this face is based on designs originally cut by the sixteenth-century typefounder Robert Granjon (1513–89). With small, straight serifs and its simple elegance, this face is notably distinguished and versatile.